W9-AUJ-699

LEAVE NO SCONE
UNTURNED

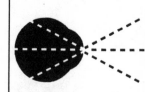

This Large Print Book carries the
Seal of Approval of N.A.V.H.

A CHEF-TO-GO MYSTERY

LEAVE NO SCONE UNTURNED

DENISE SWANSON

WHEELER PUBLISHING
A part of Gale, a Cengage Company

GALE
A Cengage Company

Farmington Hills, Mich • San Francisco • New York • Waterville, Maine
Meriden, Conn • Mason, Ohio • Chicago

Copyright © 2019 by Denise Swanson Stybr.
Wheeler Publishing, a part of Gale, a Cengage Company.

Wheeler Publishing Large Print Cozy Mystery.
The text of this Large Print edition is unabridged.
Other aspects of the book may vary from the original edition.
Set in 16 pt. Plantin.

LIBRARY OF CONGRESS CIP DATA ON FILE.
CATALOGUING IN PUBLICATION FOR THIS BOOK
IS AVAILABLE FROM THE LIBRARY OF CONGRESS

ISBN-13: 978-1-4328-6687-7 (softcover alk. paper)

Published in 2019 by arrangement with Sourcebooks, Inc.

Printed in the United States of America
2 3 4 5 6   25 24 23 22 21

*To Doris Ann Norris (1940–2018),
the two-thousand-year-old librarian.
Doris Ann was one of the first people
who welcomed me into the cozy
mystery community and was a huge
support throughout my career.
She will be greatly missed.*

CHAPTER 1

Dani Sloan's muscles strained as she lifted a heavy container of tasty dessert samples into her van's cargo area. After sliding it into place, she stretched her back. Blowing out a puff of exasperation, she scanned the street running in front of the mansion. There was no sign of her youngest employee, Ivy Drake, and there were still several more bins to load up, along with boxes of coupons and promotional brochures.

Ivy should have reported for duty half an hour ago and she was nowhere to be seen. Dani wasn't sure if she should be angry or worried. Of her three helpers, Ivy was usually the most reliable. It was usually Tippi Epstein who disappeared or had an excuse not to work her shift, not Ivy. Friends or not, she couldn't allow her assistants to walk all over her. She would have to start running a tighter ship.

Dani shook her head and returned to the kitchen to grab the next box of tasty treats. She was lucky to have escaped the rigid nine-to-five workplace and be able to focus on her passion for cooking, but there were still plenty of challenges in running her own small business.

Then again, even though her company had been up and running for four months, Dani always felt a little thrill whenever she started to load supplies into the white Ford Transit with the red Chef-to-Go logo on the side. She bit her lip. If only Ivy would get here and help.

Irritation fought with a sense of unease, but Dani shoved away her concern, and while she continued to fill the van, she thought about how she'd ended up opening her business. It had started when she'd analyzed the gastronomical competition in Normalton, Illinois, and discovered an unfilled niche.

There were plenty of catering companies, but none that also provide itinerant personal chef services to people too busy to cook for themselves, and none that sold fresh, tasty, and portable lunch-to-go meals on week-days to busy college students.

Those lunches were what brought in the day-to-day cash flow. Which is why this morning, she was focused on gaining more consumers for that part of her company.

It was seven days before classes started at nearby Normalton University, and Orientation Week Normalton, a.k.a. OWN, would officially start in a couple of hours. With students comprising the vast majority of her lunch-to-go regulars, Dani was determined to make the incoming freshmen aware of her products and entice them to become her customers.

Which made renting a table on the quad for today's OWN kickoff a necessary expense. Ivy was supposed to have helped with the preparations for the booth, then accompany Dani to work there, and she was now over forty minutes late.

Balancing an enormous container of bite-size Fowling for U sandwiches, her special turkey subs made with lemon basil hummus and balsamic onions, Dani freed one hand and opened the door of the refrigerated container. The ongoing heat wave made her glad she'd recently had the chiller built into the back of the van. She couldn't afford to have food spoil.

Once she was free from her burden, she looked at her watch. It was already ten and she wanted to have her booth set up by eleven thirty for the noon kickoff. If Ivy didn't show up in the next few minutes, she'd have to leave without her.

Sighing, Dani started to head inside to get the rolling cart with the lunch-to-go side dish samples but halted when she heard a noise from the carriage house.

The carriage house was an empty building the size of a three-car garage. At some point, when she had the money, Dani planned to turn it into apartments. However, for now, she used it mostly for storage.

That meant there shouldn't be anyone inside. Taking her cell phone from her pocket, Dani punched in 911. Holding her thumb over the Send icon, she noiselessly approached the carriage house intent to take a quick look through one of the windows before calling for help.

While she didn't want to summon the police over a raccoon or some squirrels who had found their way inside through an opening in the eaves, after having her home trashed a few months ago by an intruder, she wasn't about to take any chances. If the animal inside the carriage house had two legs instead of four, she'd back away and phone the cops.

The dirty windowpane obscured Dani's view as she tried to peer through the glass, and she searched her pockets for a tissue.

Coming up empty, she sighed and used the edge of her T-shirt to wipe away the grime.

Once it was clean enough to see through, she leaned forward and cupped her hands around her eyes. Squinting, she could just make out the shadowy figure of Ivy and a man the size of a small mountain.

Dani swallowed a scream, then relaxed when she realized that the girl was holding on to the guy's arm, not vice versa.

Ivy's captive towered over the petite young woman. He wore a long-sleeved desert-camo shirt, threadbare blue jeans, and combat boots. A thick beard covered the bottom half of his face, and a cap was pulled low over his forehead. It was clear the man was trying to leave, but Ivy continued to hold on to him as she spoke.

Anxious to find out what was going on, Dani hurried around to the carriage house door with her phone still at the ready.

As she approached the pair, Dani heard Ivy say, "I can get you the drugs."

Dani's eyebrows shot into her hairline and she jerked to a stop. *What in the heck!* Was Ivy involved in selling dope?

"Don't bother." The man's voice was raspy, as if he hadn't used it in a very long time. "Those meds make me feel like I'm a step behind everyone else and that I have to

11

summon up every ounce of energy just to function. It's like being covered in a wool blanket and being asked to run a marathon."

Ah! Ivy had been offering to get the guy his prescription. Dani sagged in relief that her friend wasn't involved in something more sinister.

"Okay." Ivy's voice changed, and she coaxed, "At least stay here. No one will be home all day and you'll be safe, Deuce. Stick around and rest. I can set up a cot for you behind a stack of boxes and no one will bother you."

"No. I gotta go." The hulking man shook his head. "Don't worry about me." He pulled loose from Ivy's grasp and backed toward the door. "I'll be fine."

"At least take the boxes of food before you leave." Ivy hurriedly grabbed a carton from the stack on the floor and pursued the retreating man. "I bet the others are waiting for these."

Neither Ivy nor her friend had noticed Dani standing in front of them, both too intent on their conversation to realize they had company. However, with the guy only a few steps away, Dani recognized it was high time to make her presence known before she startled the oblivious twosome. The guy was already jumpy, and his hypervigilant

12

aura led Dani to believe he might not be a good person to surprise.

Loudly clearing her throat, Dani said, "Hi. I'm Ivy's friend Danielle Sloan, but you can call me Dani."

Instead of introducing himself, the man froze and stared fixedly at Dani for a long moment. When she held up her hands, palms facing him, he gave a tiny chin jerk, then frantically scanned the area around her. As he was checking the perimeter, he fingered something in the pocket of his jeans. And, if Dani had to guess from the outline, the object he was touching was a large knife.

When it became clear the man wouldn't speak, Ivy moved next to him and said, "This is my friend Deuce. He hasn't shared his last name with me yet. He stopped by to pick up some food for his buddies."

"Nice to meet you, Deuce." Dani put out her hand, then quickly dropped it back to her side when he made no move to shake it. Quirking an eyebrow at Ivy, Dani returned her attention to Deuce and asked, "Do you come here often? I mean, to my carriage house."

Once again Deuce remained silent, and Ivy, an explanation falling off her tongue in a rush of words, said, "Remember several weeks ago when you catered a picnic for that motorcycle club?"

Dani barked a laugh. "Sure. Those steaks they had for me to use were the biggest pieces of meat I'd ever seen that didn't have four legs and a bell around its neck."

"Do you remember all the food that they didn't eat?" Ivy asked, and when Dani nodded, she continued, "And I asked if I could give the leftovers from that gig and our other catering jobs and lunch-to-go meals to the hungry?"

"I do," Dani confirmed. "I was glad you brought it up and mad at myself for not thinking of it when I first started the company."

"Well, I tried the downtown shelter first." Ivy scowled. "But due to some stupid health department regulation, they couldn't take the food."

"And?" Dani prompted, knowing how Ivy liked to drag out a story.

There was more to whatever was going on here, and they really needed to get to the quad soon. She glanced at Deuce, surprised that he hadn't taken the opportunity to get away, since he had obviously wanted to leave earlier. Then she noticed that he had edged a tiny bit in front of Ivy, as if protecting the young woman.

"One of the guys at the shelter told me that there was a homeless camp under the old railroad overpass a couple of blocks from the quad, and that the people there could use the food." Ivy shot Dani a sheepish glance, then continued, "So I went over there and talked to them."

Wanting to ask Ivy if she had any idea how dangerous her actions had been, Dani instead bit her tongue and murmured, "I see."

Dani was still clutching her cell phone and briefly considered calling Ivy's uncle to inform him of his niece's reckless actions. Spencer Drake was head of campus security, and after Ivy, Star, and Tippi had been kicked out of their apartment, his supervision had been part of the deal that the girls had struck with their parents in order for them to allow their daughters to live with Dani.

At first, he had just checked up on Ivy by texting Dani. But then a couple of months ago, Dani had been accused of killing one of her catering clients, and Spencer had helped her investigate the young woman's murder. Between the two of them, and with a little help from a reporter, the true culprit had been brought to justice.

At the time, it seemed to Dani as if the

handsome former law enforcement agent was attracted to her. However, once the real criminal was behind bars, Spencer had withdrawn, and he'd returned to only contacting her with a weekly text asking if Ivy was behaving.

Intellectually, Dani knew it was better this way. Her new business needed all her attention and she didn't have time for a relationship. Not to mention the baggage both she and Spencer were carrying around. He was divorced and, as far as Dani knew, still in a financial battle with his ex-wife, while Dani's previous boyfriend had left her too emotionally scarred to trust anyone.

Too bad her brain and her heart were on different pages. She missed their conversations and couldn't get Spencer out of her mind. They'd worked well together as a team and his abrupt cold shoulder had hurt her.

Was that why she wanted to call him now, or did he truly need to know about Ivy's rash behavior? Was Dani so desperate to talk to him that she was blowing this whole incident out of proportion?

Unsure of her own motives, Dani said, "Tell me a little more how this works. Does Deuce always come here, or do you deliver to the camp?"

16

"Well, generally, when we have some big events scheduled that will probably result in leftover food, I put a note for Deuce on the board at the Union and he meets me in the quad parking lot." Ivy played with one of the bright-pink wisps of hair scattered among her long, blond strands. "But with orientation week starting today, I knew the crowds and noise would be too much for him, so I told him to come here."

"So you aren't going to the camp anymore?" Dani wanted to be sure she understood exactly where the food exchanges were taking place.

"No." Ivy's lips thinned. "Deuce said it's not safe for me to go there."

"And he's right. While I'm sure that most of the residents are fine, there's probably some with mental health problems you might not understand." Dani caught the man's eye and said, "Thank you for looking out for Ivy."

Deuce dipped his head in acknowledgment as he shuffled his feet.

"Let's help Deuce with the food cartons," Dani said to Ivy as she slipped her cell phone into her pocket. Then, recalling that she hadn't seen a vehicle anywhere nearby, she asked, "Deuce, do you have a way of getting the boxes from here to your camp?"

"His cart is outside." Ivy gestured to the back of the carriage house.

Dani stacked two boxes, stepped closer to Deuce, and handed them to him. Except for the odor of stale cigarettes, he smelled clean and she briefly wondered where he showered. The unofficial homeless camp certainly didn't have any facilities.

Hefting two more boxes into her arms, Dani said, "Not to rush you, but we need to finish loading the van, drive to the quad, and set up our table before the noon kick-off."

Ivy picked up the remaining cartons, and she and Deuce followed Dani as she walked outside and rounded the building. Deuce moved past Dani and pulled out an empty flatbed cart, the kind found at home improvement and big-box stores, that had been hidden among a cluster of lilac bushes. Its normal bright-orange color had been painted over in browns, greens, and tan splotches.

Once they'd deposited their boxes on the cart and Deuce had tied them down, he jerked his chin at Dani and Ivy and muttered, "Thanks."

Dani smiled. "You're very welcome. I'm happy that people can enjoy the meals I've prepared. I absolutely hate throwing good food away."

"Isn't she awesome?" Ivy linked her arm with Dani and beamed.

Deuce ducked his head and started to push the cart down the alley.

Looking at Ivy, Dani said, "There's still one thing I don't understand." She frowned. "Why did you want Deuce to stay in the carriage house today? I mean, if he's usually okay at his camp, what is there to be afraid of today?"

Evidently overhearing Dani's question, Deuce halted his progress down the alley and turned toward her. A muscle ticked in his jaw as he scowled. "It's the zombies. They raided the camp last night around midnight, and I'm pretty sure they're coming back."

CHAPTER 2

"Zombies?" Dani voice rose incredulously and she turned to Ivy as Deuce's retreating figure continued down the alley. "Seriously?"

"First I heard of it." Ivy shrugged. "Deuce just said that the camp wasn't safe anymore and he'd have to start thinking about finding somewhere else to put up his tent."

"How delusional is that guy?" Dani asked, concerned about Ivy's safety.

"He isn't." Ivy crossed her arms. "Deuce has PTSD from his time in Afghanistan and can't deal with noise or crowds, but he isn't crazy."

"From what little I know about post-traumatic stress disorder, sufferers can have hallucinations." Dani put her hand on Ivy's shoulder.

"Actually, PTSD sufferers tend to have flashbacks where they temporarily lose connection with their present situation and are

20

transported back in time to a traumatic event. It's sort of like a daydream, but not a nice one." Ivy rolled her eyes at Dani. "And I very much doubt Deuce was in a situation where he was battling zombies."

Dani glanced at her watch and said, "We'll have to talk about this later. Right now, we need to load the rest of the samples and get over to the quad. I didn't pay all that money to rent a space for the Orientation Promenade and not be there when it starts." Frowning, she muttered, "Especially not with the recent personal chef cancellations I've had, not to mention the catering jobs that I bid on that didn't come through."

"Gotcha." Ivy patted Dani's arm. "I didn't realize that business was slow."

"Not exactly slow." Dani sighed. "It's probably just dropped off because of the pause between summer school and the fall semester." She lifted her chin. "We're busy this week and I'm sure it will pick up once classes are in full swing."

"That's right." Ivy linked her arm with Dani's. "And to make sure our lunch-to-go service is front and center throughout the week, Tippi, Starr, and I will walk through the crowds wearing sandwich boards and handing out flyers."

"That would be great! I should have

thought of that myself." Dani squeezed Ivy's arm. "Will Starr and Tippi go for that?"

Ivy shrugged. "If they balk, I'll just remind them that with fewer lunch-to-go meals to prepare during the break between summer and fall classes and no catering jobs last week, we all owe you hours."

"Awesome!" The weight that had been on Dani's chest since the personal chef cancellations eased a little. "Now, let's get going."

Ivy and Dani hurriedly packed up the remaining food and hopped into the van. The mansion was less than a mile from the NU campus, and although the streets were congested with parents delivering their offspring to college for the first time, Dani made it to the parking lot in ten minutes. Thankful that an assigned parking place had been included in the price of the booth, she and Ivy quickly unloaded the van onto a pair of rolling carts.

The midday heat made it hard to move fast. And even when Dani slowed her pace, a drop of perspiration rolled down her forehead and into her eye, momentarily blinding her.

Blinking away the sting, Dani noticed that the university had installed a temporary fake wooden path down the middle of the quad. Evidently, they didn't want the grass completely trashed by all the students and parents walking among the stalls.

As Dani and Ivy pushed their carts down the walkway looking for the location of the Chef-to-Go booth, Dani inspected the tables and stands along the way. Every organization from the swing choir to the nudist club was represented, all hoping to lure freshmen and transfer students into joining their groups.

Together with the organizations vying for the newbies' attention, merchants like Dani were trying to temp the students to part with their money. A lot of businesses depended on the college crowd to keep their books in the black.

Dani stopped, pulled the letter of instructions from her pocket, and rechecked her assigned space number. *Yep.* It was 165 all right, and she was right in front of it. Her three hundred and fifty dollars had gotten her a four-foot folding table covered in a white cloth, a couple of chairs, and a bright-blue awning.

Thankful she'd decided to pay an extra fifty bucks for the canopy — the glaring sun would have been brutal without any shade — she gestured to Ivy and said, "This is us."

"Not a bad spot." Ivy looked around,

beaming at the two fraternity brothers proudly wearing their letters in the booth to her right and the trio of guys representing the intramural soccer league to her left.

Dani snickered. "Yeah. I picked it just for your enjoyment."

She squatted in front of her cart, searching for the white banner printed with her business name and logo — a red chef's hat. Once she located it, she unfolded the sign and began attaching it to the front of the table using the Velcro tabs glued to the back of the plastic.

When Dani noticed that Ivy was just standing still and exchanging smiles with the occupants of their neighboring booths, she poked her and said, "Set up the collapsible easels. Put the pictures of the lunches we offer on one and the poster with the information regarding availability, location, and price of our lunch-to-goes on the other."

"Will do." Ivy flipped her long blond hair over her shoulder, shot the frat boys a take-no-prisoners smile, and got to work.

While Ivy put up the signs, Dani fanned flyers across the tabletop. She paused. Should she place the baskets of promotional items out now or wait until they got back with the samples?

She eyed the huge swarm of students behind the strip of yellow tape waiting for the starting horn to sound. Definitely wait.

"Let's go get the food." Dani worried her bottom lip. "But we have to hurry. If we don't make it here before they let the kids in, we'll never get through the crowd with the carts."

Ivy followed Dani's gaze and said, "Lead on. I'm right behind you."

They made a speedy round-trip and were placing platters of samples on their table by the time the beginning buzzer was sounded. As the students surged forward, the noise level was off the charts and the odor of so many sweaty bodies pressed together was enough to make a gym rat faint.

The Chef-to-Go booth was one of the few serving food and lines quickly formed. Ivy was kept busy replenishing the trays of tasty treats as they disappeared down the hungry mouths of the students, while over the excited voices of the crowd surrounding them, Dani explained the details of the lunch plan to each new group that made it to the front of the queue.

When the mob finally thinned to an occasional straggler and the frat guys once again began to vie with the soccer players for Ivy's attention, Dani hid her smile. It had only been a few months since her young friend had tried to bargain her academic talent for a chance to observe how a popular girl attracted the opposite sex.

While Dani admired Ivy's mathematical genius, her own understanding of math having stopped once the alphabet decided to get involved, she was glad to see her friend had become more socially adept. Ivy had always been beautiful, with long, blond hair, baby-blue eyes, and a bubbly personality. However, having skipped two grades, the nineteen-year-old college senior had always been one of the youngest in her class, which resulted in a certain naïveté about the whole dating scene. Dani wasn't sure if Ivy actually learned the art of flirtation from the other girl, or if she'd just gained the necessary confidence to open herself up to the possibilities.

While Ivy chatted with the boys, Dani glanced at her watch. Officially, they had another thirty minutes, but it was clear that there wouldn't be many more students coming down the walkway. Making an executive decision not to wait, she started to pack up.

As Dani began placing the remaining flyers in a box, the woman who had been working the table across from the Chef-to-Go booth approached her and said, "Hi.

Four hours of smelling all your wonderful samples has made me ravenous. I've been drooling over your food all afternoon."

"There's not much left, but feel free to try it." Dani held out her hand. "I'm Danielle Sloan, owner, chef, and chief bottle washer."

"I'm Hilary Newcastle, owner, stylist, and chief shampooer of Holy Snips." The attractive thirtysomething brunette grinned and shook Dani's hand.

"Is that the salon in the old Lutheran church?" Dani asked.

Tippi had mentioned having her hair cut and highlighted there. She'd been impressed with both the stylist and the reasonable prices. Dani had thought about stopping by herself, but with Tippi's wealthy upbringing, her idea of what was reasonable and Dani's were usually pretty far apart.

"It is." Hilary nabbed an oatmeal carmelita sample and, before popping it into her mouth, added, "The university sold it to me about four years ago. With it being on the edge of college grounds, it's the perfect site to appeal to students and staff."

"I know what you mean. Location is so important for a successful business." Dani took down one of the posters and started folding its easel. "I run my company from a place that's nearly smack-dab in the middle

27

between the student apartments and the campus."

"Well, I'd be willing to walk farther than that if these cookie things are any indication of what you serve." Hilary picked up a napkin and wiped her fingers, then grabbed a tiny paper cup full of broccoli-and-cashew slaw. After she finished eating the salad, she asked, "How did you nab such a good setting?"

"Nearly a year ago, out of the blue, I inherited a bed-and-breakfast from a woman named Geraldine Cook." Dani shook her head. "She was my late grandmother's sorority sister, and they'd made some kind of deal to look out for each other's families."

"Wow!" Hilary's eyes widened. "How lucky can you get?"

"Actually, it was like the stars all aligned for me because I was unemployed at the time." Dani shook her head again. "A few weeks before I found out about Mrs. Cook's bequest, I had resigned my position in the human resources department of Homeland Insurance. When I received that unexpected windfall, I decided that instead of looking for a new job, I'd take advantage of it and try to have the life that I always wanted."

"If you always wanted to be a chef," Hilary asked, "why didn't you before?"

"If my father hadn't insisted that I go to college, I would have attended culinary school, but —" *Oops!* She didn't want to talk about her dad so she hurriedly said, "I moved into the partly renovated mansion as soon as the will was settled and started my food company. It took more courage than I knew I had to give up the idea of a steady salary, good benefits, and a nice pension to take a chance on living out my dream, but I've never regretted putting away my suits and heels and turning my back on the corporate world."

"Good for you." Hilary smiled. "I felt the same way."

"You mean when you opened your own salon?"

"Uh-huh." Hilary tilted her head. "You know, you've got really gorgeous hair. I can tell your dark amber-blond color is natural, but how about the curls?"

"It's all me." Dani touched her ponytail. "I'm not crazy about the curls, but I don't have the time or income to get the expensive cuts I used to get that allowed me to style it any other way."

"Maybe we can work out some kind of barter system." Hilary browsed the remaining samples. "My daughter, Crystal, is turning six this coming Saturday and I'd love to have help with her party. If you waive your usual fee to cook and serve, I'll give you eight free haircuts."

"I don't know." Dani tucked the easel and poster away and started dismantling the table's banner. "I'm pretty busy this week and —"

"I'll throw in one special occasion shampoo, blowout, and style," Hilary bargained. "Good anytime for the next year and a half."

"No offense." Dani folded the banner and put it on the rolling cart's bottom shelf. "What if I don't like how you cut my hair?"

"Fine," Hilary huffed. "I'll do a demo cut for you tomorrow."

"How many are you expecting at your daughter's party?" Dani asked, tempted by Hilary's offer.

It would be so nice to get a really good cut again. And if she ever went out on an important date, it'd be terrific to have someone style her hair for her.

An image of Spencer dressed in a perfectly tailored black suit escorting her into a fancy Chicago restaurant flashed through Dani's mind. She sighed and shoved that fantasy away. His continued absence made it pretty darn clear that he had no interest in pursuing any kind of relationship with her beyond the one forced on them because of her connection with his niece.

"Thirty-two. No, wait, thirty-four including me and my daughter," Hilary answered quickly, as if she could tell Dani was weakening. "Twenty-two kids and twelve adults."

"Wow! You must have a lot of family in the area." Dani had been expecting about a third of that number, or maybe half at the most.

"No. It's just me and my daughter, but she has a big heart and didn't want to leave out any of her classmates," Hilary said with a fond expression.

"How about your daughter's father?" Dani wanted to make sure the count was correct.

"He's not a part of our lives." Hilary stared into space, her gaze inscrutable, then she winked and said, "We're better off without him. Husbands are like lawn mowers. They're hard to start, give off noxious fumes, and half the time they don't work."

"I've never been married so I wouldn't know." Dani's cheeks quivered as she tried to keep back the laughter, but a giggle escaped. And then another and another until she finally gained control and continued, "Not that you don't make it sound attractive."

"Thanks." Hilary smiled smugly. "If I save one woman from making the same mistake as I did, it's worth it."

Deciding it was time to change the subject, Dani asked, "What were you thinking of serving?" Then, afraid the woman's plans might be too elaborate, she added, "Or I could give you a suggestion based on the theme if you've chosen something already."

"I'm doing a princess motif," Hilary explained. "I rented a bouncy castle and ordered a cool smoke-breathing-dragon cake." She paused. "Could you do a sort of medieval kind of lunch, but with food kids would like?"

"Hmm." Dani tapped her chin, then smiled. "How about flatbread pizza, a cheese and fruit platter, turkey drumsticks, and mini tarts?"

"Perfect. And the kids will love eating with their hands." Hilary frowned, then tilted her head and bargained, "If you'll pick up all the food you'll need, I'll pay for it."

"Okay . . ." Dani drawled out the word, encouraging Hilary to explain.

"The thing is" — Hilary's olive cheeks turned pink — "I might have just a tiny bit of road rage when I get behind a shopping cart. I've been banned by two supermarkets."

"No." Dani's eyebrows rose. "What did you do?"

"There may have been a few incidents of ramming people in my way." Hilary smoothed the sleeves of her blouse and didn't meet Dani's eyes. "And the guy using the motorized cart was not handicapped. You should have seen how fast he jumped up and ran away when my cart clipped him."

"All righty then." Having no real response to that statement, Dani moved on. "And, if I do cater your daughter's party, I will definitely do the shopping."

"Great." Hilary smiled serenely. "What time do you want to come in for your cut tomorrow?"

Dani took out her phone and brought up her schedule. She had lunch-to-go to prepare, but the much lower numbers before classes started meant she'd be finished by twelve thirty. And although she was catering an orientation week dinner for the band, it wasn't until six.

"How about one thirty?" Dani suggested. "But I have to be back home no later than three."

"That'll work." Hilary snagged the one remaining mini beef sandwich, and as she returned to her table, she said, "See you tomorrow."

Waving, Dani started loading the dirty trays and plastic containers onto the second rolling cart. She opened her mouth to call Ivy over to help, but before she could speak, the girl's phone chirped.

Dani watched as Ivy slipped it from the pocket of her jeans and swiped the screen. Her young friend's smile gave away the caller's identity.

Ivy looked at Dani, her eyes sparkling, and asked, "Are we almost through here?"

"Yep." Dani gestured to the fully loaded carts. "You just need to help me get these to the van and you're officially off duty."

"Awesome." Ivy's thumbs flew over her cell phone's screen. "Laz asked if he can pick me up early for his family's cocktail party at the library. He wants to introduce me to his parents before the speeches start."

Lazarus Hunter's grandfather had provided the funds for NU's new library and the ribbon cutting was that evening. With Laz and Ivy seeing each other, although neither of them admitted that they were anything other than friends, Dani had been hoping to get the catering contract for the event. She'd been disappointed when she'd lost it to a more established company, but considering how many other jobs she had scheduled for the week, it was probably better for her sanity that she hadn't gotten the gig.

"Meeting the parents, huh?" Dani teased. "That makes me totally believe you two aren't dating."

"We aren't," Ivy protested.

"Uh-huh."

"Anyway." Ivy rolled her eyes. "It'll take me a while to get dressed since I still haven't decided what to wear."

"Then we'd better shake a leg." Dani scanned their booth, and once she was satisfied she hadn't left anything behind, she grabbed one of the carts' handles. Dani made sure Ivy was following her with the other cart before leading the way to the parking lot.

It only took a few minutes to reach the van, load up, and head home. The streets were still crowded, but once again the mansion's proximity to the campus paid off and they were pulling into the driveway while Ivy was still debating the merits of her blue-and-white-striped one-shoulder dress versus her pink strapless sheath for the grand-opening party at the library.

As they brought everything into the kitchen, Ivy finally took a breath and Dani was able to voice her opinion. "I like them both, but the striped dress might be a little too quirky for the occasion."

"Because of the one sleeve and the big bow?" Ivy puckered her brow.

"Uh-huh." Dani didn't want to say anything that would lessen her friend's confidence, but she also didn't want to give Laz's family any reason not to like Ivy. "Although you look absolutely adorable in the striped dress, the pink one is more elegant."

"I see what you mean." Ivy tilted her head. "How about shoes?"

"Your bone-colored sandals," Dani said without hesitation. After living with the girls for the past few months, she knew what was in their wardrobes almost as well as what was in her own. "They have a nice heel that isn't too high. You'll be on your feet for several hours and you don't want to be in pain the whole evening." Dani added, "If you want, you can wear my diamond hoops."

"Seriously?" Ivy squealed, clapping her hands. When Dani nodded, she hugged her and said, "You are the best." Darting out of the kitchen, Ivy turned her head and yelled, "I promise to be super careful."

Dani's chest tightened. It was good to see Ivy so happy. Laz was proving to be a nice guy. Dani hadn't been too sure about him when she'd first met him, especially since he'd been one of her prime suspects in his fiancée's murder. But, even though he was from an extremely wealthy family, he seemed to be down-to-earth and working hard to better himself. More importantly, he treated Ivy very well. At least so far.

After washing all the trays and plastic containers she'd used to store and serve the samples, Dani put everything away. With the kitchen tidy and ready for next morning's lunch-to-go preparations, Dani thought about what she needed to accomplish next.

She had most of tomorrow night's band dinner already prepped to cook at the venue. They had requested an Italian theme and she was making lasagna rolls, chicken cacciatore, chopped salad, and garlic knots. She planned to make the dessert, fig and parmesan cheesecake, later that night. However, there was always some chore waiting to be done and she wasn't one to sit around.

With Ivy upstairs getting ready for her big evening and the other two girls not due back to the mansion for several hours, Dani mentally ran through her to-do list. When the memory of Ivy and Deuce in the carriage house popped into Dani's head, she grabbed her clipboard. Not that she thought the homeless veteran was a thief, but with Ivy's propensity for giving stuff away to the needy, it was probably a good idea to do a thorough inventory of the supplies.

Dani changed into shorts and an old tank top, then headed out to the carriage house. When she'd realized that it would be at least a year or more before she could afford to convert the structure into apartments, Dani'd had an air-conditioning unit and metal shelving installed. The shelves were filled with all the nonperishable ingredients and disposables that she bought in bulk.

Twisting her hair into a messy bun on top of her head, Dani headed down the far aisle. Here, she kept the fifty-pound bags of various flours. To get the best deal, she had to purchase sixty bags at a time and she had a lot of money invested in these supplies.

Dani had worked her way through the first set of shelves and was busy counting bottles of spices and herbs when she heard the roar of an engine outside the carriage house. Hoping that it was either Tippi or Starr returning early and willing to help with the inventory, Dani tossed down her clipboard and hurried to the door.

Instead of Starr's cute little MINI Cooper or the sleek Lexus that Tippi's family leased for her to use, there was a beat-up Dodge

Charger idling in the driveway. One of the headlights was missing and the other bore a spiderweb of cracks. Dani couldn't tell what color the original paint job had been because of the gray filler covering most of the metal.

The dark tint on the glass made it impossible to see who was inside the car, and when the driver's side door opened, Dani instinctively took a step back. But it wasn't until she got a good look at the driver's face that she screamed.

Although she'd been worried that the Dodge's owner might be dangerous, she hadn't been expecting a zombie.

CHAPTER 3

Spencer Drake crouched behind the makeshift screen he'd constructed from loose branches and leaves, thinking about how much he hated orientation week. The first day was always bad, and with the prelaw fraternity's 5K fun-run fundraiser scheduled throughout the campus on Friday, it would only get worse.

Normalton University's administration was hypersensitive during this time of year when the new students and their parents were first introduced to the school. Yes, most of them had visited NU before deciding to enroll, but this week's experience was so much more intense and a lot less controlled than the short tour that gave only a fleeting impression and rarely allowed the potential freshman or their folks to hear any campus gossip.

During orientation week, an incident that would ordinarily be considered a minor annoyance by the powers that be could cause outright alarm. And a panicky administration quickly developed into a huge freaking pain in Spencer's butt.

Take, for instance, his current surveillance of NU's Blackheart Canal. The shallow channel was situated between the main campus and a real estate development where many of the university's upper echelon lived alongside the most successful of the business owners who ran companies that catered to the students.

There were pathways on either side of the canal and it was a popular location for the collegians to take a romantic stroll at twilight. However, recently, reports had been trickling into the security office that couples had been frightened by something lurking beneath the surface of the water.

The administration was petrified that the Creature from the Blackheart Canal, as students had taken to calling the thing they'd seen, would appear at an inopportune moment and terrify a timid freshman into withdrawing from school. Or worse yet, that freshman's parents would hear about the alleged monster and refuse to pay their child's tuition until the scary beast was caught.

As the sun dipped lower in the sky and

41

the shadows lengthened, Spencer gripped the binoculars and kept his gaze glued to the north end of the channel. It was at that location, near the aerators, that the creature had been spotted rising out of the spraying water, clutching what the kids claimed looked like an old, bent sword.

Sweat trickling down his armpits, Spencer shifted slightly, careful to avoid the thorny tentacles of the brambles growing among the trees. He snorted a derisive chuckle at the absurdity of his situation. He was a grown man and he knew there was no creature living in the canal. Whatever had been sighted was more likely to be some dumb-ass kid playing a prank than some monster from a horror movie.

And even though he knew it was a colossal waste of his time, he also knew that he'd sit there being eaten by mosquitos and inhaling the odor of decaying vegetation because it was his duty. He'd taken the job of chief of NU security, and it was his responsibility to put a stop to whoever was behind the "creature's" presence.

Hearing laughter, Spencer looked to his left. A young man was hunched into the classic Frankenstein pose and chasing his giggling girlfriend.

The guy thundered in a fake bass, "You

better run, missy, or the Creature from the Blackheart Canal will get you and drag you off to his underwater lair."

Shit! Spencer ground his teeth. All he needed was for the college kids to make this into some kind of game or urban legend. Next thing you know, a drunken frat boy would decide to dive down to find the creature's hideaway and manage to drown in six feet of water.

It really was too bad that there was no antibiotic that would cure stupid. If there were such a medication, Spencer would be willing to spend a good portion of his budget inoculating every student enrolled in the college.

When the pair disappeared around a bend, Spencer returned to watching for the creature. As he gazed at the canal, the idea of college students acting foolishly made him think of his niece and her friends and how they ended up living with Dani Sloan in her inherited mansion.

A few months ago, when Dani had become the target of a corrupt cop, Spencer had stepped in to straighten things out. He'd had no intention of forming any kind of attachment to the woman, but he'd made that decision before he saw her. Back when he'd pictured Dani as Flo from the insurance ads.

Instead, Dani had turned out to be more like the gorgeous, curvy blond from the Dove soap commercial and Spencer had had to fight his strong attraction to her. He was far from being ready for a romantic relationship and had vowed not to rush into things ever again.

Been there done that but didn't even have the T-shirt. His ex-wife had doubtlessly stolen it, along with nearly all of the rest of his assets, before running off with his best friend.

Hell! It had been the end of July before he'd finally been completely free from his ex. Even though she'd managed to make off with most of his money before he even realized she was cheating on him, up until last month, they'd still been arguing about the few possessions she hadn't been able to transfer into her name.

Thinking about how blind he'd been about his ex, he remembered something a buddy had said to him just before his wedding. Marriage is a three-ring circus — engagement ring, wedding ring, and then suffering. He'd thought the man had been joking, but he'd been wrong in discounting his pal's warning.

44

Spencer shook his head. The poor choices he'd made in his life were legion.

Just then, an image of Dani with a hurt look on her face popped into his mind. Guilt stabbed him like a steak knife driven into his ribs, and he cringed at his behavior.

Although he wasn't ready to start dating again, he had intended to keep in touch, hoping to establish a friendship with her. And if that worked out, maybe in a year or so, he'd ask her out.

Unfortunately, during the past couple of months, events had conspired to keep Spencer away from the pretty chef. Initially, he'd been tied up driving back and forth to Chicago to close on the sale of his condo. Missing paperwork had stalled the proceedings the first time, then on the second attempt, there'd been a problem with the buyer's loan, but the last Friday of July, they'd finally completed the deal.

There hadn't been much cash after the mortgage was paid off, and what there was he'd had to split with his ex. But at least he no longer had to pay for home insurance, property taxes, or HOA fees.

And when Spencer finally didn't have to travel into the city anymore, there had been one crisis after another at the college. A student had gone missing from his summer

45

school classes and his parents were unwavering in their belief that he'd been kidnapped. The father had even brought up the idea of alien abduction.

However, after an exhaustive search, the kid had turned up in Florida. He'd decided that his life's goal was to work as a costumed character in a theme park, but he hadn't thought it necessary to tell anyone about his change of plans.

Then there was the rumor trending on social media about a group of students planning to kill themselves on the eighteenth of August. Spencer and his security team had been frantically trying to track down the location of the mass suicide.

When they eventually did find out where the gruesome affair was supposed to take place and showed up on the day it was scheduled, they found a flash mob gathered to raise awareness for depression. Evidently, the security officer that Spencer had put in charge of monitoring the web hadn't done a thorough search and never saw the initial posting that described the event.

Then, just when Spencer thought he'd have some free time to drop in on Dani, this Creature from the Blackheart Canal bullshit had popped up, and the college admins had ordered him to make it his top priority. Now he was afraid it had been too long since he'd stopped by to see her.

Blowing hot and cold during the time they'd spent together investigating Regina Bourne's murder had probably already put him on the pretty chef's shit list, and doubtlessly she'd be even more ticked off after his recent disappearing act.

He'd hoped to keep up their connection, during his weekly text to check on his niece, but Dani's responses had been fairly terse. Then again, his messages probably hadn't been much better.

Hell! Maybe he should have included an emoji or two. But which one meant *I like you and want to be friends with the possibility of more someday?* Was that the cat face wearing sunglasses, or maybe the one with the hand that looks like it was waving?

Pondering how to approach Dani after two months of near silence, Spencer suddenly realized that it was dark. According to the reports he'd gotten, the creature didn't appear after twilight, and the moon was now shining down on the water. In the past hours, the only thing he'd seen were flirting couples and swarms of bugs. He was more than ready to call it a night and grab a cold one.

Spencer stood from his crouch and

stretched the kinks out of his back. Next time, he was bringing a chair. After dismantling branches and leaves, he scattered them around so that no trace of his observation spot remained.

He had just begun to slip his binoculars into their holder when his handheld radio squawked. He finished the task, hung the case around his neck, then keyed the mic and said, "Drake here. What's up?"

Robert Porter, one of Spencer's younger recruits, cleared his throat. "Chief."

"Yes?"

"I know you told us not to break radio silence unless it was an emergency." Robert's voice had gone up as if asking a question.

"I did." Spencer held on to his patience. Robert was a good kid but still a little green. "So, I assume this is an emergency."

"Uh." Robert cleared his throat again. "I think so, sir. I mean, it's pretty serious. At least, I think you'd think it was important."

"Okay." Spencer's gut tightened. What in Sam Hill had gone wrong now? "Let's hear it and I'll let you know if I agree with you."

"There's been a carjacking," Robert said, then added, "On campus."

"Has local law enforcement been informed?" Spencer tensed.

Robert's father was married to the chief of the Normalton Police Department, which could make things easier or more difficult, depending on Robert's relationship with his stepmother. Spencer had been meaning to talk to the young man about how he got along with his father's wife, but now wasn't the time to have that conversation.

"Yes," Robert answered. "I mean, no." He sucked in a breath. "Actually, the police informed us. The driver who was carjacked called them."

"Was anyone hurt?" Spencer hurriedly finished stowing his gear in his backpack and jogged toward where he'd left his truck.

"The victim didn't resist and they didn't touch her, so physically she's fine," Robert answered. "But she was emotionally shaken up."

"Not resisting is the smart thing to do in that type of situation." Spencer arrived at his truck, unlocked the doors, and threw his backpack onto the passenger seat. "The only time we recommend otherwise is if the perps tried to abduct her."

"The thing is, sir . . ." Robert paused. "I think you know the victim."

"Who is it?" Spencer kept his tone even, but his pulse raced.

"Tippi Epstein," Robert reported. "Isn't

49

she a friend of Ivy's?"

"How do you know that?" Spencer narrowed his eyes. He liked to keep his personal life separate from his job, and he was uncomfortable with the knowledge that one of his security officers brought up his niece.

There was an audible gulp, then a long stretch of silence. Spencer wondered if the young guard had dropped his radio or maybe passed out.

Just as Spencer was about to check that Robert was still there, the guy stuttered, "I . . . I must have overheard you mention something about your niece and her friends."

"You mean you eavesdropped on my private conversation with someone else?" Spencer snapped, his bad mood getting the best of him.

"No, sir!" Robert sputtered. "I would never." He hesitated, then tried again. "Maybe you said something in the break room about Ivy's friends."

"I don't hang out in the break room." Spencer felt his presence would inhibit the men and they wouldn't be able to relax.

"Then . . . then . . ." Robert groaned. "Oh hell!" There was another long silence, then he said, "Actually, I'm sort of seeing another of your niece's friends, so that's how I know about Tippi."

For a split second, jealousy burned in Spencer's chest. Was Robert dating Dani? Forcing himself to think about it rationally, he considered the facts. Dani was twenty-nine, turning thirty in November, which would make her eight years older than Robert. Would she be romantically interested in someone that young and inexperienced?

Robert was a good kid but not particularly mature for his age. His hobbies were video games and getting together with his buddies to watch sports. Would Dani want to spend time with someone like that?

No! Spencer huffed. He was an idiot. It had to be Starr Fleming. Why hadn't he thought of her right away? Robert was taking some classes at the university, a perk of being employed by the school, and he'd probably met Starr that way. She was the only logical choice. Why had he jumped straight to Dani? Was it because he was worried she'd find someone else while he was still trying to get his head together?

Realizing that, this time, he'd been the one who was silent for too long, Spencer said, "I'm coming into the office for a full report. Make sure you have it ready."

Putting his pickup in reverse, he backed out onto the street and drove the short

51

distance between the canal and his office. Less than five minutes later, he pulled into his reserved parking spot and jumped out of the truck. He hit the lock button on his key fob and headed inside.

Spencer's thoughts were on the carjacking, but as he marched down the sidewalk toward the heavy metal doors of the campus security building, he jerked to halt.

"What the f—" Spencer growled. Someone had taped a sheet of paper to the door's window. It featured a reptilian-like monster and the words *Tour of the Blackheart Canal. Guaranteed sighting of the creature. Reserve your time now. $15 per person. Two for $20. www.creaturefromtheblackheartcanal.com.*

Clearly, it was time to have another conversation with his staff about including their own perimeter in their routine patrols. Did he really have to spell out that this kind of thing wasn't allowed on campus? And that it should never have been taped to their own door?

Spencer tore down the poster, then marched into the break room. No one was there, so he took a calming breath and sent out a group text to his officers instructing them to remove all notices for the Blackheart Canal tour. A second message offered a reward of an additional day of paid vaca-

52

tion to the guard who found out the identity of the twit conducting the creature tours.

After feeding a dollar into the soda machine, Spencer rubbed his eyes while waiting for his Mountain Dew to emerge. When it finally slid into the opening, he grabbed it, popped the tab, and chugged half the can. The cold beverage eased his parched throat but did nothing for his headache.

Sighing, he proceeded to his office and dug out a bottle of ibuprofen from his desk drawer. Once he'd swallowed a couple of the capsules, he sat down and summoned Robert.

The room was tiny, with barely enough space to walk from the file cabinet to the bookcase. When Spencer had come on board, he could have claimed one of the large conference areas for his office, but since he hadn't planned on spending much time sitting on his butt behind a desk, he was fine with the smaller space.

Since assuming the chief of security position, Spencer had done little to put his personal stamp on the office or make it comfortable. But now, as the young man squeezed into the folding chair opposite Spencer's desk and perched on the edge, he wished there was a little more distance between them. Robert's obvious case of nerves triggered something inside of Spencer.

Although he'd been out of the business for more than a year, after being undercover for so long, he was finely attuned to others' emotions and he itched to grab his Glock. He wouldn't, of course, but he did casually reach down and pat his ankle holster.

While Spencer was licensed for concealed carry, the rest of campus security weren't allowed guns. They were equipped with Tasers and pepper spray but nothing more lethal. And his officers had no reason to be aware that, due to his past, Spencer was always armed.

The only person who knew exactly who Spencer had worked for or the nature of his previous job was his boss, the university vice president. And even she knew only a part of the truth. He had helped put away too many outlaw bikers ever to be entirely safe.

If it ever became common knowledge that Spencer had been the Tin Man, a member of the infamous Satan's Posse, the gang would descend on Normalton like an invading army. And they wouldn't leave until he and a lot of innocent bystanders were dead.

When he'd come out from undercover, the story had been circulated that the Tin Man had been shanked in prison and died.

There was even a small marker on an empty grave in the penitentiary cemetery to prove he was six feet under. And it was best for everyone concerned that the Tin Man was never resurrected.

Back in control, Spencer crossed his arms and said, "Report."

"At 3:12 p.m., Tippi Epstein was approached in the stadium's annex parking lot by two men wearing rubber masks over their heads." Robert shifted in his seat, his long legs bumping into the front of Spencer's desk. "They claimed to be armed and demanded her purse and her keys. She handed them over and they drove off in her brand-new Lexus. The vehicle is valued at over ninety thousand and she had about fifty in cash. The Lexus is leased to her mother. Mrs. Epstein is a DuPage County judge."

Robert paused and ran his fingers through his hair, making the black strands stand on end.

When he remained silent, Spencer said, "Go on."

"Luckily, Tippi — I mean, Ms. Epstein — had her cell in her pocket and phoned the police. When they arrived, they took her to the station. After she gave them her statement, she called a friend for a ride home."

Robert glanced up from his notes. "The police officer who caught the case then phoned campus security to inform us that a crime had taken place on university property."

"Right."

"He also told me that there have been a series of carjackings in Normalton." Robert's dark-brown eyes shone with concern. "There also have been subsequent break-ins at the residences of the victims."

"Because" — Spencer's jaw tightened — "they have the victims' key rings and wallets with their addresses."

"Exactly." Robert screwed up his face. "The officer did warn Ms. Epstein to change her locks, but he wasn't sure she took him seriously."

"Awesome. Just freaking awesome." Spencer got to his feet. "I'll head over to her place and make sure she follows through."

He'd wanted an excuse to see Dani again, but this sure wasn't what he had in mind.

CHAPTER 4

It had taken Dani only a few seconds to realize that the zombie emerging from the Dodge Charger in her driveway was really just a young man dressed in a tattered Western-style suit and wearing a lot of extremely good stage makeup. It had taken quite a bit longer for her to realize that the zombie cowboy wasn't alone.

In fact, until he opened the passenger door and helped Tippi out of the vehicle, Dani hadn't even been aware that her boarder was sitting in the Charger. Between the Charger's darkly tinted windows and the girl's absolute immobility, Tippi had been darn near invisible to anyone standing several feet away from the car.

When Dani's rush of questions had resulted in Tippi staring blankly into space and dead silence, the zombie had stuck out a large hand and introduced himself. "Hi, Miz Sloan. I'm Caleb Boyd, a friend of Miss

Tippi's from her prelaw fraternity."

"Nice to meet you, Caleb. Call me Dani." She had automatically responded to his polite introduction. The surreal scene had made her head spin and it had taken her a moment to ask, "What's up with Tippi?"

"Please excuse my appearance." Caleb touched his forehead as if reaching for an imaginary cowboy hat to tip. "Our fraternity has organized a zombie 5K run to raise funds for our organization's philanthropic cause. It's scheduled for Friday and I'm supposed to be out advertising it among the freshman and their parents."

"I see." Dani tucked away that piece of information and said, "But why isn't Tippi talking?"

"All I know is that she was carjacked. She called me for a ride home but hasn't said a word since I picked her up." Caleb edged back toward his car. "I really don't have other details and I have to get going."

After Caleb had taken off, Dani had guided Tippi into the mansion, where she had retreated to her room mumbling something about needing to be alone. Dani had contemplated contacting Tippi's parents. But the girl hadn't been hurt and it was really up to her when or if to tell her folks what had happened. If it had been Ivy, Dani would have definitely texted Spencer, but Tippi was twenty-one and Dani didn't feel right acting as if she were the girl's nanny.

Now, several hours later, as Dani sifted together the flour and baking powder for the fig and parmesan cheesecakes that would make up tomorrow night's band dinner dessert, she wondered if she should check on Tippi. She'd said she wasn't hungry when Dani called her for dinner and she hadn't come out of her room since she'd returned to the mansion.

A few seconds ago, Dani had heard the pump start running, which usually meant someone in the house was taking a bath or shower. Since she and Tippi were the only ones home, at least she knew the girl was alive.

Opening the refrigerator to check if the melted butter that she'd brushed on the parchment lining the bottom of the spring-form pans had solidified, Dani spotted a bowl of whipped cream. Maybe the girl would come downstairs if she smelled coffee brewing in the Ninja Coffee Bar. The machine had been a housewarming gift from her boarders' parents, and although Dani hadn't had time to explore all its capabilities yet, she had mastered espresso con panna, a shot of espresso with a layer of whipped cream on top.

Dani placed a small cup on the metal platform, ground the coffee beans, and loaded them into the filter basket. Adjusting the controls for a three-ounce serving, she pressed the specialty brew button. While she waited for the machine to perform its magic, she beat eggs and sugar together until they were light and fluffy. To the soundtrack of the Ninja's rhythmic hum, she slowly added milk and cream, making sure each one was thoroughly incorporated.

Next, Dani whisked in the Parmesan that she had grated earlier and then stirred in the flour mixture, finally adding melted butter, vanilla, and kirsch. After dusting the bottom of the springform pans with flour, she filled them with the batter, then placed fig halves evenly over the surface.

As she was sprinkling the top with sesame seeds, the Ninja sputtered to a stop. She placed the cheesecakes in the oven and set the timer, then carefully lifted the filled cup, breathed in the wonderful coffee aroma, and added the layer of whipped cream on top before walking out of the kitchen and down the hallway.

When the doorbell rang before she reached the stairs, Dani made a face and muttered to herself, "Who in the heck is stopping by this late? It better not be Starr forgetting her key again."

Dani considered ignoring it, but as she hesitated, the bell rang again, followed a few seconds later by several loud knocks. Frowning in annoyance, she placed the espresso on a nearby table and hurried across the foyer.

When Dani saw Spencer Drake peering through the side window, she skidded to a stop. For a moment, as he stood under the porch light, around him the whole world turned gray, leaving only Spencer still in color. Dani's chest spasmed like a defibrillator had delivered a dose of electric current to her heart and she forgot how to breathe.

Coming back to reality — the reality of Spencer's unexplained disappearance from her life — Dani was tempted turn away and pretend no one was home. Then she realized that after two months of basically ignoring her, it was highly unlikely that his visit was personal, and disappointment shot her in the heart.

Doubtlessly, as head of campus security, he was there because of Tippi's carjacking. With that in mind, she would treat him the same way she would treat any of the girl's relatives. Cordial and professional. She was his niece's landlady and nothing more.

Taking a deep breath, Dani reminded herself it wasn't as if they'd been dating. Then, plastering an impassive expression on her face, she opened the door.

When he didn't say anything, Dani said in a cool voice, "Ivy isn't here."

At her detached statement, something flickered behind his blue eyes and she noticed a slight tightening around his mouth, but his tone was neutral when he said, "I'm not here to see my niece. I wanted to make sure that Tippi told you that you need to change your locks."

"Why would I have to do that?" Dani crossed her arms and waited for his explanation.

"May I come in?"

Spencer's low voice washed over Dani like a warm drink and she reflexively moved back. Waving him inside, she said, "Be my guest."

"You're aware that Tippi was carjacked?" Spencer crossed the threshold, but then just stood there looking as if he was unsure of his welcome.

"Yes. But just the basics. The guy who dropped her off told me what little he knew, but Tippi's been holed up in her room ever since she got home." Dani glanced at the table holding the tiny cup. "I was just about to try to lure her out with espresso con panna when you rang my doorbell."

"I'd like to talk to her." Spencer seemed to hesitate, then looked at Dani and said, "But before I do, I'll tell you what I know."

"Okay." Dani gestured with her chin for him to follow her into the kitchen.

Under the brighter lights, she noticed that Spencer appeared exhausted. His handsome face was lined and there were dark circles under his beautiful blue eyes.

"Are you busy or can I . . ." He glanced at the stools lining the counter and raised a brow.

"Have a seat." Dani's cheeks burned.

She was being rude. She couldn't hold the man's lack of interest in her against him. Just because she was attracted to him didn't mean he had to share her feelings. Silently, she repeated her mantra: *Treat him like any other of the girls' families.*

"Thanks." Sitting down, Spencer took his cell from his pocket and put it on the counter, explaining, "I told my security team to call me if anything else comes up about the carjackings."

"Of course." Dani mentally instructed herself to stop making this so awkward. It wasn't as if Spencer was the first guy she'd been interested in who wasn't interested in her. She forced a pleasant expression and asked, "Would you like something to drink or to eat? I have homemade chicken potpies left over from dinner."

"That would be great." Spencer grinned. "I was on a stakeout so I haven't had a chance to eat supper." He glanced at the fridge. "And if you still have your secret beer stash, I'd love one."

Dani maintained a strict no-alcohol policy for her boarders, but she kept a supply of Corona and a bottle of wine in a compartment under a rack full of water jugs for her own use. Grabbing two bottles, she handed him the beers and an opener. As he uncapped them, she put a potpie into the microwave to heat up.

Once the food was hot, she set it in front of Spencer along with a napkin and a fork. Then she joined him at the counter, carefully leaving an empty stool between them.

As he dug into the flaky pastry, she asked, "So what's this about changing my locks?"

Between bites, he filled her in on the carjackers' modus operandi, ending with, "I take it Tippi didn't mention that the police told her the perps might use her ID and keys to break into her residence?"

"No. She actually hasn't said much to me

at all." Dani took a swallow of beer. "I've been wondering if I should call her folks."

"Hmm."

As he considered what she'd said, Spencer rubbed the sexy stubble on his chin, and Dani closed her eyes. She had to quit thinking about him as a hot guy and put him firmly in the acquaintance category. Which would be a lot easier if he didn't make a nightly appearance in her dreams. Or if he at least wore a shirt during those appearances.

Blinking to get the image of Spencer seminude out of her mind, Dani prodded, "So, do you think I should contact Mr. and Mrs. Epstein or not?"

"My first impulse is to say hell yes." Spencer shook his head. "But Tippi is twenty-one and the only thing you agreed to inform them or the other parents about when she, Starr, and my niece got kicked out of their apartment and moved in here was is if she broke your rules concerning guys and booze."

"Good point." Dani noticed that Spencer had finished his meal and hopped off her stool. After clearing away his plate and disposing of both their beer bottles, she asked, "Do you have room for some dessert?"

"What are you offering?" Spencer asked with a twinkle in his gorgeous dark-blue eyes. Before Dani could think of a response, he added, "I don't suppose you have any of your special mocha cupcakes?"

"Sorry, no." Dani walked over to the commercial-size cooler that occupied a good portion of the kitchen's back wall and slid open the glass door. Reaching in, she took out a dish covered in plastic wrap and asked, "How do you feel about sour cherry pie?"

"Warmly." Spencer beamed. "I would feel very warmly toward a piece of that pie. I used to love it."

"Used to?" Dani took off the plastic wrap and slid the plate in front of him.

"Mom doesn't bake as much as she did when my brother and I were growing up." Spencer picked up his fork, then looked at Dani and winked. "And I'd rather not have it at all if it isn't homemade."

"Well, I hope I can live up to the memory of your mom's pie." Dani's heart warmed at the affection in Spencer's voice when he talked about his mother. "Would you like vanilla ice cream on it?"

"Definitely!" Spencer waited until Dani fetched the carton from the freezer and scooped out a serving, then he dug in, moaning in appreciation as he quickly polished off the entire slice.

Although the sounds he was making made Dani wish they were in a room other than her kitchen, she kept her tone even when she said, "There's one more piece left if you want it."

"As much as I'd love it, I'd better pass." He patted his flat stomach and said, "Much more of your wonderful cooking and I'll need to double up on my gym visits." He paused as if considering the option, then said, "Although, it might just be worth it."

"Let me know if you change your mind or want to take the piece home." Dani sat back down and asked, "Anything more you can tell me about the carjacking? You mentioned that Tippi wasn't the crooks' first victim. Have there been others on campus, or have they all been in town up until now?"

"From what I can gather, previously the carjackers have stuck to the city limits. That's why I wasn't aware of them until tonight." Spencer's mouth thinned. "I need to liaison with the NPD more."

"Do you have the staff to do that?" Dani had no idea how many security officers were on Spencer's team, but her best guess was half a dozen with maybe two or three part-timers to fill in for vacations and illnesses.

"Not really." Spencer made a face. "I'd have to do it myself."

Dani opened her mouth to tell him that he already looked as if he was doing too much but snapped it closed. His well-being wasn't any of her business.

Instead, she said, "Well, if I have to change the locks, *again*" — she emphasized the last word since, a few months ago, after the mansion had been ransacked, Spencer had insisted she get dead bolts on every door — "can you give me the number of the man you called last time?"

"I . . . uh . . . already contacted him." Spencer's expression was a mixture of stubborn and sheepish. When Dani raised a brow, he quickly added, "He's a busy guy and I wanted to make sure he could fit you in first thing in the morning before you had to leave the house."

Dani started to tell him she didn't appreciate his assumption that she needed his help, then shrugged. Was she really angry? A part of her was offended at his high-handedness, but the practical side of her said *What the heck?* It needed to be done. She couldn't risk her boarders' safety. The locksmith had proven to be skillful and reasonable before so she would have used him again. And now, the locks would be changed in time for her to keep her hair appointment.

"Fine," Dani muttered, unwilling to encourage his paternalistic attitude by showing any enthusiasm or gratitude for his actions. "Just what I needed, another expense."

"I could —"

Dani's glare cut him off and they sat unspeaking until the timer beeped. Relieved to have something to do, she jumped up and hurried to the oven. She tested the cheesecakes' centers, and when she found them to be perfect — slightly springy to the touch — she took them from the oven and immediately ran a paring knife around the edges.

She wouldn't remove the side of the mold for a half hour so she turned to Spencer and asked, "Would you like another beer?"

"No, thanks." Spencer shook his head, then fiddled with his fork.

Dani waited for him to get up and leave or ask to see Tippi, but when he remained seated and mute, she searched her mind for a topic of conversation, then just as the silence was getting awkward, they both spoke.

"About —"

They stopped, then a second later, they

both said, "You first. No you."

"One of you, talk." An amused voice from the doorway interrupted their impasse.

Tippi snickered as she strolled into the kitchen holding the cup that Dani had left in the foyer. She marched over to the sink, dumped out the lukewarm beverage, and made herself a fresh cup.

"Sorry to interrupt, but my stomach's growling woke me up." Tippi darted a sly look between Spencer and Dani, a tiny smile curling her lips.

"You didn't interrupt anything." Dani frowned. In appearance, Tippi was a dark-haired little pixie, but her personality was anything but small, and she liked to stir the pot. "Are you feeling better?" Dani asked moving toward the fridge. "I can heat up your dinner if you're hungry, or make you something lighter."

Tippi immediately assumed a fragile air and said weakly, "Toasted cheese and to-mato soup might help make me feel better."

"Have a seat." Spencer gestured to the stool next to him. "I'd like to talk to you about what happened with your car this afternoon."

"I already told the police everything at least ten times." Tippi sat down and scowled at Spencer, her frail act forgotten. "And I'd like to forget it."

"I understand, but it would be helpful if you'd run through everything just once more."

"Fine," Tippi huffed. "But only because you're Ivy's favorite uncle."

"Good enough." Spencer caught Dani's eye and grinned.

While Dani fixed Tippi's supper, she kept an ear on what was being discussed. It sounded pretty straightforward. Tippi had stopped at the stadium to meet with the manager about some last-minute details regarding the prelaw fraternity's fun run. The main parking lot was full so she'd had to leave her Lexus in the annex. When she'd returned to it, two men wearing rubber Halloween masks jumped out from behind the vehicle.

They told her they had a gun and demanded her purse and keys. Once she handed them over, they piled into her Lexus and drove away. When they were out of sight, Tippi pulled her cell phone from her pocket and called the police.

"Can you describe your assailants?" Spencer asked as Dani put a steaming bowl of soup, a plate containing the toasted cheese, and a fresh cup of espresso con panna in front of Tippi. "Anything unusual about them?"

"Tall, at least six foot, and lean. The kind of body a male model might have." Tippi took a bite of her sandwich and chewed thoughtfully. "Otherwise, I couldn't see anything."

"Skin color? Accents?" Spencer asked. "Any differences between the two?"

"They were white." Tippi blew on a spoonful of soup. "I could see their wrists. I didn't hear any kind of accent and there wasn't anything to differentiate them from each other."

"What were they wearing?" Spencer asked.

"They were all in black." Tippi pursed her lips. "Their clothes reminded me of stuff cyclists wear."

"Hmm." Spencer pursed his lips, obviously trying to figure out what the carjackers' wardrobe choice might mean.

"One thing," Tippi said thoughtfully. "Both those guys had an aura of evil. Like they were a demon or something."

"Nah." The corner of Spencer's lips twitched upward. "From what I've heard about the carjackings, the perps know the area." He winked. "And Lucifer's not a local."

Tippi narrowed her eyes, clearly not

amused. But she continued eating without commenting.

After Spencer ran out of questions, Tippi said, "You know, your life really can be changed in just a few seconds by people who don't even know you."

"That's a hard lesson to learn." Dani walked over to the girl and put her arm around Tippi's shoulders. "But a good one to remember."

Tippi nodded. "Time for me to hit the hay. I'm so tired I can't think straight anymore." This time, as she headed to her room, her air of fragility was real.

When Spencer made no move to leave, Dani mentally shrugged and started washing the dishes. When she finished, she removed the sides of the pans from the cheesecakes and covered them in plastic wrap. They were best served at room temperature. Refrigerating them would dull the taste, and they were good up to three days.

As she put away the plastic wrap, a thought popped into her head and she said, "Spencer, you're aware of the homeless camp under the old railroad overpass, right? A couple of blocks from the quad?" When he nodded, she continued, "Ivy has been giving the people there our leftover food, and one of the men mentioned that they'd been having trouble with zombies raiding their camp at midnight."

"Seriously?" Spencer snickered. "I know a lot of those folks have mental health issues, and I don't mean to be insensitive, but that guy sounds full-on crazy."

"That was what I thought until a zombie brought Tippi home." Dani giggled at Spencer's look of astonishment, then hurriedly explained that the prelaw fraternity fundraiser Tippi had mentioned was actually a zombie fun run.

"I knew about the fun run, but no one told me the participants were dressing as zombies." Spencer rubbed the back of his neck. "That should have been on the paperwork they submitted to the university." He frowned. "Could I have missed it?"

Having no answer to that question, Dani continued, "Anyway, it got me thinking, maybe there really were people in zombie makeup harassing the homeless. You know, trying out their costumes before the event? Which would totally be something that should be stopped."

"I agree." Spencer stood. "Those folks have enough problems without some smart-ass kids terrorizing them." He glanced at his watch and smiled at Dani. "It's nearly midnight. Want to take a ride?"

74

CHAPTER 5

With the locks compromised, Dani didn't feel it would be safe to leave Tippi alone without the chains fastened across both doors. Luckily, Starr arrived home while Dani was still cleaning up the kitchen. Once Spencer explained about the stolen keys, Starr promised to secure the mansion and stay awake until Dani returned.

As Spencer helped Dani into his pickup, she pulled at the legs of her denim shorts and tugged at the neckline of her knit shirt. She had put on cutoffs and a tank top to do the inventory and never changed back into her more modest khakis and T-shirt. Now she fretted about the dimples in her thighs and the amount of cleavage on display.

While Spencer was occupied backing his truck out of the driveway, Dani flipped down the visor and frowned at the frizzy tangle of her hair. The passenger window was down and the breeze set her curls blowing across her face. She dug through her purse for a brush and a tie, then smoothed the whole mess into a ponytail.

Glancing over, she saw Spencer watching her from the corner of his eye and her cheeks flamed when he said, "Your hair's gotten longer."

"Yeah, I guess it was a lot shorter the last time you saw it." She slid him a sour look. "A lot changes in a couple of months."

Shoot! She hadn't meant to add that last part. She really needed a speed bump installed between her mouth and her brain.

When Spencer didn't respond, Dani refused to peek at him again and instead picked up the conversation as if she hadn't mentioned his lengthy absence. "I like my hair long so that I can put it up when I'm cooking, but it's gotten out of hand. I haven't had a chance to get to a stylist, but I have an appointment tomorrow."

"I like it this way," Spencer said, flipping on his signal and making a right turn that would take him toward the quad.

"Thanks." Dani shrugged. "But it needs a good trim to take off the split ends and give it some shape." She pressed her lips together to stop herself from rambling. She needed to accept the compliment and move on, but she couldn't stop herself from adding, "I met a woman today who offered me eight free appointments in exchange for catering her daughter's birthday party."

"Isn't she getting the better part of that deal?" Spencer frowned. "How many guests is she expecting at this birthday party?"

"Thirty-four."

"That's a lot." Spencer's eyes widened. "Catering this child's birthday has got to be worth more than just a few haircuts."

"Maybe for a guy." Dani was touched that he was concerned that Hilary might be taking advantage of her. "But a good woman's cut can cost over fifty dollars." Dani twitched her shoulders. "And all I'm doing is cooking. She's paying for the food for the party."

"Hmm." Spencer nodded, then seemed to make a decision and said, "Sorry I haven't been around for the past couple of months or so."

"You've kept up your end of the deal to check in on the girls by texting." Dani plucked at the seat belt, resisting the urge to question his apology.

"But it felt like we were becoming friends." Spencer carefully steered the pickup into the narrow dirt road leading from the quad to the railroad underpass. "I got busy, and before I knew it, months had passed. I didn't intend to just disappear like that."

"That's okay." A reluctant smile broke through Dani's previous irritation at his behavior, but she wiped it off her face. She was dying to demand an explanation but determined to keep her response casual. "Is everything better now?"

"I sure as hell hope so." Spencer gave her a sheepish grin, took a breath, and said, "I think I mentioned when we first met that things were bad with my ex?" When Dani nodded, he went on. "Unfortunately, during the past couple of months, I've been tied up driving back and forth to Chicago to close on the sale of our condo." When she raised an inquiring brow, he added, "There were quite a few screwups that kept us from completing the deal."

"Did you finally get it settled?" Dani wondered if Spencer's ex-wife was making things difficult in order to keep seeing him. It could be her way to try to win him back. Although according to Ivy, the divorce hadn't been amicable, that didn't mean his ex was ready to give up on her claim on the handsome security chief.

"Yeah." Spencer gripped the wheel as the truck bounced across a series of potholes. "But then there was one crisis after another at the college. A student went missing and his parents went ballistic. It took us forever to track him down. The kid had decided that his life's goal was to work as a costumed character in a theme park, but instead of formally dropping out of college and informing his mom and dad that he was moving to Florida, he just disappeared from his apartment in the middle of the night."

"Oh. My. Goodness" Dani could imagine the boy's folks' frantic calls to campus security. "I'll bet there's more to that story."

"Yep." Spencer shook his head. "The kid owed his roommates for the past six months' rent and didn't want to deal with the hassle if they found out ahead of time that he was leaving college."

"Nice kid." Dani snickered. "I can see how that all kept you busy."

"There was also a rumor trending on social media that there was a group of students planning to kill themselves on the eighteenth of August," Spencer interjected. "My cyber guy spent hours and hours attempting to locate where this mass suicide was going to take place. He finally found it a few hours before the incident was scheduled to happen, but when we rushed to the scene, all that was there was this flash mob gathered to raise awareness for depression." Spencer rolled his eyes. "They hoped that by implying mass suicide, TV crews would show up and give them free publicity for their cause."

"Still. Even if it was frustrating, that had to be a relief." Dani shook her head at the idea of such a tragedy. "Are things calmer now?"

"I thought so." Spencer's chuckle was humorless. "But then the Creature from the Blackheart Canal popped up and the college admins got their panties in a twist, afraid that someone might be scared into dropping out or that their parents would withdraw them from school."

"I heard about the creature, but I can't believe that they're taking that rumor seriously." Dani giggled. "I don't envy you your position. I though HR was difficult, but at least none of the employees claimed they were vampires or werewolves."

"Leading a university security team is still a whole heck of a lot easier than my last job." Spencer's expression was sober.

"Really?" Dani raised a brow.

She knew that Spencer had worked undercover for an unnamed law enforcement agency but had no idea what that involved. When he'd mentioned it last time they teamed up on an investigation, he'd said almost everything he'd done was top secret so there wasn't much he could share.

Spencer didn't respond to Dani's subtle encouragement to elaborate and she sighed. Secretive men were not something she tolerated well.

Pulling the pickup to a stop, Spencer switched off the motor, gestured to the homeless camp that sprawled in front of them, and asked, "Have you been here before?"

"No." Dani bit her lip as she gazed at the lean-tos, tents, and huge cardboard boxes that had been erected around a couple of oil drums in the center of the clearing. She noticed even more cobbled together shelters among the trees on either side of the underpass. "It looks pretty quiet though."

The only illumination came from the pickup's headlights and a distant streetlamp, but as far as she could tell, there was no movement.

"Maybe too quiet." Spencer leaned past Dani and popped open the glove compartment. Taking out a flashlight, he said, "Wait here."

"What? No! Why?" Dani grabbed his arm. "Where are you going?"

"It's only a few minutes past midnight and I'm getting a hinky feeling about this place." Spencer gently removed her hand. "There's no way every single person here should be asleep."

"What else is there for them to do?" Dani asked. "There's no TV."

"Look at those oil drums." Spencer pointed toward the middle of the camp.

"What about them?" Dani peered into the semidarkness but didn't notice anything odd about the two metal barrels he was indicating.

"They're smoldering as if someone just dumped water on the fire a few seconds ago." Spencer gestured to the thick column of white smoke.

"Oh." Now that he pointed it out, Dani could smell a combination of burning wood and the sickly sweet odor of pot. With that knowledge, she inspected the camp with fresh eyes. "And it's pretty odd that there isn't a single light flickering anywhere." She leaned out her window. "Or any sounds. Nothing moving. No one snoring."

"Almost as if when they heard my pickup heading this way, they doused the fire and are playing possum." Spencer opened his door. "I'm going to take a walk around and make sure everything's really okay. They may just be leery of strangers, but something could truly be wrong and they're afraid that we're part of the problem."

Dani hesitated, but before Spencer had taken more than a few steps, she hopped out of the truck. She clutched the tiny container of pepper spray attached to her key ring and hurried toward him. The earth beneath her feet was hard packed from the hot, dry spell they'd been having, and her sneakers made a slapping sound on the compressed surface.

Spencer scowled at her and said softly, "I told you to stay in the pickup."

"I considered your suggestion." Dani tilted her head. "And decided against it."

Spencer opened his mouth as if to argue, then sighed. "Stay close." He narrowed his eyes. "And that isn't a suggestion; it's a directive."

Dani fought against the urge to stick out her tongue and tell him that he wasn't the boss of her. Instead, she gave a single nod of agreement.

It wasn't as if she wanted to wander around by herself. Spencer was right. There was a creepy, off-putting vibe and her revved-up heartbeat thudded in her ears.

They should probably just go home. There was no sign of zombies, or any other group harassing the homeless, and it felt intrusive to be walking around their camp. Almost as if they were trespassing.

However, another part of her mind argued with the idea of leaving without finding out what was going on. When else would she have someone like Spencer as backup? And as much as she really wanted to know who or what had been messing around with the unfortunate people forced to live in such a rough and uncomfortable situation, she wasn't foolish enough to come on her own.

A second later the solution dawned on her and she murmured, "Let's find Deuce. Maybe he'll tell us if anything is wrong."

"Why would he be any more willing than the others to talk to us?" Spencer asked, doubt written across his face.

"He should recognize me from this morning," Dani explained. "And I'm counting on that reassuring him that we're not here to stir up any trouble."

"Any idea where his place might be?" Spencer swept his arm around the camp.

As Dani considered what she knew about the man, she studied the rubbish lying on the ground. There were empty beer cans, flattened food wrappers, and used condoms strewn around everywhere. From what little she knew of Deuce, she was fairly sure he wouldn't want to live among this trash.

"I'm guessing the hillside." Dani bit her lip, then added, "We could look for his cart.

It's the flatbed type used in home improvement and big-box stores but painted in a camouflage pattern." Scanning the area, she added, "It seems as if the others all have the usual smaller grocery-store kind."

"Okay. I suppose that's as good a place to start as any," Spencer agreed. "But before we head up that incline, let's do a quick sweep of the main camp."

"Sure." Dani shrugged. "Why not?"

Spencer moved forward between the rows of makeshift shelters with Dani at his side. As they walked, Spencer shined his flashlight in the area surrounding each shelter. Dani noted that he was careful to keep the light aimed at the ground so it wouldn't blind anyone peering out at them.

Several minutes later, they'd made their way through the entire main camp. Dani was herding Spencer toward the hillside campsite when he swore.

Startled, she turned to him and asked, "What happened?"

He pointed to an American flag hung upside down with a swastika painted across it and, between gritted teeth, said, "Anyone who disrespects the flag has never been handed a folded one."

Dani had never seen Spencer so angry. Giving him a chance to cool down, she scanned the area they'd been heading toward before he saw the desecrated Stars and Stripes.

Spotting an olive drab military-style tent off by itself, she said, "Look."

Spencer seemed to come out of his rage-induced trance and peered in the direction she was pointing. "Let's get closer."

The tent was halfway up the incline and obscured with leaf-covered netting stretched between four large trees. As they approached the concealed campsite, Spencer's flashlight beam caught something metal underneath the camouflaging net.

Nudging Spencer with her elbow, Dani gestured. "Over there."

Spencer squinted, then nodded and headed in the direction she indicated.

As they drew nearer, Spencer aimed his flashlight at the campsite. Dani could just make out the cart she'd seen Deuce retrieve from behind her carriage house. While most of it had been painted in a camouflage pattern, the wheel hubs hadn't, and they were what she'd seen reflected by Spencer's flashlight.

She pointed and whispered, "That looks like his."

Spencer immediately stopped walking and put his hand on her arm. "Yell his name.

Tell him who you are and why we're here."

"Deuce," Dani called out softly. "It's Ivy's friend Dani Sloan."

She paused for several long seconds, and when there was no response, she looked at Spencer, who said, "Tell him what you're doing here."

"This is Ivy's uncle. He's head of campus security and was concerned when he heard that students might be bullying you folks."

Again Dani paused, waiting for some indication Deuce had heard her. Something was definitely off and a weight seemed to be pressing on her chest, stealing her breath. Her instincts were urging her to turn around and leave as fast as her feet could carry her.

"Maybe he's a deep sleeper," she murmured. "Let's just come back in the daytime." The sound of leaves rustling in the breeze made her heart thud, and she added, "We could even contact him the way Ivy does by leaving a note on the bulletin board in the Union saying we wanted to talk to him."

Spencer shook his head. "You mentioned that Ivy told you that he has PTSD from his time in the military. There is no way a guy who spent time under fire is a heavy sleeper." Spencer frowned. "Unless he's gotten his hands on some strong drugs or a lot of booze."

"I didn't smell any alcohol on him," Dani said, then added, "That odor soaks into the skin of a serious drinker. And Ivy assures me he's not a druggie." Dani brightened. "Hey. It's possible he just isn't home right now. As you said, it's only half past twelve."

"I seriously doubt he'd leave his belongings out in the open if he wasn't here." Spencer motioned toward the battered lawn chair, rusted wrought-iron patio table, and ancient camp stove.

"I supposed you're right." Dani examined the area more closely and saw a piece of rope strung between two branches with a pair of dark pants and a long-sleeved shirt hanging over it. "When I met him, he didn't seem too trusting. Which I guess is understandable."

"Try calling out to him again." Spencer's brow was deeply furrowed.

"Deuce, please just talk to us." Dani attempted to keep the quaver from her voice. The longer she stood there, the more uneasy she felt. "If you let us know that you're all right, we'll leave."

In the ensuing silence, Dani heard movement in the shelter closest to Deuce's spot, then an angry voice that sound a lot like a growling rottweiler yelled, "Go away! We don't need no help from the likes of you two. We take care of our own."

She felt Spencer stiffen a split second before he thrust her behind him and whispered, "It's time for us to get out of here."

"Agreed." Dani clutched her pepper spray, hoping it still worked. She'd bought it when she'd had some trouble at her previous job and had felt threatened but had never had to use it before.

Before they could move, a female voice said, "Trigger, we should let them check on Deuce. We haven't seen him since group supper."

"He's always going off by himself," the male voice argued.

"But he must have come back because his clothes are on the line," the woman maintained. "And that means he's in for the night." When no one disagreed, she said, "Go ahead, you two."

"Okay!" Spencer shouted. "I'm going to check Deuce's tent." To Dani, he muttered under his breath, "Stay close and behind me."

"Got it." Dani shuffled forward, maintaining only an inch or so between her and Spencer.

He lifted the netting, ducked inside, and held it up for Dani to follow him.

As soon as she was through, Spencer called out, "Deuce, if you're okay and want us to leave just tell us and we'll go."

When there was no response, Spencer maneuvered himself and Dani to the side of the tent opening, then with his foot, he moved the flap aside.

Dani caught a hint of the scent of flowers, then as Spencer shined his flashlight inside, she peered over his shoulder and gasped.

Deuce was sprawled facedown on the floor, the back of his head was smashed in, and a long metal pipe with strangely bent ends lay by his side. The poor man was about as far from okay as possible.

CHAPTER 6

Spencer immediately closed the tent flap, put his lips to Dani's ear, and said softly, "Let me handle this." He reached into his pants pocket. "Here are my keys. Return to the pickup and do not talk to anyone until the police get here."

Numbly, Dani did what she was told. She wasn't thinking clearly and wasn't completely aware of her actions. A part of her said that she should stay and see if there was something she could do for Deuce. She'd had first aid training. But the more practical part of her whispered that the man lying on the floor of the tent needed a lot more than some Neosporin and a Hello Kitty Band-Aid.

As Dani hurriedly retraced her steps, she ignored the people who had emerged from their shelters and were asking if Deuce was okay. In truth, she barely heard them. Clouds drifted across the moon and without a flashlight, the shadows suddenly seemed threatening.

Once she got to the truck, she clicked the key fob, opened the door, and hoisted herself inside. After hitting the lock button, she leaned over, started the pickup, and switched the heat to high. It might be late August, but she was freezing.

She had just started to warm up and marshal her thoughts when a parade of police cars, with an ambulance bringing up the rear, came tearing down the dirt road with sirens blaring. Realizing that she wasn't going anywhere anytime soon, Dani texted Starr to let her know it would be a while until she got home.

Dani ignored Starr's demands for more information — she certainly didn't want Ivy hearing second-hand that something had happened to Deuce — and silenced her cell phone. Staring out of the pickup's windshield, she attempted to figure what was going on.

Was there any chance that Deuce was still alive? Could someone survive that severe an injury? Dani knew that head wounds bled a lot. Maybe he wasn't as badly hurt as he'd seemed to her.

Dani gazed at the bustling scene before her. Two EMTs had entered the tent but were already coming back out and shaking their heads at the officers questioning them. A few seconds later, they returned to their ambulance, climbed in, and drove away.

Shoot! Dani's chest tightened. No way could that be a good sign.

Strangely, unlike in the television crime shows Dani watched, the police didn't leap into action. Instead, they seemed mainly focused on keeping the campers from getting anywhere near Deuce's tent and stopping anyone who was trying to leave the scene.

But with the officers outnumbered at least ten to one, Dani saw several of the homeless slip into the surrounding trees and disappear into the darkness. It was clear they were familiar with all the escape routes and more than willing to use them.

Spencer still hadn't returned to the pickup when a white van bumped its way down the rutted path and pulled up as close to Deuce's tent as possible. It had *McClean County Coroner* painted in black with gold edging along its side, along with an insignia featuring a caduceus overlapped by the scales of justice.

Dani sagged against the seat. A coroner's van on the scene sucked away any tiny bit of lingering hope. Deuce was definitely dead.

A petite woman wearing a blue jumpsuit with *Deputy Coroner* stenciled across the back hopped out of the vehicle. She was followed by a bulky man in a similar one-piece garment, but with *Assistant Coroner* printed on his uniform. He was pushing a metal gurney with a large red duffel riding on top of the shiny black bag spread out on the gurney's thin padding.

The deputy coroner nodded to the police officer standing by the tent flap as she and her companion stepped inside. Once they were out of sight, it seemed as if the whole scene had been put on pause. The people trying to get past the officers stood motionless and the ones trying to leave stopped.

Fifteen or twenty long minutes went by before the deputy and assistant coroner emerged from the tent. The gurney was again occupied by a black body bag, but it was no longer flat. They wheeled it over to the van, loaded it in the rear, and drove away.

Then the police went back to keeping people away from the crime scene, and the campers ramped up their efforts to slip by the officers.

With nothing new to watch, Dani had

nearly dozed off when her cell phone vibrated in her shorts pocket. As she dug it out, a white panel truck with *Crime Scene Investigator* painted in gold arrived. On its tail was a newish sedan, which Dani was pretty sure was an unmarked police car. Both vehicles parked near Deuce's tent.

Keeping an eye on the CSI truck, Dani glanced at her phone and read: Ivy is home and we're going to bed. Call me when you get back and I'll go down and unchain the door. Then there was a winking emoji and another message: But if you have another place to spend the night, don't worry about making our breakfast tomorrow.

Dani shook her head at Starr's optimistic perception of the evening's activities. She typed her answer — No other place to spend the night — then searched for an appropriate emoji. Selecting a smiley face with a halo, she added: I'll be home as soon as I can.

After returning her phone to her front pocket, Dani glanced back at the scene and was temporarily blinded when eighteen hundred watts of illumination all aimed at Deuce's tent flashed on. While distracted by Starr's text, Dani had missed the placing of a dozen or more lights mounted on tripods. Nor had she seen the people wearing white

Tyvek coveralls with hoods, booties, and rubber gloves emerge from their vehicle and begin to swarm over the tiny campsite.

One was kneeling beside an unzipped wheeled duffel and another had a professional-looking camera hanging around his or her neck. A third had little yellow cones that he or she was placing at what seemed to be random spots within Deuce's campsite.

Dani realized that she'd also lost track of Spencer. She didn't see him anywhere. Where had he gone?

Panic raced through her veins, sending a low hum of electricity under her skin. It made her feel as if she needed to move. To do something. But before she could figure out what, Spencer materialized next to the pickup. He swept open the door that she'd been leaning against, startling her. Unable to maintain her balance, she tumbled out of the truck and ended up on her hands and knees on the ground. She yelped as the gravel dug into her palms.

"Shit!" Spencer helped her to stand, and when she was on her feet, he asked, "Are you okay? I'm so sorry. I didn't realize you were —"

"I'm fine." Dani cut off his apology. "I take it poor Deuce is dead." She brushed the pebbles out of her wounds. "Any idea who did it?"

"I'd like to talk to you about that, Ms. Sloan." An attractive man stepped forward and Dani realized that he'd been beside Spencer the whole time.

The guy wore a starched white shirt and crisply creased black dress pants. Although his sandy hair was neatly combed and his cheeks appeared freshly shaven, he was yawning as if he'd been sound asleep before arriving at the camp.

Dani figured he'd been yanked out of bed to handle this case, and she wondered why. She would have expected that the death of a homeless man would be dumped on whatever detective was on duty. But it appeared that the police had called in someone special.

Shoot! Her pulse thudded in her ears. Was she once again about to become the number one suspect in a murder investigation?

Realizing that she hadn't responded to the man's statement, which he could definitely construe as suspicious, Dani swallowed the panic in her throat and asked, "You want to talk to me? Why?"

"So far, we don't have any idea as to our victim's legal identity." The guy's voice was strangely soothing. "And I understand you've at least talked to him."

"Well, yeah," Dani muttered. "But only for a few minutes. I really don't know anything about him." She shook her head, then a memory popped into her mind and she said, "No, wait. I do know that he was in the military in Afghanistan."

"See, that's very helpful, Ms. Sloan. We should be able to run his prints through the military database and hopefully find his next of kin." The man beamed at her and held out his hand. "By the way, I'm Detective Christensen. But feel free to call me Gray."

"I'm Dani." She shook his hand and waited for him to continue.

"Why don't we sit in my car and chat?" The detective tilted his head toward the shiny black Chevy parked behind the CSI vehicle. "I know you must be tired and I promise this will be quick."

Dani glanced at Spencer, who nodded.

As they walked to the sedan, the detective kicked an apple core out of Dani's way. When she smiled her thanks, Spencer's grip on her hand tightened and he blocked Gray's attempt to help her into the passenger seat. After assisting her to sit himself, Spencer got in the back.

Once the three of them were settled, Gray gently prodded, "Can you tell me why you asked Mr. Drake to come here tonight and check on the victim?"

Dani drew in a deep breath and noticed the new-car smell; no wonder the interior was so pristine.

"Earlier today" — Dani paused — "I mean, yesterday, Deuce mentioned that a band of zombies had raided his camp," she said, then quickly explained, "I knew they weren't real zombies, but I was concerned the college kids were having fun at the homeless people's expense."

"That's very nice of you to worry about them." The detective's hazel eyes were kind. "I understand that your company donates its surplus food here too."

"Yes." Dani's cheeks warmed. "But I can't take credit for that. My employee Ivy Drake had the idea of giving our leftovers to the hungry and she was the one who pursued the matter."

"Drake?" Gray glanced at Spencer. "Any relation to you?"

"My niece."

Spencer's response was terse and Dani snuck a glance at him. There was a deep line between his brows, but otherwise, in the dim light, his expression was inscrutable. Had he wanted her to keep Ivy out of it? If so, he should have given her some warning.

"I'll need to talk to Ivy, but it can wait until morning." Gray's gaze landed on Dani's bloody knees. He frowned and leaned across her to open the glove compartment. Taking out a first aid kit, he handed it to Dani and said, "Here. You should clean up those scrapes and put some antibiotic ointment on them so they don't get infected. Who knows what kind of crap is on the ground around here?"

"Thanks." Dani smiled gratefully at the thoughtful detective, then grabbed a foil pouch, tore it open, and took out a moist towelette. "I wish I had more information about Deuce. He seemed to have had a rough life and I hate that someone ended it before it could get better."

"What else did he say to you when you met him?" Gray took a notepad and silver fountain pen from his shirt pocket. "Anything about any enemies?"

"No." After cleaning her knees and palms, Dani squeezed some antiseptic cream on the abrasions. "He didn't say much at all."

"Was there something besides his homelessness that made you think he'd had a troubled life?" Gray held out a plastic bag for Dani's trash.

"It was more how he acted." Dani frowned. "Tense and always on the alert, as if waiting for an attack. Ivy told me had severe PTSD."

"Hmm." Gray narrowed his eyes. "Which means it would be hard for anyone to sneak up on him. He must have known his attacker."

"Unless he was doped up or passed out from drinking," Spencer said.

His voice startled Dani. She'd been so intent on the detective's questions that she'd almost forgotten Spencer was there.

"The medical examiner will definitely screen for drugs and alcohol." Gray shot a quick look at Spencer before returning his attention to Dani. "Is there any other comment or observation you can recall from your encounter yesterday morning with the victim?"

"Not really," Dani said slowly as she stuck bandages on a few of her deeper cuts. "But he was extremely protective of Ivy."

Spencer's breath huffed out on the back of her neck and Dani resolved not to mention his niece again.

"When you two arrived here, were there any cars parked nearby?" Gray asked, and when Dani shook her head, he added, "Did you see any vehicles when you were on the dirt road approaching the camp?"

"No," Dani answered immediately.

"Everything was dark and quiet."

"Drake described his reasoning for thinking that something was off at the camp despite the calm," Gray said. "Did you feel the same way?"

"Not at first." Dani licked her lips. "But once Spencer pointed it out, I agreed with him. It was definitely too quiet for the number of people around and the thin walls of most of their shelters."

"Then you and Drake decided to look for Deuce because he would know you." Gray looked at Dani for confirmation, and when she nodded, he added, "How did you think you would recognize his campsite?"

"By his shopping cart." Dani crumpled up the wrappings from the Band-Aids and looked around for the litterbag he'd held out to her earlier. Seeing it on the floor by Gray's foot, she leaned over and tucked the trash inside. The Chevy's interior was immaculate and she wasn't about to be the one to mess it up. "Everyone else seemed to have the smaller kind."

"And you spotted it even through the camouflaged netting?" Gray jotted something down and beamed at her. "You must have excellent vision."

"I saw a glint from the metal when Spencer shined his flashlight in that direction."

102

Dani straightened. She was still nervous, but this was so much better than her last encounter with the police.

"Why did you decide to check on the victim?" Gray raised a brow. "From your description of him, weren't you afraid he might become violent?"

While Spencer explained their reasoning and the input from the homeless people who had spoken to them, Dani stared at the Tyvek-suited figures, most of who were now spread out following a trail of what looked like flattened grass up the small incline behind Deuce's tent. Had they found evidence of the attacker's route?

Gray continued to question Spencer as to why they decided to enter the tent, and Dani's mind wandered to what was happening in front of her. Normalton, Illinois, was certainly well equipped to deal with a crime scene.

Did all small cities have such up-to-date gear and so many forensics employees? The police station had recently been modernized as well, and she recalled reading in the local paper about officers attending classes. There had also been something about the purchase of new equipment.

If nothing else, the town was ready to handle any murders in its jurisdiction. Of course, although Dani thought of Nor-malton as a sleepy little college town, it did have a population of over a hundred fifty thousand when the students were in resi-dence. Which, with summer classes, was most of the year.

Focusing back on the men's conversation, Dani heard Spencer say, "Then we backed away from the tent and I called the police."

"How did the people who had been talk-ing to you react?" Gray asked.

"They wanted to know what we'd found," Spencer answered. "But I sent Dani to the truck and refused to answer their ques-tions."

Dani frowned. He'd *sent her to the truck?* Well, yeah. But putting it that way sounded as if she were his daughter or his pet poodle.

"Can you describe what you saw?" Gray tapped his notepad with his pen.

After Dani told the detective what she'd seen, Gray gazed out the windshield for a long time.

Finally, he nodded to himself and said, "I guess that's all." He paused, then smiled at Dani. "Well, one more thing. I need to get your address so I can stop by tomorrow to talk to you." He paused. "Oh, and I'll need Ivy's as well."

Dani tensed and she felt as if she was going to suffocate. The last time a police officer had been in her home, things hadn't gone too well for her. That detective had been an abusive jerk who had tried to pin a murder on her.

As if reading her mind, Spencer put his hand on Dani's bare arm and a strange calm radiated from her chest and drifted throughout her body, as if she'd been injected with an antianxiety medication. Her hot skin cooled, the roar in her ears quieted, and she could breathe again.

Putting her hand over Spencer's, Dani inhaled and reeled off her address, then said, "And Ivy lives with me."

Gray jotted it down and said, "Are you and the young lady roommates?"

"In a way." Dani explained, "The place I own had been in the process of being renovated to become a bed-and-breakfast when I inherited it, but I didn't want it as a B and B. Instead, I use the kitchen for my cooking business."

"Okay." Gray tilted his head. "So how did you end up with a boarder?"

"Actually, I have three. Ivy, Tippi, and Starr." Dani chuckled at the memory of the trio showing up at her door. "They were less than a month from finishing their junior year at NU and were horrified that their parents were insisting that, due to the behavior that had gotten them evicted from their shared apartment, they either had to move back into the dorms or pay for tuition and living expenses themselves."

"I can see their point." Gray's tone was sympathetic. "Living in a dorm your senior year would really suck."

"Yeah." Dani nodded. "They knew me and that I had just inherited the mansion because I had lived in the apartment next door to the girls. And although I was quite a bit older, I'd drifted into a sort of big-sister relationship with them."

"I doubt you're that much older." Gray's eyes twinkled.

"Thank you." Dani smiled her appreciation. "Anyway, the girls made me an offer that I realized I couldn't refuse. It took some negotiation, but in the end, I scored rent money and three part-time employees."

"Sounds like a win-win for all four of you." Gray patted her hand, then said, "Well, I suppose it's time to let you get home. I'm sure it's way past your bedtime." He chuckled and added, "I know it's past mine."

The detective got out of the sedan, walked around the car, and opened Dani's door. She was surprised that he escorted her back to Spencer's pickup and helped her inside. Spencer had followed them, and from the look on his face, he wasn't too happy with Gray's actions.

After the detective returned to his own vehicle, Dani waited for Spencer to say something. But he was silent as he started up the truck and drove her home.

When they arrived at the mansion, Dani reached for the pickup's door handle, but Spencer cleared his throat and she hesitated.

Finally, he said, "I know Detective Christensen is coming off as a nice guy. But there's no way in hell he became the Normalton Police Department's lead detective by playing fair with suspects. Watch your back."

Dani gulped. "Do you think that he thinks that we murdered Deuce?"

"Probably not." Spencer's eyes drilled into Dani's. "But you didn't have to give him the whole story about your inheritance or why Ivy and the girls are staying with you. Next time, be careful of what you say."

CHAPTER 7

After some discussion, Spencer agreed it was best if Dani told Ivy and the others about Deuce's death. They talked about it a little more and decided there was no use waking the girls to give them that kind of information. The sad news could wait until morning.

Although it wasn't easy, Dani was able to avoid Starr's questions when her boarder unchained the door and let her inside the mansion. Knowing her mumbled excuses wouldn't have worked if Starr hadn't been half-asleep, Dani quickly made her way upstairs.

She was once again thankful that the mansion's previous owner had created a secluded oasis on the third floor. The cozy sitting room filled with comfy furniture, the spacious bedroom with the amazing walk-in closet, and the huge spa-like bathroom straight out of HGTV were wonderful, but the big advantage was the suite's location on an entirely separate level from the others' living quarters.

Dani cherished the privacy that the suite provided. She loved having the girls around, but there were times she needed some space and this was a good example.

After a quick shower, Dani stumbled into bed and fell asleep almost before her head hit the pillow. She'd been afraid the events of the night would scroll through her mind on an infinite loop and keep her awake, but evidently exhaustion trumped emotions.

When she woke at 6:00 a.m. to the blaring alarm on her cell phone, Dani felt muddled. Lack of rest made her question if she and Spencer had really gone to the camp and found Deuce murdered. Or had the whole scenario just been a figment of her overactive imagination?

Dani's question was answered after she hurriedly pulled on a pair of black yoga pants with a red Chef-to-Go T-shirt and checked her messages. She found a voice-mail from Gray Christensen, and if the detective wasn't a part of her dream, then neither was the rest of the nightmare. Sadly, Deuce was really dead.

Gray's message said that he would like to stop by to talk to Dani and Ivy at nine and asked if they would be home.

When she called him back, he picked up on the first ring and greeted her, then said, "I hope you're not feeling any ill effects from last night."

"Thanks. I'm . . ." Dani trailed off. Gray's warm tenor seemed genuinely interested in how she was doing. She'd been about to fob him off with the standard answer that she was fine, but instead, she found herself telling him about her fatigue and disorientation.

"That's completely reasonable," Gray sympathized. "You had quite a shock seeing Deuce like that and then very little sleep."

Dani opened her mouth to reply, then snapped it shut hearing Spencer's admonishment not to fall for the detective's nice-guy routine.

"Thank you for your understanding." Dani kept her tone neutral. "I'm calling to tell you that nine o'clock should work for us. Ivy is scheduled to help me with the lunch-to-go preparation this morning. So if you don't mind us continuing to assemble the meals while you talk to us, we'll both be available at that time."

"Terrific." Gray chuckled. "And if there's any chance at samples, I don't mind at all. I'm told your food is outstanding."

"That's nice to hear."

Dani wondered who the detective had been talking to about her. She hoped his conversation with her mysterious fan hadn't been because Gray was investigating her as a suspect in Deuce's murder.

After chatting for a few more minutes with the detective, Dani said goodbye to him and headed to the kitchen. As she walked down the stairs, she thought over Spencer's warning. Her instincts said that Gray's behavior was genuine. But why would Spencer be so concerned if he didn't have some information about the man that Dani didn't know?

Mulling over the question of Gray's true personality, she was startled when the doorbell rang and she tripped on a step. Clutching the railing to keep from tumbling down the stairs, she caught her breath and scowled. It was too early for visitors.

Dani carefully made her way down the rest of the stairs, then rushed across the foyer and peered through the window. She recognized the locksmith from their encounter a few months ago and she hastily let him inside. She'd forgotten that Spencer had arranged for all the dead bolts to be changed first thing this morning.

After greeting the locksmith and exchanging pleasantries about the weather — it continued to be hot — and the local baseball team — they continued to lose — Dani left the man to his work and hurried down the hallway. If she didn't get some caffeine in her system soon, her head would explode.

Dani walked straight for the Ninja Coffee Bar and started a pot of French roast. Inhaling the rich aroma as it started to brew, she took four bowls out of the cupboard and set them on the counter in front of the stools. From the fridge, she grabbed blueberries, soy milk, and pumpkin puree. Once she'd put them near the stove, she stepped into the small pantry adjacent to the kitchen and picked up old-fashioned rolled oats, brown sugar, and a bottle of cinnamon.

Once she had her ingredients lined up, Dani poured herself a mug of coffee and started making breakfast. Removing a large saucepan from the shelf, she put it on the stove, turned on the burner, and put in three cups of the oats. Then she stirred in six cups of the milk, a cup and a half of the purée, and two teaspoons of the cinnamon.

As Dani cooked, she realized that aside from the ticking of the refrigerator, the kitchen was eerily silent and surprisingly chilly. Even though it meant something had gone wrong with his work, she was almost happy when the locksmith let loose a stream of profanity.

The oatmeal was just coming to a boil when Dani's three lodgers shuffled into the kitchen and took turns pouring themselves cups of coffee. They then plopped on the stools and blinked sleepily.

Turning the flame on low to let the oatmeal simmer, Dani refilled her own mug, then turned to the half-awake young women and said, "I have some sad news."

"Starr told me you and Uncle Spencer were going to check on the homeless camp and then you called and said you were delayed but wouldn't say why." Ivy clutched her cup to her chest. "What happened?"

"Well . . ." Dani stalled, unsure how to break the news.

She'd never told anyone someone was dead before. Deuce wasn't exactly a loved one, but Ivy was extremely tenderhearted and would be devastated. In hindsight, Dani should have rehearsed her speech.

"Yoo-hoo," a female voice trilled from the hallway, interrupting Dani's thoughts. "I hope it's okay. Your locksmith let us in."

"You know it is." Dani smiled as Frannie Ryan appeared in the doorway, beaming.

Frannie was a little taller than the average woman and a lot curvier than was fashionable, but she had an abundance of confi-

113

dence that Dani greatly admired. Frannie had told Dani that she attributed that self-assurance to counseling she'd received from her school psychologist friend, Skye.

One thing about living in a college town with its plethora of young, beautiful, and predominately thin females was that it was hard for anyone who wore a double-digit size not to feel huge. Dani often caught herself wondering if her ex might not have cheated on her if she looked more like those young women.

Shaking off those self-defeating thoughts, Dani grinned as Frannie marched across the kitchen, trailed by an extremely tall young man in his early twenties. His slender build emphasized his height and he reminded her of a young Jeff Goldblum.

Dani had met Frannie when the rookie reporter had shown up to investigate Regina Bourne's murder. Since that time, they'd become friends.

Shooting Frannie a questioning look, Dani asked, "Why are you here so early in the morning?"

"Because of what happened at the homeless camp, of course." Frannie waved an iPad in the air, and with a triumphant smile, she announced, "I am finally officially off obits and the Miss Fortune column. As of today, I'm assigned to investigative reporting." Crossing her arms, Frannie looked at Dani. "I hear you and Spencer discovered the body."

Frannie's words struck with the force of an ax blade and Ivy, Starr, and Tippi all shrieked in unison.

Five pairs of eyes focused on Dani and she froze, trying to gather her wits. No one spoke and their intense stares made her feel as if she were a gazelle surrounded by a pride of lions.

Finally, Dani stuttered, "Who's your friend, Frannie?" She had a good guess as to his identity, but asking gave her a chance to think.

Frannie narrowed her eyes suspiciously at Dani's change of subject, but the young man stuck out his hand and said, "I'm Justin Boward, Frannie's boyfriend." He raised his chin. "I'm finishing up my class work at U of I online while I do an internship at the *Normalton News* in their e-pub department."

He pushed his short, nut-brown hair off his forehead and reached into his pocket for a handkerchief to clean his glasses. As he wiped the lenses, his long-lashed brown eyes blinked, taking in the scene before him. When his gaze landed on the three pajama-clad girls on the stools, he blushed and quickly looked away.

Evidently, Ivy was neither embarrassed nor distracted by Justin's presence and she demanded, "You said body? Did someone die?"

"I'm sorry to tell you this" — Dani took the girl's hand — "but we found Deuce lying on the floor of his tent. It looked as if he'd been hit over the head with a large metal pipe, and he was dead."

"Did you know the deceased?" Frannie whirled on Ivy. "Were you friends?"

"Uh," Ivy faltered. "I wouldn't say friends. I mean, yes, I guess maybe we were friends." Her blue eyes beseeched Dani to take over.

"Ivy had been working with Deuce to distribute the leftover food from our events to the homeless population at the camp." Dani herded Frannie and Justin toward the table and gestured to the others to join them. She looked at Frannie. "How about we all have some breakfast? I made an extra-large batch so there's plenty. While we eat, I promise I'll tell you everything I know."

"Perfect." Frannie turned to Justin. "Dani is the best cook ever."

While they ate their oatmeal and drank glasses of orange juice, Dani explained how she and Spencer had ended up at the homeless camp and described the scene when they arrived. When they were all finished with their food, she finally told them about finding Deuce.

Frannie immediately asked, "So do you have any idea who killed him?"

"How would I?" Dani twitched her shoulders in a shrug. "I'd only met the man once before."

"How about you?" Frannie focused her intense interest on Ivy.

"Everyone at the homeless camp seemed to like him a lot." Ivy sniffled. "He protected them from scavengers and provided them with food."

"Maybe those vultures that were preying on the homeless took him out. We need to interview the campers. They can identify the predators and we can hunt those sharks down." Frannie warmed to her idea like a batter taking a few practice swings. "We should —"

"I think we should look into the folks who harassed the campers the previous night," Justin interrupted, his tone thoughtful. "There might be some bad blood there. They might have thought the homeless would be easy pickings and not expected to go up against someone like Deuce."

Dani tilted her head to look at the young

man. He was so quiet it would be easy to forget he was around. But intelligence shone from his eyes, and she was sure it would be a mistake to underestimate him.

Starr had been silently playing with the silver bead on the end of one of her braids, but suddenly, she said, "If Deuce had been killed that first night, I'd definitely look at the fake zombies."

"But you're saying," Dani jumped in, "that for one person to come back by him- or herself the next evening, sneak into the camp, and stealthily attack Deuce, it doesn't really fit group dynamics."

"Huh?" Ivy wrinkled her brow. "Why not? That would be the safest way."

"True." Dani shrugged. "But if someone in that original gang had felt humiliated or threatened by Deuce, he or she would have wanted to take him out while his peers watched him or her do it. They'd want to prove that they were the baddest guy or chick."

"Right." Starr got up. "Anyway. I've got to bounce. I'm showing a group of freshmen around the science department at eight and if I'm late, I'm afraid one of them might blow up the chemistry lab."

They waved her off, and Dani looked at Ivy. "And we better get started on today's lunch-to-go sacks. Thank goodness the desserts are already done and the sides I have scheduled are fairly quick and easy."

Dani was about to mention that Detective Christensen would be arriving in an hour to talk to them, but then she glanced at Frannie and decided to keep quiet. The young reporter would insist on staying if she knew the detective on the case was stopping by, and all Dani needed was Gray thinking she'd called in the media to get free advertising for her business. She didn't want to end up on his suspect list.

"I guess that means you want us to leave." Frannie shot Dani a look that said she knew that Dani was holding something back, then started for the doorway. "Text me if you hear anything that we can use for the paper." Frannie suddenly stopped and grabbed Justin's hand. "Despite Dani's theory, we should definitely investigate the group that attacked the homeless camp Sunday night. Think of the headlines. 'The Zombie Apocalypse Is Here. Armageddon Comes to Normalton. Protect Your Brains.' "

Dani laughed as Frannie dragged a reluctant Justin down the hall, but then she noticed that Tippi was frowning and asked, "What's wrong?"

"I'm worried that my frat's philanthropic cause will get lost in the chaos Frannie plans to stir up." Tippi rushed to the door. "I'd better get dressed and get over to the office ASAP to warn everyone so we can do some damage control."

Dani called toward Tippi's back, "Look on the bright side. Frannie's article on the fake zombies harassing the homeless camp might get your zombie fun run a lot of exposure."

Once everyone was gone, Dani told Ivy about the detective's upcoming visit. Ivy was unusually quiet as they went to work making the components for the lunch-to-go sacks.

While they chopped, mixed, and assembled the meals, Dani tried to think of what to say to her. It had been different when Regina was murdered because the girl had been so unlikable, but Deuce was a lot more sympathetic. Clearly, Ivy was having a difficult time with the news.

They were nearly finished making the two entrées — Let Veggie Entertain You, a roasted zucchini, red pepper, yellow squash, mozzarella, and sun-dried tomato mayo wrap, and the Cheesy Piglet, a ham-and-cheddar sandwich with honey mustard — when the doorbell rang. The locksmith had finished and departed twenty minutes ago, so it was probably Gray.

After washing and drying her hands, Dani hurried to the foyer and opened the front door. The attractive detective greeted her with a warm smile and commented on how much he liked the antique decor as she led him down the hallway.

Dani thanked him, then introduced him to Ivy and suggested he have a seat at the counter. He hopped up on one of the stools and didn't try to hide his interest as he examined the kitchen.

"This is a really sweet setup," Gray said, running his hand lovingly across the stainless island that contained two commercial stoves, a griddle, a broiler, a salamander, a sink, a pot filler, and a built-in ice container all integrated in the countertop.

"Do you like to cook?" Dani asked, carving the remaining slices of meat from a ham.

"I love to." Gray's hazel eyes twinkled. "But clearly, I'm outclassed."

"Well . . ." Dani smiled at his envious tone. "The kitchen doesn't really make the cook, but this one sure helps." She gestured to the pass-through window near the back door and said, "I had to have that installed in order to make selling the lunches-to-go practical, but everything else came with the house. I'm not sure why Mrs. Cook thought she'd need anything this elaborate for a bed-and-breakfast, but I'm sure thankful she had it remodeled this way." She glanced over her shoulder and added, "Even the restaurant-size refrigerator was here, and it's a dream come true for storing the perishables I need for my personal chef and catering services."

Ivy had been observing the exchange between Dani and Gray, and Dani saw her begin to relax. Her fingers flew as she expertly folded the whole wheat tortillas around the vegetable filling.

"Okay." Gray grinned. "Enough kitchen envy, back to business."

Dani saw Ivy tense and hurriedly asked, "Have you found out Deuce's real identity yet? Or anything about him before he came here?"

"Not yet." Gray took out his notebook and flipped it open. "But we hope we'll get a hit on his prints from the military database soon."

"He mentioned growing up not too far from Normalton." Ivy scrunched up her face as if trying to remember something. "I think part of the name was something like Coal or Clay or Carbon."

"That's great." Gray jotted down a note.

"Anything else he told you?"

"Hmm. Let me think." Ivy wrinkled her nose. "He wasn't much of a talker."

"I'd have to second that." Dani wrapped the ham bone up, placed it in the fridge to use for soup, and turned to the wheel of cheddar. "I thought he might be mute at first."

"Did he ever say how he ended up in Normalton?" Gray asked, accepting the sliver of cheese Dani handed him and popping it into his mouth.

"I asked him why he didn't go home after getting out of the military and he got real quiet." Ivy's blue eyes filled with tears. "Then he said that when he got back from his last tour of duty, he no longer had a home."

CHAPTER 8

When Spencer returned to the campus security building after his early morning meeting with his boss, he was still thinking about her request that he address the faculty tea and nearly missed the girl sitting in a corner, curled into a tight ball, and hidden behind a large plant. It was only because she took a sobbing breath as Spencer passed by that he spotted her.

Her eyes were wide with shock. He used a soft voice when he said, "Can I help you?"

The girl leaped to her feet and plastered herself against Spencer's chest, crying as if the world were coming to an end. She reeked of stale sweat and the sickly sweet odor of marijuana, which might explain some of her behavior. However, Spencer knew that it was just as easy to smell that way by being near someone who had been puffing away so she might not have been smoking pot herself.

He peeled the girl off him and looked her over. She didn't appear physically harmed, no bruises or cuts, and her clothing seemed intact.

"Can you tell me what happened?" Spencer asked, and when she didn't respond, he tried a few other questions, but she just stared mutely into space.

There was no indication of what was wrong with her, and all he could conclude was that something had happened that scared her into a near-catatonic state.

Realizing he wasn't going to get any answers from the girl, he used his cell phone to call Lavonia Jools, the only female member of his team. Even if Lavonia wore her uniform like it was a suit of armor and hadn't demonstrated an ounce of maternal instinct, it was fortunate that she was on days this week and was already in the building.

He definitely wanted a female witness to offset any false accusations. The girl had already thrown herself into his arms and he wasn't taking any chances of getting caught in a "he said, she said" mess. If nothing else, his years undercover had taught him to protect himself.

When Lavonia arrived a few minutes later, she didn't have much better luck than Spencer at getting the young woman to talk.

But after the fifth or sixth time Lavonia asked her name and if she was injured, the girl cleared her throat and said, "My name's Cindi Streicher. I'm not hurt and I don't need an ambulance."

Cindi allowed Lavonia to guide her up the stairs and into Spencer's office but then just shrugged when he asked her any questions.

Spencer gazed at the young woman sitting across from his desk. She was rocking back and forth, her ragged nails digging into the chair's padded armrest, and staring out the window as if in a trance.

Spencer ground his teeth in frustration. He'd only gotten a couple hours of sleep and he wasn't at his best. Not that being well-rested would help. His past undercover assignments hadn't given him a lot of practice dealing with hysterical young women.

He glanced at Lavonia, who silently shook her head. She'd been an army MP before coming to work for Spencer and probably had even less experience than Spencer with calming down weeping girls. At least he was occasionally around his niece and her friends, but Lavonia had mentioned that she had no family in the area and lived alone.

Spencer's mind wandered as he waited for Cindi to gather her wits and talk. He was startled when she finally said, "I need to use the restroom."

"Lavonia will take you. While you're away, how about if I get us all a cup of coffee?" Spencer was dying for a hit of caffeine.

"Tea for me, please?" Cindi gave him a watery smile. "Two sugars."

"You got it," Spencer said. "Maybe we'll get lucky and there'll be muffins too."

As the women headed toward the bathroom, Spencer rose and went to get their drinks. The smell of tuna fish and hot dogs hit him when he entered the break room and he made a mental note to have the cleaning crew put out some air fresheners.

After starting the coffee brewing, Spencer put a cup of water in the microwave for Cindi's tea. Then as he searched the break room cabinets for a tea bag, he tried to imagine what could have happened to the young woman. She claimed that she hadn't been assaulted and wasn't physically hurt, so what did that leave? She must have seen something that upset her.

As his brain reeled off a list of all the awful possibilities, his thoughts wandered to Dani. She'd been a trooper when they'd found Deuce dead. Followed instructions.

Kept her emotions contained. And shown more concern for others than herself. She really was something.

During their last investigation together, he'd realized that he could count on Dani. She knew how to act in any situation and behaved as a true partner, not someone in need of his protection.

In a way, he was surprised that he'd noticed that about her. He hadn't paid much attention to women since his divorce, but Dani was such a unique mix of smart and caring that he noticed everything about her. And even though she never did exactly what he thought she would do, a trait he normally found annoying, she'd always managed to charm him.

When he'd gone over to Dani's place to speak to Tippi and make sure the mansion's locks were replaced ASAP, it had been a relief that she'd been so reasonable. He'd been expecting that she'd give him the cold shoulder at best, and overtly hostile at worst.

True, Dani had been cool at first, but her natural warmth had quickly taken over. And as soon as she'd offered him food, he knew she'd forgiven him.

A loud gurgle from the coffeepot, signaling that it had finished brewing, pulled him from his thoughts, and he was suddenly aware of the faint hum of the soda machine, as well as the low voice of the dispatcher coming from her cubicle. Up until then, he could have sworn the place was silent.

After retrieving the cup of hot water from the microwave, he plunked a tea bag into the liquid and added two packets of sugar. Then he poured two mugs of coffee and carried all three cups to his office.

Cindi and Lavonia had already returned from the restroom and were sitting in their chairs, so Spencer distributed the hot beverages and announced, "Sorry, no muffins. Last shift must have eaten them all."

Taking his seat, Spencer waited until everyone had had a sip of their drinks, then looked at Cindi. The harsh overhead lights emphasized the deep, purple shadows under the girl's eyes, making her look almost as if she had twin shiners.

He leaned forward and asked, "Are you ready to tell us what happened?"

Cindi took a deep breath and said, "Last night, my boyfriend and I took one of those tours they've been advertising."

"Tours?" Spencer asked, wracking his brain to think of what organization might be conducting orientation activities in the evening.

"The ten o'clock one of the Blackheart

Canal," Cindi explained. "They guarantee that you'll see the creature." She made a face. "I didn't really want to do it, but Craig kept pestering me."

"That's interesting," Spencer remarked. "The reports I've gotten claim that the creature doesn't appear after twilight."

He clenched his jaw. Now he remembered seeing that flyer and thinking they needed to shut those tours down before someone got hurt. Evidently, something had already happened. But what?

"I told my boyfriend that but he wouldn't listen." Cindi shook her head. "He said the later tour would be scarier than the seven o'clock one."

"Right." Leaning forward, Spencer encouraged, "So you went on this tour and . . ."

"Nothing. We were led to a spot near the canal and told to sit on some blankets that were spread behind a line of bushes." Cindi sighed. "Then we waited and waited and eventually my boyfriend and some others got impatient."

"What did they do?" Spencer asked, hoping it wasn't something violent.

"They demanded the dude running the tour give them their money back, but the guy refused." Cindi was back to staring out the window. "He said there was another spot where the creature had been spotted and he'd take us there, but it was a bit of a hike."

"Did you go?" Spencer really wanted her answer to be no, but he knew that wasn't what had happened. Because if it had, she wouldn't be sitting in his office about to have another panic attack.

"I didn't want to." Cindi wrapped her fingers around her cup and gazed at the contents as if it held all the wisdom of the universe.

"Where did the tour guide take you?" Spencer asked, pulling a pad of paper toward him and searching his desktop for a pen.

"I'm not sure." Cindi put down her tea. "We walked for a long time."

"Did you head in the direction of the campus or the houses?"

"It was toward the campus." Cindi closed her eyes as if trying to remember. "But we veered off before we got to the quad."

"Did you go north or south?" Spencer grabbed a diagram of the campus from his drawer and put it in front of Cindi. "Can you show me where you walked?" He pointed to the canal. "This is where you started, and you must have gone on this path to head for the campus."

Cindi turned the map this way and that, then shook her head. "I have no idea. It was really dark and I was pretty freaked out."

Spencer asked, "When you reached the place the guide led you, what happened?"

"By the time we got wherever in the heck it was the guy took us, it was eleven thirty. I'd been up since 5:00 a.m. — I have a part-time job as the early morning receptionist at the university's health club — and all I wanted to do was go back to the dorm and go to bed." Cindi frowned, then shrugged. "But my boyfriend gave me something that he said would give me an energy boost."

"And you just took it?" Spencer scowled. "Did you even know what it was?"

He examined the girl. She'd said she was a sophomore, so she was probably nineteen. He rolled his eyes. When was this old-enough-to-know-better crap they kept talking about supposed to kick in? Considering some of his own decisions, he was hoping no later than thirty-two.

"A doctor prescribed it." Cindi glared. "For my boyfriend's ADHD."

"Yeah, right. That makes it so much better," Spencer muttered darkly. "Taking someone else's meds is always a good idea."

Lavonia shot him a look that said *Back*

132

down, and Spencer realized that he needed to watch it or the girl would clam up and they'd never get the whole story.

After a long pause, Cindi said, "Well, anyway, one of the others started passing around a bottle of tequila and I took a few sips. Then we all just sort of chilled."

"Like how?" Spencer asked, biting his tongue to keep from commenting about adding alcohol to the stimulant she'd already taken.

"We had climbed down this little slope and the tour dude spread out the blankets behind some tall weeds and told us to be quiet."

"And?" Spencer prompted. "Did you see the creature? Is that what upset you?"

"I don't know what I saw." Cindi nibbled at her thumbnail. "Between the pill and the booze, it's all a little blurry."

Ignoring all the warnings he wanted to shout at the girl, he counted to ten and said in as gentle of a voice as he could muster, "How about you close your eyes and try to remember what scared you." When Cindi complied, he continued, "Pretend you're a TV reporter. Now describe what's happening."

"I was half-asleep when a noise made me sit up." Cindi's head lifted. "It sounded as if

133

something was running up the hill."

"And then what?" Spencer murmured softly, afraid he'd pull the girl from her memories if he said too much or spoke too loudly.

"A second or two later, this . . . this thing rushed past where we were sitting." Cindi's breath hitched and her voice shook with emotion. "I was afraid it would see us and attack, but at first, it wasn't looking in our direction."

Cindi stopped speaking and Spencer encouraged, "But then . . ."

"Then the thing turned its head, and when we saw its horrible face, people started screaming." Cindi shivered. "The thing skidded to a halt, then swung around and came right at us."

Spencer and Lavonia exchanged a worried glance, but they both remained silent.

"For a split second, we all froze." Cindi's lips trembled. "Then the tour guide yelled *run,* and as if the ice encasing us had suddenly melted, everyone took off. My boyfriend and I got separated, and I found myself alone at the top of the incline."

Spencer nodded, trying to recall where the ground was sloped near campus.

Cindi blinked rapidly. "I didn't know which way to go, but I knew I had to keep moving. I could see some lights that I hoped were the campus so I decided to follow the railroad tracks in that direction."

"That was really good thinking." Lavonia patted the girl's arm and Cindi grabbed the security guard's hand and held on to it.

"But I'd only gone a few steps when that thing appeared out of nowhere."

Spencer seriously doubted that it had magically materialized out of thin air. It had probably just crested the hill at that instant.

"That thing was so close to me I could feel its scorching breath." Cindi's grip on Lavonia's fingers tightened until the girl's knuckles were a dead white and the veins on the back of her hand stood up like a topographical map. "It reached out, but before it could grab me, I stumbled and fell down the other side of the incline."

"Can you give me a description?" Spencer finally asked the question he'd wanted to ask from the start. After a few seconds, when Cindi didn't answer, he elaborated, "What did this thing look like?"

"That was the worst part of all." Cindi shrank back in her chair and Spencer's scalp prickled. "From the neck down, it seemed almost human, but its face was just a mass of tentacles with two bloodred eyes staring out."

■ ■ ■ ■

Spencer had needed to be patient, but he'd finally gotten Cindi to give them a halfway decent idea of the thing's appearance. It had helped when she said she was an art major and that she'd do better drawing the thing she'd seen rather than try to describe it.

The sketch she'd produced was of a creature covered in black from its neck down, with human-looking legs, torso, and arms. Looking at it, Spencer could understand how a drugged and boozed-up kid had ended up scared into a nearly catatonic state.

After Cindi again assured Spencer that she had no physical injuries and didn't want to talk to a mental health professional at the student counseling center, he had gotten her contact information and had Lavonia escort the girl to her dorm. The security guard would stay with Cindi as long as the girl wanted and report back to Spencer if there were any new developments.

Once the two women departed, Spencer called in one of his part-time guards to take the remainder of Lavonia's shift. Until the replacement reported in, Spencer would cover her assigned area.

Grabbing a utility belt loaded with all the necessary gear and filling a to-go cup with coffee, Spencer hurried out to the patrol car. Thankfully, Lavonia wasn't on bicycle duty. He settled behind the wheel and drove out of the parking lot, heading toward the quad.

Spencer rode through Lavonia's route at a steady fifteen miles an hour, noting that even with the orientation week activities taking place, the campus was surprisingly quiet. There were a few small groups trooping from building to building, and some students dotted the lawn, but nothing like what it would be once the fall semester started on Monday.

Relieved that everything appeared to be under control, Spencer considered what Cindi had reported. And as it all began to take shape in his mind, he pulled over and fished his cell from his pocket. Scrolling through his screen until he found the recording app, he swiped it, put the phone on the seat next to him, and steered the car back onto the road.

"Taking into consideration the victim's drug- and alcohol-influenced state of mind, from both her description and her drawing, it is safe to assume that the thing she saw was a person wearing a Halloween mask and black spandex leggings and a turtleneck."

Spencer paused the recording while he thought about what he'd just said. Something about that description rang a bell. His lack of sleep was making him fuzzy, but it was on the tip of his tongue. He took a gulp of his coffee, put the cup back in the holder, and waited for the caffeine to enter his bloodstream.

Of course! Spencer thumped his forehead with his palm. How could he be so dense?

Tapping the screen of his cell phone to continue recording, Spencer said, "A recent victim of a carjacking described her two assailants as wearing rubber masks and dressed in black clothing that reminded her of a cyclist's. One possibility is that the 'monster' that Cindi Streicher stumbled upon was one of those carjackers escaping after a failed attempt to steal another vehicle. That means I need to check with the police department and determine if there was an attempted car theft in that time period."

Spencer picked up his cup, took another sip of coffee, and returned it to the holder. "Another urgent question is the location of Cindi's encounter. She mentioned following railroad tracks, which would have to be somewhere on the north part of the campus. She stated that they first walked toward the quad, then veered off until they reached the slope."

Visualizing the college map, Spencer mentally followed the girl's trail. He suddenly stiffened and gripped the steering wheel. Spencer's jaw clenched as he said, "It is highly likely that the tour guide led the group to the embankment behind the homeless camp. And in that case, it is a distinct possibility that Cindi and the others either ran into Deuce's murderer as he or she was fleeing the scene of the crime or the 'monster' was a witness to the crime."

CHAPTER 9

As Dani turned into the parking lot of Holy Snips, Hilary's hair salon, she checked her watch and discovered she was running late for her appointment. There had been more lunch-to-go customers than she'd expected and she had ended up having to put together a couple dozen extra meals at the last minute without the help of her assistant.

That, in addition to all the visitors that morning, had her seriously behind schedule. She'd considered canceling, but thoughts of Spencer had persuaded her to show up for her cut and style. Not that she expected anything to happen between them, but a tiny inner voice whispered that there was no harm in trying to look her best.

Pulling the van between two freshly painted yellow lines. Dani jumped out and hurried toward the salon. As she jogged toward the door, she observed the pristine asphalt of the newly paved lot and pursed her lips. What would it cost to resurface the mansion's deteriorating driveway?

Even in her rush to get inside for her appointment, Dani took a second to admire the old stone structure that housed the salon. It had a lot of quirky charm and she could see why Hilary had chosen it for her business.

Originally, the building had been a Lutheran church. But a few years ago, the congregation had moved to another location. One that could accommodate the growing number of parishioners.

As she approached the entrance, a warm breeze carried a light, sweet scent, making Dani glance to either side. She was impressed by the perfectly manicured shrubs and the bed of colorful flowers. She could identify chrysanthemums, impatiens, and daisies, but not the ones with the wonderful fragrance.

Dani stepped into the vestibule and a less pleasant odor assaulted her nostrils. The smell of hair spray and nail polish remover made her nose twitch and she paused, attempting to hold back a sneeze.

Hearing raised voices coming from the next room, Dani was hesitant to move forward. She could tell that one person was male and the other sounded like Hilary, but background music was too loud for her to make out what they were yelling about. Still, the tenor of the discussion was pretty darn clear. Someone was royally ticked off.

Dani was torn. Should she wait until they were finished shouting at each other, or should she walk in as if she had no idea what was going on? Either her presence would defuse the situation or it would make things super awkward between her and Hilary.

Finally, she cleared her throat as loudly as possible and slowly made her way through the lobby, giving the pair a chance to stop arguing before she got to where they were standing. Stepping into the reception area of the salon, she saw that she'd been right. The female voice she'd heard was Hilary's, and the stylist was squared off with a young man who looked to be in his late teens or early twenties.

The guy was wearing skinny jeans, a half-tucked blue collared shirt, and a sullen expression. He glanced at Dani as if she were something he'd scraped off the bottom of his shoe, then turned back to Hilary and muttered something below his breath. She gave a short nod and pointedly looked toward the exit.

Giving Hilary a defiant glare, he stomped

contemptuously past Dani and sneered, "Put your eyes back in your head. Show's over, lady."

Without another word, the young man marched away, a scowl on his face. His departure was punctuated by the slam of a door, and both Dani and Hilary jumped at the sound of glass shattering.

"Damn!" Hilary grimaced. "That window will be a bitch to replace. This place is so old, nothing is a standard size."

"I'd make that guy pay for it," Dani said. "Maybe you should call the police and file a complaint so you have some leverage."

"My insurance will cover it." Hilary sighed. "It's not worth the hassle of getting the cops involved over something so minor."

"But what if he comes back and assaults you?" Dani shivered.

The salon's air-conditioning must have been set to arctic, and the chill settled on her skin like an ice blanket. She rubbed the goose bumps that had popped up on her arms, wishing she were wearing long sleeves like Hilary.

"Not to worry." Hilary's expression was distinctly unimpressed.

"Do you know him personally, or is he just an unsatisfied client?" Dani tilted her head, puzzled that the stylist was so blasé about the broken glass, not to mention her own safety.

"He's just a spoiled kid who is used to getting his own way." Hilary adjusted her silky white blouse. "I can handle him."

Dani admired the woman's stylish shirt but wondered how she could work without ruining the delicate material. Shrugging, she examined her surroundings. Although the theme was along the lines of shabby chic, Dani could tell the furnishings were anything but inexpensive.

Looking around, Dani saw a frosted door on her right that had *Spa* etched on it, and to her right, an archway that led into the styling areas. She couldn't detect any activity in either of the spaces.

Dani nodded toward the rest of the salon and asked, "Am I your only customer?"

"Yep." Hilary smiled. "At least for another half hour. Then my staff returns from lunch and we're fully booked through closing." Today, the salon owner's dark-brown hair was in a sleek bun at the back of her head and she absentmindedly smoothed the sides. "In fact, we're so busy, I'm looking to add more employees. I have an entire second level that could be remodeled into work spaces."

"Wow. That's impressive." Dani glanced

at the ceiling, imagining the room up there. "I recall you mentioned that you'd only been in business a few years, and you're already able to expand." She pursed her lips. "I doubt Chef-to-Go will be growing at that same rate."

"Well . . ." Hilary squeezed Dani's arm. "I think you and I are destined to be good friends, so if you ever want to talk expansion strategy, I'd be happy to give you some tips."

"Thanks." Dani beamed. "I can use some friends closer to my own age. My BFF is married with kids and I don't get to see her as often as I'd liked."

"Awesome." Hilary smiled. "Now, let's start getting you beautiful for your boyfriend."

"I'm not currently seeing anyone." Dani shook her head. "My ex turned out to be a creep and I don't have time to find someone new right now." Her cheeks burned as an image of Spencer flashed through her mind. "Besides, I'm not sure I can trust a man again."

"You don't have to get serious. Just find one to take you to nice places." Hilary gave a wry laugh. "My philosophy is that men are like bank accounts. Without a lot of money, they don't generate much interest."

Dani giggled, then sobered as she thought about the guy Hilary had been arguing with earlier. Although she'd tried to forget about the scene she'd witnessed, there was something about the man that made her uneasy. Losing her internal argument to let the issue go, she decided to try one more time to convince Hilary to make a police report. After all, she'd feel terrible if something happened to the stylist that she could have prevented.

"Uh, about that guy who broke the window," Dani said slowly, "are you dating him? Because if so, you really should file a complaint. Just in case he becomes violent."

Dani thought he seemed too young for Hilary, but his appearance could be deceiving, or the stylist might just like younger men if they were rich enough.

"He's nothing to me. Just a jerk who's never satisfied." Hilary's tone was impatient, but a second later, it was softer when she said, "Although I really do appreciate your concern."

"Okay." Dani had no choice but to drop the matter. She wasn't sure Hilary was telling the truth — the argument had sounded pretty heated — but it really wasn't any of her business and there wasn't much else she could say.

"Now, let's get started on your new look." Hilary took Dani's elbow and guided her to the shampoo area. She uncapped two bottles and held them out to Dani. "Would you prefer a floral- or fruity-scented shampoo?"

Dani marveled at how serene the stylist appeared. If someone had been yelling at her and broken her door, she'd be a basket case. In contrast, Hilary's hazel eyes were calm and she seemed eager to get to work.

"I'd prefer one with no fragrance if you have it. My sense of smell is really keen." Dani took the seat Hilary indicated and squirmed to find a comfortable position while the stylist tied a nylon cape around her neck. "And I like to keep it as sharp and unaffected as possible for my cooking."

"No problem." Hilary took out a small bottle and held it up so Dani could see the label, which read *Fragrance-Free.*

While Hilary washed Dani's hair, the two women chatted about Normalton and the university. When Hilary finished, she led Dani to a styling chair, then stepped back and examined her from several angles.

Picking up a pair of shears, she opened and closed them a couple of times, then asked, "What kind of style did you have in mind?"

"Nothing shaved on one side," Dani said

quickly. "Those types of cuts look cute on some of the younger, edgier women but aren't anything I can pull off. I need to look professional."

"I agree." Hilary selected a comb. "But what do you like for yourself?"

"I need to keep it long so I can put it in a ponytail or bun when I work."

"Okay." Hilary waved the shears in Dani's direction. "Anything else?"

"Bangs just look weird on me, so not that. Maybe some layers for definition. And anything that will cut down on frizziness would be terrific." Dani was getting frustrated. What she wanted was hard to put into words. "You're the expert. Why don't you tell me how I should wear it?"

Hilary had the grace to look a bit chagrined. "You're right. I just wanted to make sure you were happy so you'd agree to our barter deal."

"Wait a second." Dani dug her phone from her pocket and swiped through several photos until she found what she wanted. "Here's a picture of how I used to get it cut. Can you replicate that style?"

Taking Dani's cell from her, Hilary enlarged the photo. "Absolutely."

Hilary grabbed a section of Dani's hair and held it straight up, but before she could take the first snip, Dani heard the front door open and her heart raced. What if that angry guy had returned and this time he had a gun?

Dani held her breath until a delivery person jogged into sight. Feeling almost lightheaded, she exhaled loudly. A UPS guy had never looked so good to her before. And some of those men were pretty darn hot.

The man put down a stack of large packages and held out an electronic clipboard. Looking at Hilary, he said, "Sign here, Ms. Newcastle, and then I'll get the rest of the boxes from the truck."

"Thanks." She scribbled her name, knelt by the box, and slit the tape. "I've been waiting for this." She lifted out a child-size pink satin jacket with puffy sleeves and a stand-up collar outlined in gold. Next from the carton was a matching pink ball gown with a sweeping hoop skirt, star details scattered across the shiny material, and petals at the waist. Finally, Hilary held up a glittery gold belt with a flower appliqué.

"Is that for your daughter's princess birthday party?" Dani guessed.

"Yes." Hilary beamed. "Isn't it exquisite?" She grabbed the remaining two boxes and tore them open. "Phew!" She held up a sparkly pink crown, gold wand, and gold shoes. "I was afraid these were missing, which would have just ruined the whole fantasy."

"Uh-huh," Dani agreed, though she thought it would have been fine.

A costume like that had to cost close to a hundred dollars, especially with all the accessories. It seemed a bit excessive to Dani for one day's use, but who was she to judge what a mother spent to make her child happy?

Once the delivery guy had brought in the remaining packages and left, Hilary continued to reveal the contents of each box, holding up each item for Dani to admire. There was a princess castle piñata with all the candy and trinkets to fill it; a banner reading *Happy Birthday, Princess Crystal;* favors; matching plates, napkins, and cutlery; and a princess treasure chest cooler.

Mentally keeping a running total of what Hilary must have spent, Dani gasped. It had to be well over five hundred dollars. Did the stylist save all year for this party or go into debt for it? Then again, Hilary had said her salon was doing very well. She could probably spend a lot of money on her daughter's party without blinking an eye.

Nearly fifteen minutes later, Hilary put all the items back in their cartons, stacked them out of the way, and turned back to Dani. It was a relief when Hilary finally began to cut her hair. Dani was on a tight schedule. She'd only budgeted an hour of her day for the salon appointment and, between the angry guy at the start and the delivery, a lot of time had already been wasted.

Hilary worked silently for a few minutes before saying, "I understand your company donates leftover food to the homeless camp."

"Where did you hear that?" Dani had no idea anyone outside of the girls and herself knew about those donations. And now Gray and Spencer, of course. Heck, she'd only found out yesterday.

"Tippi mentioned it this morning when she was in for a cut." Hilary continued snipping off pieces of hair. "She was concerned that her friend Ivy might be in danger. Those people can turn on you pretty quickly."

"Those people?" Dani wasn't sure she liked the way Hilary said that.

"No need to take offense." Hilary caught Dani's eye in the mirror. "But you have to admit that a lot of them are mentally ill."

"That's true," Dani admitted. "But having mental illness doesn't mean someone is a bad person."

"But it can make them dangerous."

"Sometimes," Dani agreed. "Anyway, Ivy only dealt with one man, and he picked up the food and took it to the camp, so she didn't go there." She paused. "At least after the first time."

"That's good." Hilary finished cutting and then took out a blow-dryer.

"Unfortunately, we'll need to find another go-between." Dani sighed.

"Yeah, Tippi said the guy Ivy had been dealing with passed away yesterday." Hilary grabbed a large round brush and twisted a section of hair around it. "What happened to him?"

Dani wrinkled her brow. Was it okay to reveal Deuce had been murdered? Gray hadn't told her she couldn't talk about it and Frannie was already writing the story, so it was probably all right.

"We're not sure." Dani decided to err on the side of caution and not give many details. "Ivy's uncle and I went to visit him about a concern he had mentioned to me earlier that day, but by the time we found him and called the ambulance, he was gone."

"How sad." Shaking her head, Hilary switched off the dryer, put it and the brush down, then picked up a curling iron. "But maybe it's for the best. That had to be a horrible, horrible way to live."

"I suppose." Dani shrugged. "But there's always that chance that things will get better. He could have found a job. Or possibly family could have taken him in and helped him get back on his feet."

"That's highly unlikely." Hilary shook her head. "Chances of either of those things happening are about a million to one."

"Odds are worse on the lottery." Dani didn't believe for one minute that Deuce was better off dead. "And yet people still buy tickets."

"Hmm." Hilary didn't appear convinced. "Anyway, what I started to say was that you might not realize it, but a lot of folks in Normalton are none too fond of having a homeless camp here."

"I'm not surprised by that." Dani crossed her arms. "No one wants to be reminded that there's a segment of our society living in such difficult circumstances."

"Especially near the college kids," Hilary said. She added, "They panhandle everywhere and some of them really get in your face."

"I know, and that can be frightening," Dani said in her best HR voice, "but if you just keep walking, it's fine. I've never heard of any of the Normalton homeless becoming violent or attacking anyone."

"It probably just hasn't been reported." Hilary finished curling Dani's hair, brushed her off, and removed the cape. "But what I was getting at was, is it true that the personal chef and catering side of your company generally caters to the wealthier citizens in town?"

"Yes. Them and various college organizations and clubs." Dani hesitated as an unwelcome thought occurred to her. "Are you suggesting that donating food to the homeless could hurt my business?"

Unable to sit still, Dani jumped out of the styling chair and paced. Was that why the Rockwells and the Wallaces had canceled? Was it why she hadn't gotten the job for the library party?

"Who knows what anyone will do when pushed." Hilary busied herself sweeping up the curls of hair on the floor and didn't make eye contact. "But I know I wouldn't want to alienate my best clients by supporting something they felt was a blight on their community."

Dani forced herself to stand still and take a calming breath. This was something she needed to think about before she made any decisions. She hated the thought of kowtowing to that kind of peer pressure and felt guilty for even thinking about it, but Hilary was right. The upper middle class made up her entire personal chef clientele. She couldn't afford to lose the income from that part of her business if they decided to boycott her.

Unwilling to continue the discussion with Hilary, Dani walked over to a mirror and examined her image. The stylist had done an amazing job. Instead of a frizzy mess, her dark-blond hair was curled away from her face with smooth waves down her back.

"Oh my goodness!" Dani turned to Hilary. "I love what you did."

Hilary beamed. "Then we have a deal for the catering next Saturday?"

"We do." With a flourish, Dani held out her hand. "Eight cuts and one special occasion shampoo, blowout, and style in exchange for me cooking and serving the food at your party."

"Deal."

The two women shook hands and Dani headed for the exit. She paused in the archway. "If that guy who broke your window calls for another appointment, you should really turn him down."

"And you should really think about just

how much the people in Normalton hate that camp and the homeless people who occupy it."

CHAPTER 10

After leaving the hair salon, Dani couldn't resist making one detour before going home. She'd gotten an alert from her favorite resale shop that it had recently acquired a box of mint condition mid-century salt and pepper shakers. Ever since Dani had discovered Geraldine Cook's stash of these little vintage condiment dispensers in the mansion's attic, collecting them had become her newest obsession.

Luckily, Retro Relics was only a couple of blocks from Holy Snips and there was a parking spot right in front of the store. As Dani got out of her van, a strong breeze blew her hair into her eyes and she sighed. She hadn't even been able to keep the sleek new look an hour before it was messed up.

The wind had gotten a lot stronger in the few minutes it had taken her to drive from the salon to the shop, and she looked up at the sky. Dark clouds hovered to the north and she hoped they were bringing some much-needed rain and cooler weather.

The lemony fresh scent of furniture polish greeted Dani as she pushed open the door. Like the store's pretty pink exterior, the inside of the shop was done in welcoming pastels. Its layout invited browsing and Dani wished she had more time.

The whole place could fit into the mansion's first floor with room to spare, and as Dani walked down the center aisle, she gave the merchandise on display a quick scan. She'd promised herself that she'd be in and out in ten minutes — fifteen tops — so she didn't stop to look at any of the enticing offerings.

As she neared the rear of the store, faint fifties music came from the open door of a storage room. Dani increased her speed, steadfastly ignoring all the cool clothes on the racks. Rose, the owner of Retro Relics, had said she'd keep the salt and pepper shakers at the back register for Dani if she got to the store by that afternoon.

When Dani approached the checkout, Rose strolled out of the storage room and beamed at her. "You made it."

Rose was an elegant woman in her late sixties or early seventies. As always, she was impeccably dressed and coiffed. Her silver

158

hair was in a stacked pixie bob and she wore a blue floral print Diane Von Furstenberg wrap dress with navy pumps.

"I really shouldn't have taken the time. My schedule is packed and I still have a gig this evening, but you know how to lure me into your trap." Dani eagerly examined the counter. "Where are they?"

"I tucked them out of sight until you arrived." Rose grabbed a plastic bin and set it in front of Dani. "Here you go. I think there are several you'll like."

Dani swiftly sorted the shakers into yes, no, and maybe rows. Back into the box went the fish, owls, ducks, and mice with cheese. She already had those. Next to be rejected were the shell-encrusted souvenir Hawaiian ones. They were cute, but they didn't fit into her collection.

The definite yeses were the T-bone steaks, metal milk cans, metal flat irons, bucket and brush, and stove and coal. She was on the fence about the wooden donkey and the golden half hearts.

It was clear that Rose had been paying close attention to Dani and noticed her indecision because with a sly look in her direction, the shopkeeper said, "You can have all seven pairs for seventy-five dollars." When Dani didn't respond, she tapped a pair with her bright-red nails and coaxed, "The flat irons and milk jugs are worth at least fifteen apiece."

Knowing she had to make up her mind and get home, Dani countered, "True. But steaks and the donkeys are probably closer to three dollars, and the bucket and brush and coal and stove around ten."

"That leaves the broken heart." Rose tipped her head. "I can't find it online so I'm gambling it's in the mid-dollar range, but who knows?" she singsonged. "Maybe the reason I can't find it is because it's so rare."

"Hmm." Dani stroked her chin. The half hearts were calling to her, but she didn't know why. "Who brought these in to sell?"

"She wasn't one of my regulars." Rose shook her head. "And the woman definitely didn't want to chat. She was in and out of here in five minutes."

"I wonder if they're stolen," Dani mused. "I'd hate to think that someone was missing their treasures and I had them on my shelf."

"I'm pretty darn sure there's not a lot of demand for hot salt and pepper shakers," Rose snickered. "By the way she was dressed, it seems more likely that the woman was cleaning out a deceased relative's house and in a hurry to get back to finish the job."

"I suppose." Dani sighed. It didn't really matter. It wasn't as if she could track down the real owner, and she had to make a decision. "Okay. I'll give you seventy-five for the seven of them."

She handed over her credit card. Rose ran it, then wrapped the shakers in tissue paper and put them into a plastic bag. Cradling the sack to her chest, Dani whistled "Tutti Frutti" along with the music as she hurried to her van. Five minutes later, she was home, and after changing into her chef jacket and pants, she started pulling together what she needed for the band dinner.

While she worked, she kept thinking about Rose's theory concerning the shakers' origins. It made her think of Deuce and his belongings. Who would clean out his campsite, and where would his things go? If they never found out his identity or located any family, would they end up forever in the police evidence locker?

Shaking her head sadly, Dani began to load her van for the event. It was already past three thirty and once again her scheduled helper was nowhere to be found, but this time it was Starr who was late, not Tippi or Ivy. Starr was usually the most reliable of the three girls. If she was starting to blow off her shifts, Dani would know she'd been too lenient with her employees. She would have to call a meeting and lay down the law. Maybe come up with some consequences for tardiness and no-shows.

Ten minutes later, just as Dani slid the last container of supplies into the back of the van, Starr's Caribbean-aqua MINI Cooper turned into the driveway and skidded to a stop. Starr immediately burst out of the car, her dark skin shiny with perspiration.

Spotting Dani, Starr ran toward her and panted, "Sorry I'm late."

"Me too." Dani narrowed her eyes. "It's beginning to feel as if you girls are treating your jobs as an optional activity instead of an obligation." She crossed her arms. "And it has to stop."

"That's not fair." Starr put her hands on her hips. "I've never not been on time before. Tippi is the one who's always late."

"True," Dani conceded. "But all of you have left early or been on your phones texting instead of working." She uncrossed her arms and gestured to the van. "Get inside. We need to get going."

Once they were driving toward the quad, Starr took a breath and said, "I really am sorry. Robert and I were with his friends playing this cool new game and it was three o'clock before I realized it." She smoothed her denim skirt. "From now on, I'll set the alarm on my phone. It won't happen again."

"I'd appreciate that." Dani turned down the alley next to the Normalton University Union. "But I think it's time for all of us to have a talk and agree to some job guidelines and consequences."

"You're probably right." Starr hung her head. "We do sort of take advantage of your good nature sometimes and I, for one, am sorry."

"Thank you." Dani pulled the van up to the service entrance at the rear of the building, switched off the engine, and reached over and squeezed Starr's knee. "I'm grateful that you've noticed that, and I have to admit some of the problem is my fault." Dani jumped down from the vehicle and headed toward the back.

"Right," Starr called after her, then hopped out of her side and joined Dani at the rear of the van. "You need to be meaner."

The band dinner was being held at the Union, a utilitarian brick building at the head of the quad. The dinner was a gathering of the director, incoming performers, and the new musicians' parents. Dani's contract called for no more than seventy guests and a social hour that started at six, where guests could help themselves to antipasto while getting to know one another.

Dani and Starr quickly hauled the food and equipment into the service elevator and rode to the Union's top floor. This level was often rented out for meetings and private events, and the band dinner was being held in a suite of rooms connected to a small kitchen.

Once they had all the supplies spread out on the stainless-steel counters, Dani dug into the pocket of her chef's pants and flipped the keys to Starr. "Go ahead and park the van in the adjacent lot." As the girl walked away, Dani shouted, "And don't forget to put the temporary event parking permit on the dashboard this time. It's in the glove compartment and I can't afford another parking ticket." When Starr waved without looking back, Dani yelled, "And make sure it shows through the window. All we need is to be towed."

After Starr left, Dani pushed through the kitchen's swinging doors to inspect the area where the guests would gather before dinner. Like most rental spaces, it was no-frills and bland, and she wondered if she needed to start adding decor items to her catering price list.

As Dani had specified, there were several bistro-height tables scattered around the room. They were covered in white cloths but nothing else to make them feel festive. A nice centerpiece would go a long way to perk up the atmosphere.

Instead of formal hors d'oeuvres, which her client had declined, Dani planned to put trays of cheeses and deli meat slices layered with roasted vegetables and drizzled with herbed olive oil on each of the tables.

With no liquor being served, soda dispensers with stacks of plastic cups were arranged along the far walls. And for the purists, bottles of water stood in large tubs of ice on stands at the back.

Far from satisfied with the look of the predinner space, Dani walked next door and scrutinized the dining area. At least there, someone had put an effort into the decorations. The band uniform colors, which were also the university colors, had been used as a theme.

Placed evenly around the floor were nine round tables covered in red cloths and set with white napkins. Vases of white carnations with large black plastic musical notes arranged among the flowers were in the center of each of the tables.

Pleased that the rooms were ready for the food to be served, she returned to the kitchen to start preparing the meal. Once again, at her client's request, the menu was fairly simple. Although everything was already assembled and ready to cook, she would still need to be on top of things from the beginning. At least both Ivy and Tippi were coming to help with the dinner service.

At quarter to six, the band director pushed open the swinging door, shoved his head into the kitchen, and said, "If you want to put out the antipasto trays now, the kids and their parents should be arriving shortly."

Graham Jones was a large man in his early forties with a deep, resonant voice. He looked as if he would be more at home coaching football than conducting a band, but rumor had it that he was considered one of the best college directors in the Midwest. And having heard the band play, Dani certainly believed that assertion.

It was said that larger, more prestigious schools had tried to lure Graham away from Normalton University, but none had succeeded. He often stated that he was happy where he was and had no intention of taking any of the offers of more money or fame.

"Terrific." Dani smiled at Graham and

gestured for him to join her over by the counter, where eight trays were lined up and ready to go. "Would you like a sample before I take them into the other room?"

"Don't mind if I do." Graham reached for a toothpick from the container in the center of the platter and stabbed a rolled-up slice of meat. He popped it into his mouth, and after he chewed and swallowed, he moaned, "That was amazing. What exactly was it?"

"Mortadella with a drizzle of herbed olive oil." Dani beamed. The Italian sausage made of finely ground, heat-cured pork contained small cubes of pork fat, whole black peppercorns, olives, myrtle berries, and pistachios. It was a bit pricey but totally worth the cost. "There's also prosciutto and Genoa salami, as well as aged provolone, smoked gouda, and spiced Havarti cheeses."

"I recognize most of the veggies." Graham scratched his bald head and pointed to a light green pepper. "But what are those?"

"Peperoncini," Dani answered. "You've probably seen them as a side to Italian beef sandwiches. It's considered a sweet pepper, but can be a little hot if you aren't used to those kinds of foods."

Graham winced. "Then I'd better not let my wife catch me eating those. The doctor told me to lay off spicy foods." He grabbed

167

one and winked. "But I love the heat, and what she doesn't know won't hurt me." As he chewed, he looked around the kitchen and nodded to Starr, who was busy brushing rolls with a mixture of garlic butter, minced parsley, and coarse ground sea salt asked, "Do you need a hand getting the trays out?"

"Thanks, but I've got a cart and my servers should be here any minute." Dani started loading the platters next to the bread and cracker baskets already on the cart's shelves, then jerked her chin toward the other room and said, "But I think I hear voices so I better get this out there before they eat the napkins."

Graham chuckled and held the door for Dani as she pushed the trolley over the threshold. There were already a few students and their parents milling around, and she quickly distributed the antipasto trays and the baskets of rosemary crackers and slices of Italian bread.

She waved at Graham as he swooped in to schmooze with the parents and kids, then hurried back to the kitchen. A few minutes later, Ivy and Tippi arrived. She sent them with Starr to the dining room to start placing ice into glasses and pouring water. When they finished with that, they would put out the plates of chopped salad.

Dani checked the lasagna rolls and chicken cacciatore. Both needed another thirty minutes. Satisfied that the food was under control, Dani grabbed a bottle of water, sat on a stool, and checked her cell.

She'd felt the phone vibrating earlier but hadn't had time to respond. There was a voicemail from Gray asking to come by the mansion the next afternoon around two so he could ask Dani some more questions. There was also a text from Spencer asking if he could talk to her and the girls after they finished their catering job.

She returned Gray's call and left him a message saying that she'd be available until 4:00 p.m. After that, she had to leave for a personal chef job.

Next, she texted Spencer to tell him that they would probably get home between ten thirty and eleven and he was welcome to stop over after that time.

Glancing up from her phone, she observed the girls loading the carts with salad plates and heading to the dining room with them.

Dani looked back at the rest of her messages and smiled. All the other calls were from potential customers looking for quotes. She'd have to wait until tomorrow after the lunch rush to talk to them, but it was good to see the number of people interested in her business was picking up again. The previous couple of weeks had been slow and she'd been worried.

Glancing at the time on her cell, Dani saw that it was a couple of minutes past seven o'clock. She hastily stood, smoothed her chef's jacket, and entered the party room. She announced that dinner was served and trotted back into the kitchen.

As per Dani's prior instructions, Starr and Ivy returned from the dining room to help Dani plate the main course. Dani had allowed twenty minutes between the salad and the entrée, which left thirteen minutes, and she needed all hands on deck to get the food ready to serve while it was still hot.

As the three of them went to work lining up the empty dishes along the counter so they could be filled, Dani realized one of her helpers was missing and asked, "Where's Tippi? Don't tell me she's still putting out her salad plates."

Ivy ducked her head and remained silent, but Starr raised her chin and said, "She's flirting with one of the assistant band directors." When Ivy frowned, Starr turned on her and snapped, "I don't know about you, but I'm sick of doing her job and I'm not going to cover for her anymore."

"I'll take care of it." Dani scowled and made a mental note to call a meeting sooner rather than later. "But for now, these plates need to be completed and served."

Just as they were finishing, Tippi strolled into the kitchen, giggling. "Marcus is so cute. He's a graduate student in the music department." When neither Dani nor the other girls responded, Tippi huffed and grabbed one of the carts stacked with plates. "Guess I'd better get these to the tables while they're still hot."

Starr rolled her eyes and followed Tippi with the other cart while Ivy remained and continued to help Dani fill the plates.

After a few minutes of silence, Ivy asked, "Any news about Deuce?"

Dani shook her head. "Detective Christiansen is stopping by tomorrow with a few more questions. Maybe he'll have some information to share." She shrugged. "But the police usually play things pretty close to the chest, so I wouldn't get my hopes up."

"Well . . ." Ivy's eyes twinkled. "Detective Dreamy does seem to have a crush on you, so he might be a bit more willing than usual to give us the scoop."

Dani snorted. "He does not. He's just really into cooking."

"He's really into something." Ivy giggled. "And it's not just your cupcakes."

CHAPTER 11

While the entrees were being served, Graham gave a quick welcome speech. Once everyone had their food, Dani returned to the kitchen to plate the dessert, leaving her helpers to refill water glasses and bread baskets.

Thirty minutes later, the guests were presented with the fig and parmesan cheesecake. While the girls poured coffee, Dani walked through the dining room.

It had become her practice to socialize a bit near the end of each catering gig, as it gave her a chance to hear what people thought of the food. Also, dressed in her bright-red chef jacket, it was obvious she was the cook, so anyone who enjoyed the meal and might have a job for her in the future could stop her and ask for her business card.

As Dani neared one of the tables, she overheard the parents chatting about the benefit of belonging to the marching band. It was an interesting topic and she paused to listen to the discussion.

An attractive woman wearing a pretty black-and-white dress said, "From what I've read, playing music affects the brain. There's something about the math involved that keeps the brain active and growing and can even help alleviate or prevent depression."

Dani wrinkled her brow. Was she too old to take up an instrument?

"And don't forget, Kim, how marching and playing helps develop neurological multitasking," a handsome man with silver hair added. "Not to mention the discipline that's needed to attend rehearsals, memorize the drills and the music, and work as a team."

Hmm! Dani pursed her lips. Maybe her boarders should join the band.

A woman with long blond hair flicked a strand behind her shoulder, and said, "But, Greg, I think the friendships that occur are the most important things that our kids get from being part of the band."

"I like that they learn resilience," another parent responded. "Our kids learn making a mistake or having a setback is not the end of the world. That no one is, or expected to be, perfect all the time. And that criticism can actually help them become better."

Nodding her agreement and wishing that more of the job applicants that she'd worked with in her stint in human resources had been in a school band, Dani resumed her stroll between the tables.

She stopped again as she approached Graham's table. He and his wife were surrounded by several other diners. Hearing lowered voices and observing darting glances, Dani's heart skipped a beat. Were they complaining about the food she'd served? The fig and parmesan cheesecake might have been a tad too unusual for this group and might not have been the best choice. Maybe she should have stuck with good old tiramisu or cannoli.

Ducking behind a tall rack holding the dirty dishes, she eased off the caddy's brake and inched it forward. She still had to strain to hear what was being discussed, but from what she could gather, the people talking to Graham were all locals, some of whom were on the university's payroll.

It wasn't a surprise that the folks who lived in Normalton would send their kids to the college. The savings from living at home would be enormous. Then there were the people who actually worked for NU. The tuition break for employees' children would be motivation enough.

An elegantly dressed woman finished touching up her lipstick and loftily informed the group, "I really wasn't at all shocked to hear that someone had been murdered in that homeless camp." She gave an exaggerated shudder. "My husband has been telling Mayor Boulder for the past six months that he should send the police in to disband that horrible place."

A man holding two dessert plates in one hand and using the other to shovel cheesecake into his mouth as fast as he could, snorted.

Crumbs flew from his lips as he pontificated, "Kristina, Kristina, Kristina, your husband has the mayor in his back pocket. If he truly wanted that homeless camp gone, it would be gone. But he doesn't give two hoots about Normalton or what an unsightly place like that camp does to our community's reputation."

Kristina tucked the distinctive silver Dior lipstick tube into her purse and said, "That's not true, Reverend. When that homeless woman tried to snatch my purse and then spit on me, Steven begged Mayor Boulder to clear those people out. But he claimed the media would crucify him. And that they'd just move to another spot in town."

"Now that is probably true." An older woman sighed. "Besides, a lot of those homeless campers are young couples and families searching for work and housing. It's not fair to take away what little security they have just because we're offended by their poverty."

"That's bull hockey, Marsha!" The reverend finished both of the desserts in his hand and grabbed another untouched plate from the table. "Most of those freeloaders are druggies and alcoholics."

"And mentally ill." Kristina's voice sank to a whisper and Dani had to abandon her hiding spot and move closer to hear her next remark. "Some of those guys are *not* in their right minds."

"Which means we should help them, not try to drive them away." Marsha frowned. "What would your parishioners say, Reverend?"

"The Lord helps those who help themselves." The reverend stuffed another bite in his mouth. "And my congregation agrees with me."

Graham finally spoke up and said, "It's easy to say we should help them, and I agree we should, but if they don't trust you, there's very little you can do for them." He paused and took a sip of water. "A friend of mine is a member of a veterans group that has been trying for a number of years to build that trust."

"How?" Marsha asked, moving closer to where Graham was seated.

"The members go out to the camp and leave boxes of toilet paper, water, canned food, and sleeping bags." Graham smiled. "And inside those boxes are pamphlets with information about the services that are available to the homeless vets. Still, only some take advantage of the shelters and the government programs they could utilize."

"Yeah." A tall, thin man wearing a perfectly tailored suit crossed his arms. "Because they're too lazy to even do that," he sniffed. "And are they really even veterans?" The man chuckled meanly. "If so, I'll bet it isn't of any war we've ever heard of."

Dani shot a glance at Graham's wife, who was nodding her head. Mrs. Jones seemed as if she agreed with the guy arguing with her husband, but she kept her mouth shut, her lips compressed into a thin, hard line.

"That kind of statement does nothing but reveal your own ignorance. The actions of the homeless have nothing to do with laziness, and they certainly don't need to lie about being veterans." Graham frowned at the guy who had spoken. "Some have been through hell. They just want their space and to be left alone."

"What makes you such an expert on the homeless?" the reverend demanded.

Graham rose from his seat, faced the minister, and declared, "Because my brother was one of them." When everyone gasped, he added, "When Lou came back from serving in Desert Storm, his PTSD was so severe he couldn't stand to be near people, so he just dropped off the grid. Thank goodness he still wore his dog tags or we might never have known when he passed away. He was in a camp in Oregon very similar to the one in Normalton, and one of the outreach groups that were trying to assist the people there informed us of his death."

Dani sighed. It was too bad that Deuce hadn't been wearing his dog tags. Had he been hiding his true identity?

Noticing that people were starting to leave, Dani pushed away thoughts of the murdered vet. It was time to clean up. She began pushing the rack of dirty dishes toward the kitchen but only made it about halfway before the reverend hurried up to her.

The clergyman panted, "I wanted to tell you how much my wife and I enjoyed your food."

"Why, thank you." Dani hadn't appreciated the man's opinions about the homeless, but she tried to infuse some warmth into her voice anyway.

"By the way, I'm Reverend Flynn." He held out his hand. "Do you have a card?"

"I do." Dani took one out of the pocket on her sleeve and gave it to the reverend.

"You know a lot of local companies donate their time and resources to my church." Reverend Flynn fixed his gaze on Dani and waited expectantly.

"How nice for you and your congregation." Dani gave him a stiff smile. "Parishioners of my church do the same to support it."

"Wonderful." The reverend's frown spread wrinkles across his face, making Dani reestimate his age from late forties to late fifties. "Of course, the smaller churches don't have as much need as one of our size. Perhaps you'd like to attend one of our services to see all we have to offer."

"That's a generous offer, but I'm happy with my church." Dani ground her teeth but continued to smile. "Please excuse me, Reverend Flynn. I need to finish up so I don't keep my helpers out too late."

Dani tried to move the cart forward, but Reverend Flynn stood in the way. She

180

cleared her throat, but he didn't budge. Staring slack jawed at her business card, he turned it over and over in his pudgy, well-manicured fingers.

He didn't seem to notice that he was blocking her path, so Dani backed up and went around him. She certainly wasn't going to wait to see what about her card had him so entranced.

As Dani approached the swinging doors, she heard Starr say, "No. You're wrong, Tippi. We don't want to hear your excuses. Just stand there silently in your wrongness and be wrong."

"Is that right?" Tippi snapped.

"Hell to the yeah," Ivy chimed in.

"In my defense," Tippi whined, "I was left unsupervised."

For a moment, Dani was shocked that Ivy and Starr were reprimanding their friend. Then she recalled the conversation that she'd had with Starr. Evidently, she'd shared Dani's dissatisfaction with their work habits with Ivy and the pair had decided to take matters into their own hands.

Dani smiled. Maybe she wouldn't have to call a meeting to lay down the law after all. Still, as much as she didn't want to do it, any improvement in the girls' behavior would only be a temporary fix if there were no consequences for their actions.

Dani pushed through the doors and was pleased to see that the girls had already made a good start on the kitchen. Even after hearing Starr and Ivy rebuking Tippi, Dani was still shocked when Tippi hurried over and grabbed the dish rack from her.

Without a word, the girl pushed the trolley toward the dishwasher and began to load the dirty plates into the hulking appliance. Dani scanned the area. Starr was packing the Chef-to-Go carts with equipment and trays of leftover food, while Ivy was spraying the counters and other surfaces with a bottle of commercial grade kitchen cleaner.

Their initiative was a pleasant surprise. Usually they waited for her to tell them what to do.

Beaming at her helpers, Dani said, "It looks like you three have everything under control in here, so I'll go make a final sweep of the event space to see that we haven't forgotten anything. Once I finish out there, we can start the dishwasher and haul our stuff out to the van."

"Don't we have to wait for the dishwasher to stop and put the plates and silverware away?" Ivy asked scrubbing at a stubborn stain.

"Not this time." Dani hooked her thumbs

in the waistband of her pants. "I added a clause in the contract that the Union's custodial staff would be responsible for that."

Starr tilted her head. "You're really getting the hang of this, aren't you?"

"I'm trying." Dani grabbed a bin and thumped the swinging doors open with her hip.

Checking the perimeter, she found a couple of dirty plastic glasses that folks had left hidden among the decorative plants and wedged between the chairs. She put them in the trash can and went into the dining room.

Someone had turned off the overhead lights and she let out a frustrated sigh. Dani was fumbling along the wall looking for the switch for the fluorescents when she heard the door behind her squeal open. Her pulse kicked into high gear and she swung around. There was a bulky outline blocking the brightness from the hallway and she tensed, ready to make a run for the kitchen.

Before she could move, the figure crooned, "I was hoping you'd come back."

Swallowing a scream, Dani backed up. The light switch poked her in the shoulder and she reached behind her, thrusting the toggle upward. Once her eyes adjusted to the sudden brilliance, she saw Reverend Flynn marching toward her with an angry look on his face.

He was clutching her cherry-red business card and demanded, "Are you the one feeding the homeless?"

"Why do you ask?" Dani shuffled a few feet to her right.

She still wanted a clear shot at the kitchen doors. The man might be a member of the clergy, but her skin crawled at his nearness and she wasn't at all sure that he wouldn't hurt her.

"I heard that some new catering business was giving their leftovers to those people out at the camp," Reverend Flynn said, not bothering to answer Dani's question. "Is it your company that's doing that?"

Dani loved living in a place the size of Normalton. It didn't have the frantic energy of a city; it also wasn't a small community like Towanda, where she'd grown up. Until now, she would have sworn that Normalton didn't have the same kind of grapevine as her hometown. But evidently the news of Ivy giving food to the homeless had spread.

The reverend must have grown impatient for an answer because he gave her a nasty glare and snarled, "It is you, isn't it?" When Dani nodded, he barked, his voice heavy with derision, "Don't you know that if you feed a stray, it keeps coming back?"

"So I said they're people, not dogs. I'll give them food if I want to. And that's when he threw my card at me and stomped away." Dani finished her story and took a long sip of her merlot.

She was sitting in a large booth at Flame's Wood Oven Grill and the aroma of garlic, melting cheese, and oregano made her mouth water. She was always hungry after a catering job, and she couldn't resist when she'd read Spencer's text offering to take her and the girls out for pizza after their gig.

The decision had been unanimous. Once Ivy, Tippi, and Starr heard about Spencer's invitation, they had all declared they were starving too. So once Dani and her helpers had finished at the Union, they headed for the van. Fifteen minutes later, they'd met Spencer at the restaurant.

After placing their orders and being served their drinks, Ivy had said, "Tell Uncle Spence what happened with that reverend after the dinner." Before Dani could respond, Ivy had screwed up her face and declared, "If I were a bird, I sure know who I'd poop on."

185

After his niece's pronouncement, Spencer had insisted on Dani telling him what had happened.

Dani had reluctantly taken him through the entire incident. So far, his only reaction was a tightening of his jaw.

Finally, he took a swallow of his beer, then, clearly forcing himself to remain impassive, asked, "Any idea who's been telling everyone about your charitable endeavors?"

"I don't think it's been any big secret." Dani recalled that Hilary had stated that Tippi told her about the leftovers and looked at each of the girls. "Have you guys mentioned that we've been donating the food to the homeless camp?"

"Of course." Ivy nodded her head so vehemently, her eyes nearly crossed. "It's a great example of how being charitable and extending a hand to those who are down and out doesn't have to cost a lot. I've been trying to get other businesses to help in the same way."

Dani exchanged a worried glance with Spencer. After hearing that group at the band dinner's opinion of the homeless "problem," she was afraid that Ivy's good intentions might get her in trouble.

"I mentioned it to my father," Starr said.

"He's decided to organize a mobile medical unit to go to the camp and treat people there."

Dani blew out a breath of relief. Starr's father was a thoracic surgeon and extremely well respected. If Dr. Fleming was planning to help out the homeless, it meant the whole community didn't feel negatively about them.

"I talked to my prelaw fraternity about it this morning." Tippi lifted her chin. "We're donating part of the proceeds from our fun run to the Normalton Mission's homeless outreach program. They bring services out to the camp rather than making the homeless come to them."

"Well, I guess that answers the question of how the reverend heard about Chef-to-Go donating food." Spencer's tone was resigned.

He raked his fingers through his coal-black hair and Dani forced herself to look away from the flex of his biceps. Although she'd like him to be more, he'd made it clear that he was just a friend, and it wasn't nice to drool over a friend's muscles.

Just then, the pizza arrived, and while everyone filled their plates, Dani searched for a new topic of conversation. She was tired of talking about the reverend's reaction to her choice of charity.

Waiting for her slice of pepperoni and mushroom to cool so she could eat it without incinerating her tongue on the lava-like cheese, Dani asked, "What was it you wanted to talk to us about, Spencer?"

He swallowed the bite he'd just taken, then turned to Tippi and said, "Can you describe the Halloween masks that your carjackers wore?"

Tippi grimaced. "Well, it was really scary." She curled her lips. "Actually, it looked like a mass of tentacles, not a face at all."

When Spencer was silent, Dani asked, "Why do you want to know about the mask? Do you have a suspect?"

"No." Spencer shook his head. "There's no special reason. I just forgot to ask before."

"Really?" Dani raised her brows skeptically.

Spencer refused to meet her eyes, but his expression had a look of I-may-not-be-telling-you everything-but-I'm-not-admitting-it.

Instantly, Dani knew he was keeping something from her. And after her ex-boyfriend's massive deception, she was sick and tired of men who didn't tell the truth.

CHAPTER 12

At precisely seven fifty-five on Wednesday morning, Spencer walked into the NU security building. He did a quick reconnaissance of the small vestibule and was relieved that there were no sobbing females huddled along any of the walls or hiding behind the plants.

Pleased that things were back to normal, at least for the time being, he crossed the short distance to the stairs and climbed to the second floor. His good mood continued when he found that his desk was clear of any of the annoying unicorn-themed message slips Carly, the new dispatcher, favored.

Adding to his contentment, the break room was empty, which meant all his guards were out making rounds. Maybe things were finally calming down on NU's campus.

After topping off his travel cup, Spencer ducked into Carly's cubicle and said, "I'll be at the police station for the next hour or so. Phone me immediately if you get any unusual complaints."

"Uh, okay." The young woman looked up from the textbook she was reading and blinked at him from behind her oversize, pink-framed glasses. "You mean something weird like the creature?"

"Exactly." Spencer ground his teeth. He was so sick of hearing about the Creature from Blackheart canal, he could spit nickels.

The dispatcher was a recent addition to his staff and Spencer was still debating whether the position was worth the cost to his budget. They needed someone to answer phones and relay messages, but he wasn't sure if there was enough work to justify her salary. She seemed to spend more time studying than doing her job.

Putting budgetary concerns out of his head, Spencer headed to his pickup. On the ten-minute drive to downtown Normalton, he reviewed the material he wanted to discuss with the police chief.

He'd asked to meet with her yesterday afternoon to share his thoughts on what Cindi Streicher had revealed, but Chief Cleary hadn't been able to fit him into her schedule until this morning. He'd wanted to insist that he had vital information, but he'd had to face the fact that he was no longer a hotshot undercover agent. To the police, he was nothing more than a security guard, and most cops didn't think much of what they called rent-a-cops.

Spencer supposed that he could have passed his information on to the detective handling Deuce's murder. But there was something about Gray Christensen, something that Spencer couldn't quite put his finger on, but it bugged the crap out of him.

If he were honest with himself, it was probably because the guy had been flirting with Dani. Spencer knew that deep down inside, once he got his head on straight, he wanted Dani for himself, and Christiansen had definitely been coming on to her. What kind of cop did that at the scene of a crime?

In addition to pure jealousy, Spencer *was* worried that the detective was trying to trick Dani into lowering her guard and saying something that might get her into trouble.

Having finally admitted to himself that he was falling for Dani, Spencer parked his truck in the public lot opposite the police station and jogged across the street. Technically, he was jaywalking and he should have used the marked crossing, but it was at the end of the block and he was in a hurry.

Still, his actions made him recognize that he had held onto some of the bad habits he'd acquired when he was undercover. Rationalizing his less-than-admirable behavior was one of them. That was something about himself he would have to improve.

Slowing, Spencer examined the police department's square brick structure. Like most other municipal buildings, it had absolutely no personality, but he tended to be hyperaware of his surroundings and gave the exterior a thorough inspection before pushing open the glass door.

As soon as Spencer stepped into the sterile beige vestibule, he wrinkled his nose. The headache-inducing stench of heavy-duty cleaning products hung in the air. Looking around, he noticed the public restrooms on either side of the small space and appreciated that the odor of bleach was preferable to the alternative.

When Spencer entered the police station proper, he was surprised at the silence that greeted him. The last time he'd been there, the visitor seating section had been overflowing. The plastic chairs had been full and people had been sitting on the floor and leaning against the wall. But today, the waiting room contained only a couple of folks filling out forms.

Without the college student population, Normalton's population was barely above fifty thousand, but due to the three universities and the town's vintage car and motorcycle collection, there was usually a lot of activity. With orientation week at all three schools, Spencer was surprised at the emptiness of the police station. He would have expected more of a crowd during this kind of prime troublemaking time.

Turning his attention to the dispatch area, Spencer saw a single uniformed man perched on a stool staring at his cell phone.

Walking up to the counter, he caught the man's attention and announced, "Spencer Drake to see Chief Cleary." When the officer didn't react, Spencer added, "I have an eight thirty appointment."

The guy swiveled toward the computer and clicked a few keys, then said, "You're on the list. Do you know where her office is?"

"Thanks, I do." Spencer jerked his chin in acknowledgment and strode toward the elevator.

After a short ride, Spencer emerged into an empty waiting area situated across from the office of the chief's administrative assistant. He knocked on the closed door and entered after someone called out, "Come in."

Stepping over the threshold, Spencer saw

that not much had changed from his previous visit. The front two-thirds of the room were still lined with rows of gray metal file cabinets and shelves containing thick red, yellow, and blue three-ring binders grouped by color.

The only difference from last time was that instead of a surely teenager manning the desk, an attractive woman in her late twenties was sitting behind it.

He nodded to her and said, "Spencer Drake to see Chief Cleary."

The woman looked him up and down. With a sultry chuckle, she held out her hand and said, "I'm Suzette Boulder, the chief's PA. She's on the phone right now, but she'll be with you momentarily."

"That's fine." Spencer shook the woman's hand, but when he tried to let go, she dug her long, scarlet-tipped nails into his flesh and held on. He tugged his fingers free and said, "I'll just take a seat in the other room."

"No need to go so far away." The corners of the woman's bright-red lips tilted upward. "You can wait right here." She waved at a chair in front of her desk. "I see the position of NU security chief has been significantly upgraded. The guy in charge when I was there had to be a hundred years old."

"How did you know I was head of security?" Spencer frowned. He'd thought he had kept a fairly low profile, at least off campus.

"I Googled you when I saw your name in the chief's schedule."

"I see." Spencer sat down, scooting the chair backward to avoid inhaling her heavy rose-scented perfume.

"But there were no pictures." Suzette pouted.

That was a relief! Spencer blew out a breath. Still, he'd better get a tech at his old agency to sterilize his media presence again. He needed to request that they do that every few months.

"If I'd have known you were this hot, I would have worn something prettier."

Suzette's annoying voice broke into his thoughts and Spencer was barely able to stop himself from squirming. He wished the chief's assistant would have let him wait in the other room. He'd rather cool his heels reading an out-of-date magazine than fend off a woman like her. There was no denying she was nice looking, but he wasn't attracted to predatory females. And Suzette definitely gave off that kind of vibe.

She had clearly expected Spencer to compliment her, and when he remained silent, she tossed her hair and asked, "Are you from this area originally?" When he shook his head, she continued, "Is your wife from around here?"

In what Spencer was damn sure was a practiced move, Suzette leaned forward, resting her arms on the desktop and treating him to a view of her cleavage. He shook his head again, hoping she'd take that to mean he was married and stop batting her lashes at him.

Narrowing her eyes, she said, "You sure don't talk much." Then in a voice that oozed like melted rubber, she said, "The strong, silent type doesn't usually appeal to me, but for you, I'll make an exception."

"I find that I learn a lot more if I'm not trying to fill every available silence with words." Spencer kept his expression blank.

Trying to ignore the annoying woman, he looked around the room. There was a thin coat of dust on the shelves, and in the corner, a philodendron with brown, curled-up leaves appeared near death. Things had certainly changed. The last time he was in this office, the plant had been green and healthy and the shelves sparkling clean.

Suzette rapped on the desktop. "Earth to Spencer. I'm bored. Let's talk about something interesting."

This office wasn't as small as his own, but suddenly it seemed the size of a linen closet. He tugged at his tie, wondering if he was becoming claustrophobic. But he'd once hidden in a casket without feeling this closed in, so he doubted it.

Spencer crossed his arms and said, "I prefer to keep my mind on business."

"Seriously?" Suzette widened her un-naturally blue eyes and sulked. "What's the fun in that?" She examined him from head to toe. "And I bet you and I could have some fun."

Scooting her chair away from the desk so that Spencer had a clear view of her entire body, Suzette ran her palms down the hips of her tight white skirt, then toyed with the buttons on her silky black blouse and crossed her legs, dangling one of her high-heeled black sandals from her toe.

When she turned to retrieve her phone from behind her, her long black hair rippled in waves down her back. Spencer's lips twisted. She reminded him of his ex. Maybe that's why she didn't do a thing for him.

Suzette faced forward and gazed at Spencer, waiting for a response, but when he remained impassive, she shot him an offended look, and her voice rose incredulously. "You're turning down *this*?" She jerked her thumb at her substantial chest.

"Yep."

"Fine," Suzette sneered. "You couldn't handle me even if I gave you the instruction booklet."

"That's probably right." Spencer shrugged. "And I don't want to try."

Fuming, Suzette picked up the phone, pressed a button, and in a clipped voice said, "Your eight thirty is here." Banging down the receiver, Suzette picked up her cell and, without taking her eyes from the device, said, "The chief will see you now."

"Thank you." Spencer rose from his chair and walked over to the chief's door.

He knocked and the chief swung open the door. Spencer had met Meredith Cleary during a previous murder investigation involving an NU student and he smiled at the attractive fortysomething woman who ushered him inside.

"It's nice to see you again." Meredith waved her hand to an impressive oak credenza and asked, "Would you like a cup of coffee?"

"No, thanks." Spencer sighed. "I'm about at my caffeine limit."

"Sadly, I completely understand." Meredith smoothed an ash-blond curl back into the sleek bun she wore at the back of her neck. "I'm never sure if I've had too much coffee or not enough."

Spencer chuckled.

Meredith waved at the chairs opposite her desk and said, "Sit down." She settled in her own seat and glanced at the closed office door. "I hope my new admin didn't keep you waiting."

"Uh . . ." Spencer wasn't sure where the chief was going with that remark.

"I can see from your face that she did." Meredith narrowed her steely gray eyes. "Did she tell you that I was on the phone?" When Spencer nodded, she continued, "I'm really going to have to do something about her."

"Oh?" Spencer was about to ask what the chief meant when she said, "I knew I never should have hired her, but her father begged me to give her a job and I owed him a favor. She was fired for coming on to her last employer, evidently she has some kind of compulsion that makes her to try to seduce any attractive guy she meets, and he thought working for a woman would solve that problem."

"He didn't take into consideration all the men around a police station?"

"He was desperate and not thinking."

Meredith shook her head. "But I'm going to have to let her go. It took me a month or so to tumble to the fact that she delayed sending in my appointments if the man was good-looking. I spoke to her and gave her one more chance." Meredith winked at Spencer. "I knew you'd be a good test as to whether she could keep her promise to behave."

"Thanks." Spence chuckled. "I think. What would have happened if I took her up on what she was so blatantly offering?"

"From the way you talked about that caterer the last time we spoke, I figured you wouldn't be in the market for someone like Suzette."

"I see." Spencer smiled to himself. The chief was a true diplomat. Someone who could tell you to go to hell and make you think that you'd enjoy the trip.

Meredith pursed her lips. "What really worries me is if one of my officers falls for her routine. That scenario would be a lawsuit waiting to happen."

Spencer nodded but didn't know what else to say so remained silent.

"So what can I do for you, Spencer?" Meredith laced her fingers. "You mentioned a possible connection between the carjackings and the murder of that homeless man."

Spencer appreciated the chief getting down to business. He needed to return to campus as soon as possible. Pulling a notebook from his suit pocket, he flipped it open. "I don't want to take up too much of your time, but I had an unusual encounter yesterday."

"Oh?" Meredith gestured for him to continue. "I'm all ears."

Spencer closed his eyes briefly to help him remember every detail. Once he was certain of his memory, he described Cindi Streicher's visit to the security building. He attempted to repeat verbatim what the student had told him about her experience. About halfway through his narration, Meredith pulled a legal pad toward her and started to take notes.

When Spencer paused, Meredith asked, "What are your conclusions?"

"Taking into consideration Cindi's drug-and-alcohol-influenced state of mind, from both her description and her drawing" — Spencer withdrew a folded sheet of paper from his breast pocket and handed it to the chief — "I think it's safe to assume that the thing the girl saw was a person wearing a Halloween mask."

"Agreed." Meredith tapped her pen on her lips, screwing up her face in thought.

"Why does what you've told me sound so familiar?"

"Because a recent carjacking victim described her two assailants as dressed in black clothing that reminded her of a bicyclist's and wearing a rubber mask." Spencer leaned forward. "Does that description match what the other carjacking victims reported?"

"I believe it does." Meredith turned to her computer and her long, elegant fingers flew across the keyboard. A few seconds later, she lifted her eyes and said, "Yes. All the victims described their attackers in exactly that same manner — tight black clothes and a rubber mask."

"That means one possibility is that the monster that Cindi Streicher stumbled upon was one of these carjackers escaping after a failed attempt to steal another vehicle." Spencer looked at the chief. "Was there another theft reported Monday night?"

A few more clicks of the keyboard and the chief said, "Nothing that night."

"I suppose a carjacking might have been thwarted and the attempted theft not reported," Spencer said slowly.

"That could certainly be the case." Meredith fiddled with her wide gold wedding band. "People often don't want to bother us even when they should."

"Yeah." Spencer nodded his understanding. The same thing happened with the students and campus security. "Anyway, the other important piece of information is the location of Cindi's encounter. I think she was on the slope behind the homeless camp." He waited a second for the chief to realize what that fact might mean, then continued, "That makes me suspect that Cindi and the others might have either run into Deuce's killer as he or she was fleeing the scene of the crime or was a witness to his murder."

Meredith pulled a document up on her computer monitor. "The timeline the student described does mesh with Detective Christensen's report. The monster that ran past her could have just killed that homeless man."

"Speaking of Christensen . . ." Spencer paused, trying to find the best way to word what he was about to say. "I'm curious as to why your lead detective is on this case."

"You don't approve of Detective Christensen?" Meredith arched a brow. "Now why would that be? As you said, he's our lead detective — he's the best we have. And he's a lot more polished than the last detective your little group had to endure." She snapped her fingers, then said, "Oh, that's it. Gray is a little too handsome and charming and you don't want him around the caterer or your niece."

"That's not it at all." Spencer concentrated on adjusting the crease in his trousers. He wasn't about to admit to the chief that her guess was exactly why he didn't like the guy. "It just seemed like he is a lot of horses for a case like this."

"I could spin you a load of bull crap about every murder of a Normalton citizen deserving equal treatment, but the truth is that as soon as I was notified that there'd been a murder in the homeless camp, I knew it would end up being a high-profile investigation."

"And you sure didn't want someone like Mikeloff in front of the TV cameras," Spencer guessed.

"Happily, I no longer have to tolerate that man." Meredith's smile was fierce and Spencer saw beneath her polished facade to the woman who had fought her way up the police ladder and smashed through the glass ceiling to become chief. "Against my wishes, the police board gave Detective Mikeloff the option of retirement or undergoing a full investigation of how he bungled the Regina Bourne case. Of course, Mikeloff chose to take his pension and run." She frowned. "I wanted to nail him to the cross, but the board wasn't sure we had enough to bring him down and get rid of him."

"At least he's gone. And I'm sure you're keeping an eye on him, ready to pounce if he does anything illegal," Spencer guessed. Meredith was silent, but the gleam in her eye was answer enough, so he let it go and asked, "Has Christensen discovered Deuce's legal identity yet?"

Tapping a gold pen against her palm, the chief gazed at Spencer and said, "As I told you previously, we don't usually discuss an active investigation with anyone outside the department. However, having made an exception last time after reviewing your employment record and talking to people in law enforcement who vouched for you, I'm inclined to share with you again. *If* you can tell me why you're interested in the case."

"Two reasons," Spencer answered quickly. "First, the homeless camp is right up against university property, which is obviously in my purview." The chief nodded her head for him to continue and Spencer said, "Second, I'm concerned that the carjackings, which are also beginning to impact the campus, are somehow connected to the murder."

"Detective Christensen will certainly be looking into that." Meredith nodded. "And I'll email you what little we have regarding the victim's identity." She smiled and said, "Before you ask, we're still waiting for the medical examiner's report, but death was due to blunt force trauma, which caused a fatal brain injury."

She stood, indicating Spencer's appointment was over. Once Spencer rose from his chair, the chief walked him to the door, shook his hand, and said goodbye.

As Spencer rode the elevator to the PD's main floor, he thought about the meeting with Chief Cleary. It had gone well, but he felt uneasy about something.

His mind sifted through his concerns until he figured out what was bothering him. Was there another clue buried in Cindi Streicher's experience that he'd missed?

CHAPTER 13

Dani grabbed the last baking sheet from the dish drainer, dried it off, and slid it into its assigned slot in the cupboard next to the oven. Some would say that she was more than a little OCD about her kitchen, but Dani preferred to think of herself as extremely organized.

Yes, she'd drawn up a diagram showing the correct location for every pan, dish, utensil, and small appliance, but she liked everything to be in the right spot even if the girls were putting things away. Searching for what she needed while she was in the middle of a recipe annoyed her to no end.

Gathering up the dirty dish towels, dishcloths, and pot holders, she walked into the laundry room at the back of the house. She had an hour or so before Detective Christensen was due to arrive, which was enough time to get a load of linens washed and in the dryer.

As she filled the machine, added detergent, and started it up, Dani's mind automatically tallied the chores she hadn't gotten around to yet. She'd returned all the messages left on her voicemail regarding future catering jobs but hadn't been able to contact a plumber to fix the leaky faucet in Ivy's bathroom.

With an image of her next water bill increasing by the second, she mentally moved that task to the top of her list. Well, maybe not the very top. That spot was reserved for the electrician she needed to find. The light switch in her sitting room made a buzzing noise every time she flipped it on or off and she was afraid she would get electrocuted one of these days.

Although the mansion may have been mostly renovated when she inherited it, any building its age would always have some things in need of repair. However, Dani would never give up the house's old-fashioned charm for brand-new construction.

Finished in the laundry room, Dani headed down the hallway toward the staircase. She wanted to take a quick shower and change into something a little nicer than her threadbare denim cutoffs and faded Maroon 5 T-shirt, but the sound of raised voices stopped her before she reached her goal.

Tippi had finally called her parents that morning and told them about being carjacked — probably because she'd had to report the theft to her insurance and was afraid the company would inform her parents. As a result, Mr. and Mrs. Epstein had arrived as Dani and Tippi were beginning the lunch-to-go cleanup. The Epsteins had greeted their daughter with affectionate hugs and tender concern, but evidently in the last half hour the visit had become less loving.

Cringing, Dani hesitated but then shook her head. Even if she sympathized with Tippi's situation, it wasn't her business. Dealing with one's über-successful parents was never a pleasant proposition. And from what Dani could hear coming from the parlor, neither Mr. nor Mrs. Epstein were happy with how their daughter had handled things after the carjacking.

Dani could commiserate with Tippi's plight. She still hadn't told her own father about her change in career, and it had been a good nine months since she'd made the decision to quit her HR job and open her culinary business. Of course, she hadn't seen him in that time. They'd spoken on the phone once or twice, but she wanted to explain her choice in person.

Still, although she knew her father would be disappointed in her once again, she needed to tell him. Her dad would see leaving the position at Homeland Insurance to become a chef, even one that owned her own company, as a complete waste of her education and his money.

Dani had never been able to come anywhere near to meeting her father's standards. None of her accomplishments were enough for him — not even graduating summa cum laude — and her physical appearance was a constant disappointment.

In her dad's eyes, Dani didn't come close to her mother's perfection. He didn't understand that living up to the memory of the gorgeous woman he'd loved and lost at such a young age was an impossible goal for his daughter to meet. She just didn't have her mother's movie star face and model-like body.

The closest she'd ever come to gaining her father's affection and approval had been when she'd started dating Kipp Newson. Her dad had been so impressed that Dani was involved with such a handsome, successful doctor that she'd continued to see the scumbag long after she should have come to her senses and broken up with him.

Heck! Even in the beginning of her relationship with Kipp, deep down in her heart, Dani had known that the situation was too good to be true. There was no way someone like Dr. Kipp Newson would really be interested in someone like her — a less than beautiful, less than thin, less than up-and-coming corporate minion, whose greatest achievement was a perfectly golden-brown beef Wellington.

But it had taken Ivy discovering Kipp's second Facebook page and showing Dani his engagement picture featuring another woman for her to accept that all her fantasies about a future with him were just that — fantasies. Once she came to terms with that, she was able to cut him loose, but the breakup had cost her. Both her self-esteem and her relationship with her dad had sunk to an all-time low.

Dani was jolted out of her musings when Tippi ran into the hallway, grabbed her hand, and tugged her toward the parlor as she begged, "Please, please, please come help me talk some sense into my parents."

"What's the problem?" Dani asked as Tippi towed her down the corridor.

Rounding the corner into the parlor, Tippi pointed to the elegantly dressed couple perched on the settee and said, "They want me to leave school and move home until the carjackers are caught."

"That's for you and your parents to decide." Dani tried to free her hand from Tippi's grip. "It's really not any of my business."

"No." Mrs. Epstein waved to the pair of cream damask Louis XV armchairs that matched the settee. "We'd appreciate your perspective."

"Uh . . ." Dani stuttered, staring at the stylish woman. Tippi's mother was a county judge, and Dani was never sure whether she should call her Mrs. Epstein or Your Honor. "Really?"

"Please." Mr. Epstein glanced at his wife and then at his daughter, whose lips were set in a hard line. "We'd like to hear your thoughts."

Dani walked across the Oriental rug, Tippi following at her heels, and took a seat. "I'm glad to discuss this with you, but truthfully, I'm not sure how much help I'll be."

Taking a moment to gather her thoughts, Dani was vaguely aware of the sound of the washing machine chugging away in the laundry room and the scent of Mrs. Epstein's lavender perfume.

"Whenever you're ready," Mr. Epstein

prompted her, his words short and clipped.

Dani faced Tippi's parents over an ornate gilt-and-marble coffee table. The formality of the room made her wonder briefly if she should offer them tea and crumpets.

Mentally shaking her head at her foolishness, Dani said, "I don't know too much about the carjackings, but from what Ivy's uncle has said, none of the victims have been harmed."

"So you're telling us that our daughter is safe here in Normalton?" Mrs. Epstein demanded, her voice reminding Dani of Mrs. DePaul, her high school's strictest teacher.

"I . . . I —"

"You have the right to remain silent." Tippi rolled her eyes. "Because anything you say will be misquoted and used against you."

Dani glanced at the young woman slouching in her chair and wondered how she managed that position on such a stiff piece of furniture. The parlor and the dining room were the only two places in the mansion that had been left furnished with their original antiques. The parlor was the smallest room in the house, designed to be used for receiving ladies as they made their calls and not much else.

Realizing that Mr. and Mrs. Epstein seemed to be waiting for her to continue, Dani said, "No, I cannot guarantee your daughter's safety, but as per Mr. Drake's suggestion, all the locks on the mansion have been changed, so the criminals can't use Tippi's keys to get inside the house."

"How much did that cost?" Mr. Epstein pulled a small leather notepad and a slim gold pen from his inside jacket pocket. He flipped the pad open and said, "We'll send you a check to reimburse you."

"Thank you. That's so nice of you." Dani blinked in surprise. "You don't have to do that, but I appreciate it." She should turn them down. Getting robbed wasn't Tippi's fault. It wasn't as if she'd lost her keys because she was careless. But still, the Epsteins had offered and it would be rude to turn down their generosity. "I'll get you a copy of the bill before you leave."

Mrs. Epstein trained her shrewd brown eyes on Dani. "I hear that in addition to the carjackings, there are also reports of some kind of creature roaming the Blackheart Canal area."

"Mr. Drake seems to believe that the creature is an urban legend started by intoxicated students," Dani said. "The campus rumor mill says that the creature only comes out an hour before twilight and sticks to the paths around the canal. I'd say, even if there's any truth to the stories, as long as Tippi agrees to keep away from the Blackheart Canal during that time period, she should be perfectly safe from whatever is causing that particular piece of gossip."

Before her parents could respond, Tippi said, "No problem. I have no interest in walking anywhere near that smelly place."

"Moving on." Mr. Epstein made a note on his pad. "Tippi wants us to provide her with another vehicle. In your opinion is a car a necessity for her education or just a convenience?"

"Well . . ." Dani could tell from Tippi's expression that she wanted her to say having a personal vehicle was essential, but she had to be honest. Choosing her words carefully, she answered, "I'm not sure that I can make that kind of determination. What I can say is that while we do have an adequate bus system and the mansion is in walking distance from the campus" — Dani paused when Tippi shot her a thunderous look, then continued — "I'm not sure I'd feel comfortable riding the bus at night or walking back here after dark."

"Good enough." Mr. Epstein turned to his daughter. "We will provide you with a modest older car that will not be attractive to thieves."

"Daddy!" Tippi's whine was truly a thing of horror. "I can't be seen —"

"It's that or nothing," Mrs. Epstein snapped. When her daughter nodded and sank back in her chair, she turned to Dani. "One last thing."

From the look on Tippi's face, Dani knew that this was the deal breaker. She straightened her back.

"On the drive down here, I received an email from one of my law school friends who works in the area. She tells me that there was a murder in a homeless camp near the school and that you have been donating your surplus food to that place. Is that true?"

"Yes, it is." Dani had an idea where this was going, and she wasn't happy about it.

Mrs. Epstein pulled down the hem of her beige skirt. "As I'm sure you can understand, and as I'm certain Ivy's and Starr's parents will agree" — she brushed off an imaginary piece of lint from the matching jacket — "we must insist that you cease that particular charitable endeavor while our daughter is in residence here. And that you have nothing more to do with that camp."

"No." Dani shook her head. With the

216

murder and what she'd heard at the band dinner, she'd actually been thinking about doing just that, but no one was going to order her to quit feeding people.

"Then Tippi will need to move home until we can find her alternate living arrangements." Mrs. Epstein tilted her head at Dani. "Do you really want to lose the income from the rent we pay for her to live here or her hours of help with your business?"

Later, as Dani stood in the shower, she wondered how she would have answered Mrs. Epstein's question if Tippi hadn't thrown a fit before Dani could respond. The girl had leaped to her feet and accused her parents of everything from child abuse to arson.

During her stint in human resources, Dani thought she'd heard and seen people lose their minds, but they didn't compare to a spoiled daughter being told no one of the few times in her life. And by the time Tippi was through screaming at her folks, they had grudgingly agreed she could stay at the mansion if she had nothing personally to do with distributing the leftovers to the homeless.

Tippi had readily agreed, but on their way

out the door, Mrs. Epstein had urged Dani to reconsider her donation policy. She had pointed out that her generosity could end up losing her paying customers.

All of this churned through Dani's mind as she finished showering and dried off. After applying a light coat of bronzer and sweeping her lashes with mascara, she turned her attention to her hair.

There was no way she had the time to make the curly mass look anything like it had when she'd left the hair salon. Instead, she braided it into a loose fishtail. She would add a headband before she left for her personal chef gig later that afternoon.

Wiggling into a pair of khaki capris, she frowned. They seemed a little tighter than the last time she'd worn them. It was too bad she couldn't donate fat like she donated blood every two months. Of course, she could stop sampling her own cooking so much, but that would never happen — she had to test her recipes to make sure they tasted right. At least, that was what she told herself.

As she was sliding her feet into a pair of tan sandals, the doorbell rang. There was no one else home — Ivy was somewhere with Laz, Starr was on sandwich-board duty at the quad, and Tippi had left soon after her parents' departure, saying she had to pick up her zombie costume — so Dani hurried to answer it.

Once she had looked out the peephole and was assured that her visitor was who she was expecting, she swung open the door and said, "Detective Christensen, come on inside. Would you like something to drink?"

"Didn't I ask you to call me Gray?" The detective's hazel eyes twinkled as he stepped into the foyer.

"Yes, you did." Dani's cheeks warmed. "That's an unusual name. How did your parents choose it? Is it short for something?"

"My mother's maiden name was Grayson, but my dad thought it was too long to be paired with Christensen, so they compromised."

"Compromise is good in a marriage." Suddenly, feeling like she'd been too personal, Dani fidgeted with the buttons on her shirt. "Not that I'm married, or have been married, but it seems like it would be."

"Mom and Dad have some pretty loud disagreements, but, yeah, they always manage to find the middle ground." Gray smiled fondly.

"Well, anyway, Gray is a nice name." Dani couldn't seem to stop herself from saying whatever stupid thing popped into her head.

"Grayson comes from Scotland and was originally from the name Grier, a pet form of the given name Gregory, which means watchful." Gray shrugged. "Life would have been easier if they'd called me Greg."

There was an awkward silence and Dani realized he'd never answered her about the drink. "So, would you like to sit down and have a cup of coffee or a glass of water?"

"Actually, I was hoping you'd agree to take a ride with me to the homeless camp." Gray shoved his hands into the pockets of his crisply creased dress pants. "We're not making much progress in the investigation," he admitted. "And maybe if you walk me through your actions just before you found the victim, something will spark."

"I only have an hour," Dani hedged. The last thing she wanted to do was relive discovering poor Deuce with his head bashed in.

"I'll set the alarm on my watch and we'll leave as soon as it goes off."

"Okay." Dani sighed. "Just let me grab my keys and cell phone." She paused. "Wait! Can I also bring a couple boxes of leftovers from last night's catering gig?"

"Good idea." Gray nodded. "Always nice to bring a gift when you're visiting some-one's home."

Dani stared at him. Was he mocking her? No. From his expression, he seemed sincere. Could he truly be that nice a guy?

Gray accompanied Dani to the kitchen and helped her pack the cartons of food. Carrying both containers, he guided her to his car. As she buckled her seat belt, Dani couldn't help but relive the last time a police officer had arrived at the mansion and lured her into accompanying him somewhere. That jerk had interrogated her for hours and the whole time she'd felt like she was a few words one way or another from landing behind bars.

Could she trust this detective? Spencer had warned her not to, but then he'd turned around and lied to her last night over pizza. So maybe Spencer was the one she shouldn't trust. Because so far, Gray had been nothing but sweet, thoughtful, and open with her.

Glancing over at the driver's seat, Dani noted that the detective's cheeks appeared to be freshly shaven and his aftershave was subtly masculine, a combination of ginger, citrus, and amber. It would be conceited to think he had cleaned up just for her, but then again there were no wrinkles in his white dress shirt.

Before she could blurt out something

stupid, Dani dug her nails into her arm and asked, "What have you found out about Deuce so far?"

"Not much." Gray twitched his shoulders. "I'm hoping we'll have a confirmation on his identity by end of business today. The tip that he'd been in the military was extremely helpful."

"Then why is it so hard to find out his real name?" Dani asked.

"Unfortunately, it looks as if he was Special Forces, which makes his records top secret. We have to jump through a lot of hoops to get information on him."

Seconds ticked by while Dani thought about Gray's words. "So you have nothing until the military's red tape is unraveled?"

"If he is who we think he is, he was discharged because of a diagnosis of personality disorder, which is often what soldiers with PTSD are labeled." Gray scowled. "It frequently results in Bad Conduct Discharges because of behaviors they can't control. And a less-than-honorable discharge keeps vets from getting help from the VA."

"Oh my gosh!" Dani's head felt as if it were going to explode with the unfairness. "How wrong is that?"

"Beyond wrong."

Dani took a deep, cleansing breath — anger wouldn't help anyone. "Could his past in Special Forces be why he was killed?"

"I'm leaning toward no." Gray steered the car onto the dirt road leading to the homeless camp. "I think if it had been anything to do with the military or covert operations, either his body would never have been found, or his death would have looked accidental."

CHAPTER 14

Dani gazed through the windshield at the homeless camp sprawled in front of her. It looked even more heartbreaking in the daylight. The trash was more visible, the shelters more rickety, and the surroundings more desolate.

It was as if all vestiges of comfort and ease had been stripped away and all that was left were the very basics needed for survival. Pieces of insulation were nailed to the outside of the shacks, cardboard walls were reinforced with thin strips of wood clearly scavenged from discarded pallets, and a series of electrical cords were duct-taped together and ran from a pole at the top of the hill.

The cord ended at a makeshift table made from a wire spool. There it was connected to a power strip with half a dozen outlets. A woman sat next to the table, keeping an eye on the devices being charged there.

Dani had heard that one of the churches had been giving prepaid cell phones to the homeless and she'd wondered how they kept them running. Admiring the campers' ingenuity, she hoped the electric company didn't catch on and turn off the juice.

While Dani had been lost in her observations, Gray had parked the car, got out, and came around to open her door. As she swung her legs free of the vehicle and stood up, she rubbed at the ache in her chest. What had happened in these people's lives to bring them to this place where each day was a struggle to stay alive?

It was another scorching day and Dani used a tissue to wipe the sweat from her forehead. The blazing sun beat down relentlessly on the hard-packed earth and she gazed at the shelters cobbled together among the trees on either side of the underpass. They were minimally better off than the ones on the flat ground. Their occupants had some shade from the foliage and most were at least living in tents meant for outdoors use.

Unlike the night of the murder, people were visible and their voices drifted to where Dani lingered near the car. She strained to hear the words, but they were too far away.

"Everything okay?" Gray put his hand on

her back. When she nodded, he asked, "Ready to walk around?"

"Yes. No. Wait." Dani grabbed his arm. "I don't want to intrude on these people."

"I fully respect their rights, but I have to treat this like any other crime scene." Gray gently removed her hand. "If the murder took place on your street, there would be officers canvasing the neighborhood. They would search your yard and interview you."

"But this somehow feels worse." Dani bit her lip. "They can't hide inside and refuse to open the door because they don't have anything but flaps or boards."

"We're not going into their residences, and if they wish to retreat, we won't follow them." Gray pointed to a few who were in the process of doing just that. "We're just going to walk around in the common area."

"All right." Dani peered at the group who remained, then remembered the leftovers and said, "At least we brought them some food."

Gray nodded and retrieved the boxes from the back seat. "Let's distribute the meals and see if anyone is willing to talk to us."

"I assume your officers have already questioned the residents and not had much luck." Dani raised a skeptical brow. "What makes you think they'll be any more willing to tell us anything?"

"First, you're not a cop, and second, I'm not in uniform." Gray shrugged. "But maybe more importantly, one of the challenges with investigating a homicide at a homeless camp is that the inhabitants tend to come and go. Which means there could be people here today who weren't here when the officers were canvasing."

"Good point." Dani moved toward the clearing.

"They may be leery of strangers," Gray cautioned. "So don't make any sudden moves in their direction or try to get too close to them."

"Okay." Dani's steps faltered, but she forced herself to keep walking. Surely, she was safe with an armed officer at her side and the aroma of garlic and tomato sauce spreading before them like a white flag.

Gray gave her an approving look and said softly, "So, let's go back to the night you found the victim's body. Where did you go and what did you notice?"

Dani closed her eyes for a moment. "We made a quick circuit of the clearing area, but the fire was out in the barrels and no one was around."

"No one at all?" Gray asked. "Did you hear anything?"

"Nope. The fire barrels were smoking, but everything was completely silent." Dani shuddered at the memory. "There was a creepy vibe."

"Hmm." Gray stopped a few feet from where a girl who appeared to be in her late teens sat on the ground with a large white dog across her lap. He gestured to Dani, who tried to look harmless. "My friend here is a chef and she has some food from the dinner she catered last night. Would you like some?"

"What's the catch, Po-Po?" The teen's gaze was both hungry and distrustful.

"None at all." Dani stepped forward. "My name's Dani. What's yours?"

Even though the temperature was in the nineties, the girl wore faded jeans and an army jacket zipped all the way up. Her white-blond hair was tucked under a base-ball cap and large sunglasses covered most of her face.

Sadness tugged at Dani's insides as she compared this girl's circumstances to the students who bought her lunch-to-go meals. Whatever had caused this young woman's homelessness had to have been an awful situation.

The girl stared at Dani as if deciding whether to answer, then muttered, "Atti."

"Nice to meet you, Addy." Dani started to hold out her hand to shake but recalled Gray's advice about keeping her distance and shoved it into her pocket instead.

"Not Addy." The girl's tone was disgusted. *"A-T-T-I."*

When Dani didn't respond, Atti added, "You know, 'cause I got an attitude."

"Gotcha." Taking one of the boxes from Gray's arms, Dani put it on the ground and dug inside. She grabbed a take-out container, handed it to the girl, and said, "Hope you like Italian."

Atti ignored Dani's words and opened the foam tray. She plucked a fork from the backpack resting by her side and dug into the lasagna roll. After a few bites she looked up at Dani, jerked her chin at the pit bull in her lap, and asked, "You got anything for Khan?"

"Does he like chicken?" Dani asked, surprised at the dog's good behavior — he hadn't tried to get into the girl's food as she ate.

"Khan's not picky." Atti patted the animal on his broad head and he gave her a wide doggy grin. "Deuce used to say that in the army, you learned to eat whatever was in front of you or you starved."

"Was Khan Deuce's dog?" Dani asked as

she located a container with chicken cacciatore inside and handed it to the teenager.

"Yep." Atti fed the dog pieces of chicken. Without looking up at Dani, she said, "I promised Deuce to take care of him if . . ." She took a breath. "You know . . ." She glanced up, her eyes glossy with unshed tears and unspeakable sadness. "If Deuce wasn't here."

Gray squatted down and said, "So you and Deuce were friends." When the girl nodded, he asked, "Were you here the night he died?"

"No." Atti scowled. "I was staying at the stupid shelter in town."

"Why were you there if you don't like it?" Dani asked. This girl was around Ivy's age and there was no way Ivy would stay somewhere she didn't want to without an extremely compelling reason.

"After those goons from the college came out here scaring everyone with their zombie act, Deuce insisted I stay at the shelter until it was safe here again." Atti glared at Gray. "Have you talked to that bunch, Five-O? You guys are out here harassing his friends when it was probably those scumbags who killed Deuce."

After determining that Atti didn't seem to

know anything more about Deuce or his death, Dani left her with a piece of cheesecake, and they moved on. While the others were happy to get the food Dani passed out, they were even less inclined to talk than Atti.

Giving up on finding anyone willing to share information, Gray steered Dani away from the area around the burn barrels and said, "Can you retrace the path you and Drake followed once you decided to look for Deuce?" Gray swept his arm around the camp.

"I'll try." Dani walked between the rows of makeshift shelters built on the level area, with Gray following a step or two behind her. As they walked, Dani tried to remember their exact movements. "We wanted to be respectful and not seem like we were looking into anyone's home, so Spencer kept his flashlight aimed on the ground and I wasn't able to see much of my surroundings."

"Did you sense anyone watching you?" Gray asked several minutes later after they'd made their way through that part of the camp.

"I didn't see anyone then, but I did hear a few rustling sounds that might have been a person keeping track of us." Dani closed her eyes. There was something else she'd noticed. What was it? *Oh, right.* The people who had yelled at them. "Did Spencer or I tell you when you first interviewed us that once we approached Deuce's space, a man and woman spoke to us? We didn't see them, but the man ordered us to go away and the woman told him to let us check on Deuce because they hadn't seen him since supper and his shirt and pants hanging out on the line indicated that he was home for the night."

"Hmm." Gray stroked his jaw. "You reported the man and woman talking to you, but I don't think either of you mentioned the clothes."

Dani took an automatic step toward Gray. "Do they mean something?" Realizing that she was too close to him, she moved back.

"I'm just wondering why his shirt and pants hanging on the line meant he was home for the night." Gray continued to stroke his chin.

"Maybe he only owned one set of clothing?" Dani hazarded a guess.

"No." Gray's brow furrowed. "In addition to the black tactical pants and shirt on the line, when we searched his tent, we found a pair of jeans, a couple of camo BDUs, and several T-shirts."

"BDUs?"

" 'BDU' stands for 'battle dress

uniform,' " Gray explained. "They're camouflaged fatigues. Civilians can purchase certain types of them, but the vic's were military issue, as was the tactical gear."

"If he had other clothing options, why were the neighbors convinced his pants and shirt hanging from the line meant he was in for the night?" Dani mused.

"I need to find those people who talked to you and Drake." Gray heaved a sigh. "So far, no one has admitted that they were the ones."

"The couple was in the tent closest to Deuce's spot," Dani offered.

"That tent was vacant when we started processing the scene." Gray scrubbed a hand over his face. "And when we came the next day for a second canvas, the tent was gone and the only thing left was a patch of flattened grass and a broken folding chair."

"The woman called the guy something like Tiger or Digger or —" Dani squinted. "I told you that, right?"

"Yes, but no one admitted to knowing anyone with a similar name." Gray shook his head, took a deep breath, and said, "Before those people spoke to you, how did you end up at the vic's tent?"

"Spencer and I headed up the small hill leading to the railroad overpass." Dani led him in that direction. "We wanted to take a look at the shelters among the trees, and once we got closer I spotted an olive drab military style tent sort of off by itself."

"What made you notice it?" Gray asked as they approached the netting surrounding Deuce's tent. "As I recall, it was pretty well concealed."

"I would have missed it if Spencer's flashlight beam hadn't shined on something metallic," Dani explained. "It turned out to be Deuce's cart."

"So you two walked toward the hidden campsite . . ." Gray encouraged.

Dani continued, "We stopped here, just outside the netting, and Spencer told me to yell Deuce's name and tell him who I was and why I was there."

"When the vic didn't answer, why didn't you two just leave?" Gray asked.

"I wanted to, but Spencer was determined to check on him," Dani admitted. "There was something in my gut telling me to get out of there."

"And?" Gray's soothing tenor encouraged Dani to continue her story.

"I tried calling out to Deuce again." Dani shivered at the memory of the eerie silence. "But the longer we were there, the antsier I felt."

"Was that when the vic's neighbors started yelling at you to go?"

"Yes." Dani licked her lips. "We were about to leave when the woman convinced the guy and us that Deuce should be home. That's when Spencer decided to check inside his tent."

"Did you go with him or stay beyond the netting?" Gray asked.

"I followed Spencer." Dani made a disgusted face, feeling a bit like a coward. "At that point, I felt safer sticking close to him."

"You have good instincts." Gray moved aside the police tape draped over the netting and motioned Dani to precede him inside the campsite. "Now you're both approaching the tent. Did you notice anything unusual? Maybe you heard or saw something?"

"I don't think so, which isn't too surprising." Dani rolled her eyes. "We weren't exactly trying to be stealthy. Spencer called out to Deuce that we just wanted to make sure he was all right, but if he wanted us to leave, he could let us know and we'd go."

"Right." Gray nodded in agreement. "If the killer was still around, he'd have to be pretty stupid to allow you to see or hear him."

"And truthfully . . ." Dani paused. "We

235

weren't thinking like witnesses."

"Bystanders rarely realize they are witnesses until after the fact."

"Of course." Dani winced at her stupidity. She usually wasn't so dumb.

Gray patted her shoulder sympathetically and said, "Go on."

"When Deuce didn't respond, Spencer moved to the side of the tent opening," Dani said. "Then he used his foot to push the flap aside."

"So the opening wasn't zipped shut," Gray said thoughtfully. "It hadn't occurred to me before, but a guy like the vic, ex-military with PTSD, would have definitely secured the flap."

"No, it wasn't." Dani hadn't thought of that either. "When Spencer shined his flashlight inside, I looked over his shoulder." Dani demonstrated by pushing aside the flap and poking her head inside, freezing when a dim recollection flitted across her mind. Trying to catch that memory, she said absently, "That's when I saw Deuce lying on the floor with the back of his head smashed in."

"Was it immediately after you'd both seen the vic and realized he'd been assaulted that Drake sent you to wait in his truck?" Gray asked.

"Yes," Dani said distractedly. "Spencer closed the flap and gave me his keys. He said he'd call the police and I wasn't to talk to anyone until they got here."

"So —" Gray started.

But Dani finally remembered what had caught her attention. "I smelled flowers when Spencer first opened the flap. Were there any in the tent? Or maybe a deodorizer?"

"No. Nothing like that."

"Then . . ." Dani stared at Gray. "I think the last person in that tent with Deuce was a woman wearing a floral perfume."

CHAPTER 15

On the drive back to the mansion, Gray and Dani discussed her theory that Deuce's murderer had been a woman. Dani was impressed that the detective took her opinions seriously and was willing to listen to her ideas. He asked thoughtful questions and seemed equally impressed with her observations.

Hardly any men in her life had treated her with such respect. Certainly not her father or her ex-boyfriend or her boss at Homeland Insurance. With the exception of Spencer, Dani was hard-pressed to come up with any another male over the age of sixteen who acted as if her thoughts were important.

Dani frowned, recalling her doubt about Spencer's honesty when he'd questioned Tippi about the details of the carjacker's mask. Was he another guy she'd have to add to the naughty list?

When Gray turned onto her street, Dani

shoved away her concerns about Spencer and checked her watch. It was 3:59 and she was anxious to get home to start organizing her supplies for that evening's personal chef gig. She had wanted to be on her way by four to allow a cushion in case she got lost, but it would take her at least twenty minutes to pack up her equipment and load everything into her van.

Her clients, referred by Frannie, were a new couple who lived an hour north of Normalton. Dani wouldn't have ordinarily taken a job so far away, but the woman had sounded desperate. So, against her better judgment, she'd agreed to make the drive.

Evidently, the woman's boyfriend had invited several of his colleagues for dinner, and she wanted to impress them with a meal as good as one they could get in any city restaurant. Unfortunately, although she'd told her beau that she was a whiz in the kitchen, in actuality, she didn't know how to boil water, let alone whip up a gourmet supper.

The woman had finally admitted her lack of culinary skills and her boyfriend had told her to figure something out. Hiring Dani had been her last hope to avoid embarrassing herself in front of the guy's business associates.

As Gray pulled into the mansion's driveway and parked the unmarked police sedan, he interrupted Dani's thoughts by tapping his fingers on the steering wheel. She glanced at him and saw that he was staring at the car's ceiling.

Finally, Gray said, "If the vic was killed by a woman, I don't think she was from the homeless camp."

"Because it's doubtful someone scrabbling to get by would waste their money on perfume?" Dani asked, unbuckling her seat belt and reaching for the door handle. She really needed to get her stuff together and hit the road or she'd never make it in time. "I was thinking about that and I realized that it could have been a bottle someone threw out or even a sample from a store."

"It's not the cologne that makes me believe the perp isn't from the camp." Gray unfastened his own belt. "It's the trail of flattened foliage we found behind the vic's tent. It leads up the incline all the way to the railroad tracks, not back into the camp."

"Whoever was wearing the perfume could have been so freaked by what she'd done, she wasn't thinking and just wanted to get away." Dani exited the car and walked up the ramp to the mansion's back door. "Once the police arrived, I saw an awful lot of the homeless escaping up that hill."

"People tend to run toward the familiar when they panic, not away from it." Gray followed Dani into the kitchen and shook his head. "And the pathway we found was too near the vic's tent to have been used by anyone from the camp trying to flee from the cops."

"Both good points." Dani shifted from foot to foot. "I hate to rush you, but I have to go."

"How about I help you load up before I leave?" Gray asked. "It's the least I can do for taking so much of your time."

"You don't have to do that." Dani grinned and held out her key ring. "But if you really don't mind, you can load up the van with those cartons." She pointed to a stack of bins and added, "I'll be out as soon as I grab my chef's coat and put on a headband."

"Sounds like a plan," Gray said. "Do you have more or is this it?"

"The stuff that wouldn't be hurt by the heat is already in the van," Dani said, then raced into the hallway and up the stairs.

It took her less than ten minutes to get ready, but by the time she got outside, Gray had all the bins secured. Dani noticed that even after their tour of the homeless camp and loading up her vehicle, his dress shirt was still crisp and his pants had a razor-like crease. Didn't the man sweat?

Gray handed over the keys and said, "Let me know if you think of anything else about the vic or hear anyone talking about him."

"Will do, and thanks for the help." Dani slid behind the wheel of the van and turned on the ignition.

She waved, backed out of the driveway, and headed toward I-55. Her last view of the detective was him standing immobile with a thoughtful look on his face.

Putting the murder investigation out of her mind, she concentrated on the drive, growing more and more alarmed as she realized that Frannie had underestimated the time she'd told Dani to allow. Frannie had told her that it would take less than sixty minutes to get from Normalton to Scumble River, but it took almost an hour and a quarter.

Dani was close to hyperventilating by the time she pulled up to the address she'd been given. A strikingly beautiful woman in her early thirties paced on the front porch of the sprawling two-story brick house. When she saw the van, she squealed, clasped her hands to her chest, and ran over to greet Dani.

Nearly yanking Dani from the driver's

seat, the woman hugged her and gushed, "You must be Dani. I'm Emmy. I am so, so, so glad to see you. I told Simon I could try to cook something and we could just serve a lot of wine to cover up the bad food. But he said booze wasn't the answer." Emmy put her hands on her hips, wrinkling her nose. "And I said, then the question sucks."

Dani chuckled and freed herself from Emmy's embrace. The woman's lily of the valley cologne was overwhelmingly sweet and Dani inhaled a breath of fresh air before she said, "Sorry I'm late. It took me longer to get here than Frannie said it would."

"I bet you drive the speed limit." Emmy smirked. "Frannie, not so much."

"Well, anyway, we'd better get everything inside so I can set up." Dani looked at the shapely blond dressed in a short silky robe that hardly covered her assets. Her hair was in hot curlers and her face was bare of makeup. "You had said that you'd be willing to help me since none of my employees were available at the last minute."

"I am," Emmy assured her, tightening the belt of her silk kimono. "Just tell me what to do."

Dani walked to the back of the van and pulled out the two carts. "First, we load these with all the supplies and equipment and wheel them into the kitchen." She demonstrated by putting a bin on the cart. "I have more than usual since you said I'd better bring all my own pans and utensils, as well as china, crystal, silverware, and linens. Normally, I use what's available."

"My boyfriend, Simon, doesn't generally prepare his own meals so he doesn't have much in the way of cooking paraphernalia or any of the stuff to set a nice table."

"I see." Dani continued to unpack the van.

Emmy followed Dani's example, and a few minutes later, the two women had the carts loaded, but when Dani started toward the front, Emmy said, "It would probably be easier to go in through the garage. There's a ramp there because the previous owner was in a wheelchair, and it's closer to the kitchen."

Without waiting for a response, Emmy led Dani along the route she'd suggested and into a mudroom lined with shelves and hooks. As Dani followed her employer, she quickly reviewed the menu, hoping that she would be able to have everything ready in time.

The mushroom pizzetta appetizers were ready to pop in the oven. The salad of fall greens with raisins and walnuts just needed to be tossed and drizzled with olive oil and balsamic vinegar. And she could whip up the creamy baked parmesan polenta and brussels sprouts with spicy, lemon-infused olive oil in a little over an hour.

Luckily, the dessert was nearly ready to serve. Dani had made the lemon buttermilk cake the night before and the pistachio mixture for the ice cream was ready to go into her trusty Cuisinart.

However, the tricky part was the main course. The cider-brined pork loin should be roasted for an hour and allowed to rest for fifteen minutes. Add ten minutes to preheat the oven, and with dinner scheduled for seven, if there was any hope of the meat being done in time, it had to go in as soon as the oven was ready.

Entering the kitchen, Dani was blasted by hip-hop thumping out of the iPod docked on the counter. She wanted to put her hands over her ears but instead hurried over to the larger of the double ovens and set it to three hundred and seventy-five degrees. She turned the smaller oven to four hundred, then glanced around.

French doors led to an enclosed porch containing bronze wrought-iron furniture with black-and-tan plaid cushions. Through the screen, she could see a cute Westie playing in the fenced-in backyard.

Emmy followed her gaze and said, "That's Toby."

"What?" Dani couldn't understand what the woman was saying over the music.

Marching over to the counter, Emmy turned off the iPod and repeated, "That's Toby. Thank your lucky stars that the weather's nice or he'd be 'helping' you in the kitchen. That dog is Simon's pride and joy and spoiled rotten."

"Phew!" Dani smiled. "I love animals, but not around my food."

"Okay." Emmy straightened her shoulders. "I have to allow thirty minutes to get dressed and do my hair, and the guests will arrive at six thirty for cocktails, so you have me for half an hour. What do you want me to do?"

"How about setting the table." Dani pointed to a couple of large containers. "Everything you'll need is in those two green bins."

"Sure." Emmy picked one up, then said, "I couldn't believe that Simon didn't have any of this stuff." She wrinkled her nose. "Who knew that when he had me over for that romantic dinner right after we met that he'd rented everything and got the food from Truth in Joliet?"

When Emmy left for the dining room,

Dani noticed that without the woman's heavy perfume in the air, the house had a sterile odor, almost as if it were a model home being shown to potential buyers. It was really none of her business, but how other people lived fascinated her. Shrugging, Dani began to arrange her equipment and food.

The pork tenderloin was still in its brine. Yesterday, she'd combined a quart of water with a cup of granulated sugar and half a cup of salt, then brought it to a boil. Once the sugar and salt had dissolved, she'd added another quart of water and two quarts of apple cider. After the mixture cooled to room temperature, she'd added the tenderloin, which had then spent twelve hours in the refrigerated brine.

Once the pork was in the oven, the ice cream maker was churning away, and a pot of water was simmering, Dani went to check on Emmy. The rooms she could see from the hallway were extremely tidy. She stepped into the living room and noticed that even the bookshelves were orderly. They held mostly nonfiction and biographies and were organized according to size. With the lone exception of a couple of mass-market romances, they were all hardcover. Did the paperbacks belong to Emmy?

Realizing that she had gotten distracted, Dani swiftly walked over to the dining room. Warm light spilled from the chandelier over the table, which had been set with the crisp white linen tablecloth that Dani had provided. Mrs. Cook's delicate Waterford china, sparkling crystal, and sterling flatware were in place, and tall candles in silver holders graced each end of the long table.

When Dani nodded in silent approval, Emmy raised a feathery brow, and her sapphire-blue eyes twinkled. "I'll bet you didn't think I would know how to set a proper table, did you?"

"I never doubted you for a second," Dani fibbed. "It looks lovely."

"Thanks. I Googled it." Emmy held up her phone. The humor left her expression and she said, "I really appreciate you coming all this way to help out. It's important that this evening goes well. I need to show Simon that I can handle a sophisticated dinner party with his stuffy business friends or I think our relationship is doomed."

"Everything is under control," Dani assured the blond. "Do you want to serve the appetizers with drinks before sitting down to eat or as a first course?"

"Which is classier?" Emmy asked. "Since

the front went through and the weather's cooled off a little, I thought it would be nice to have drinks in the screened-in porch." She chewed her thumbnail. "Or maybe I should stick to the living room."

Dani felt sorry for Emmy. "What's your boyfriend's profession?" Emmy seemed so out of her element and Dani hated seeing a woman twist herself to become something she wasn't just to make a man happy.

"He owns the local funeral home and he's also the county coroner." Emmy tugged on her short robe. It seemed as if she had just grasped that it might not be appropriate to wear out of the bedroom. "His colleagues are attending a coroner's convention in Chicago and Simon is one of the speakers. They're here from all over the state."

"Well . . ." Dani paused, then continued, "Not to stereotype, but I'd have to go with the living room. If they're coming in from a professional convention, I'm guessing they'll be in business attire and even though the weather isn't as hot, it's still a bit humid. Also, they'd probably rather eat their appetizer at a table."

"Right." Emmy shuffled her bare feet. "I should have thought of that."

"Why should you when you can hire a personal chef for that kind of thing?" Dani smiled at her. "Now, we'd both better get cracking. You need to go get dressed and I need to get cooking."

As Emmy ran up the stairs, Dani returned to the kitchen and started making the creamy baked parmesan polenta. She turned the burner to high under the six cups of water and two teaspoons of salt that she'd started simmering earlier. Once it began to boil, she turned it down to medium and added a cup of polenta, whisking continuously until it thickened.

Then she added four tablespoons of unsalted butter, three eggs, and a cup of grated parmesan. When the mixture was smooth, she poured it into a buttered baking dish and sprinkled parmesan over the top. After sliding it into the oven that already contained the tenderloin, she set the timer for a half hour. Ten minutes later, Dani put the mushroom pizzetta in the oven next to the polenta. The shelves were now officially full.

Just as Dani picked up her knife to trim the brussels sprouts, she heard the front door open and a male voice call out, "Emmy, we're here."

The kitchen and dining room were on one side of the house, with a hallway between them and the living room on the other side. It was open enough that Dani could make out the initial introductions and then the clink of ice cubes and people chatting, but nothing else.

Turning her attention back to her cooking, Dani sprinkled spicy lemon olive oil, garlic, sea salt, and pepper on the sprouts, then tossed them until they were coated. She placed them in a baking dish and put them into the smaller oven.

Dani had twenty minutes to get the salad plated and the dishes for the other courses lined up. She finished that just as the timer for the mushroom pizzetta sounded. She was arranging two slices on each of eight small glass dishes when Emmy came into the kitchen.

The woman was wearing a black sleeveless swing dress scattered with white blossoms. The sweetheart neckline was modest and the flared hem floated an inch above her knees. A flowered headband held back her perfectly curled blond hair. She was a knockout.

"If you're ready, we'd like to sit down to dinner now." Tension showed on Emmy's beautiful face and her smile did nothing to hide it.

"Go right ahead," Dani said.

As Emmy nodded and left the kitchen, Dani began to load the appetizer plates on one of the serving carts. Once she had all eight, she pushed the cart into the dining room.

She assumed the handsome, auburn-haired man at the head of the table was Simon. Emmy was seated at the foot and between them were three people on each side — five men ranging in age from early thirties to late sixties, and a fortyish woman.

The guests barely glanced at Dani as she slid their plates in front of them, although Simon did give her a head nod and a thank-you.

Fifteen minutes later, as Dani served the salad course, she overheard snatches of conversation. From what she could piece together, the guests were discussing various cases that they'd found interesting. Emmy looked a little greener each time the coroners attempted to top each other with more and more gruesome details, and when Dani heard a rapid tapping, she looked down to see the blond's foot bouncing off the table leg. Evidently noticing the direction of Dani's gaze, Emmy's eyes widened and she place both feet firmly on the hardwood floor.

A quarter hour after that, Dani brought in the entrées and sides, and Emmy's face was whiter than the flowers on her pretty dress.

Her boyfriend didn't seem to notice either her distress or her lack of participation in the discussion, and Dani wondered how those two had ended up dating. They didn't seem to fit, and she'd bet the story behind that relationship was a doozy.

Mentally shaking her head, Dani returned to the kitchen to plate the desserts. When she came back into the dining room with the cake, the female coroner was leaning toward Simon, her perfectly manicured fingers on his arm.

The woman's voice was intimate when she said, "I understand you had an interesting case four or five years back." Simon raised an elegant brow, and she added, "The quadruple homicide just outside of Clay Center. Isn't that in your county?"

"Yes, it was." Simon's jaw twitched. "It was definitely a sad, sad case. An entire family was nearly completely incinerated."

The woman withdrew her hand and stirred cream into her coffee. "It's a shame that the police never solved that case." She had a sleek, self-satisfied appearance that grated on Dani's nerves.

"The county sheriff didn't have much to work with." Simon's expression was frozen. "The remains were only able to be identified by some bone fragments in the master and a single tooth in each of the other bedrooms. They weren't even sure how many people had been in the home when it burned down, and only figured it out when a neighbor informed them he had seen Mr. and Mrs. Olhouser, their daughter-in-law, and granddaughter enter the house at 6:00 p.m., which was about half an hour before the fire marshal determined the fire had been started."

How awful! A chill raced up Dani's spine.

"Why was the case classified as murder and not accidental death?" one of the male coroners asked.

"They were able to determine that it had been arson." Simon fiddled with his fork. "But there was no way to tell if the Olhousers were already dead or if they died as a result of the fire."

Dani glanced at Emmy, who definitely looked as if she'd had enough. Dani was surprised that the guests had been able to eat while they discussed such horrific topics, but it probably came with the job.

After serving the cake and ice cream, Dani asked if they needed anything else. No one had any requests, so she retreated to the kitchen. While she packed her equipment, she tried to put the conversation she'd overheard out of her mind. There had been no mention of the grandchild's father or any other relatives, and she wondered how someone ever recovered from losing their entire family like that. That had to damage them emotionally for the rest of their lives.

CHAPTER 16

It had been close to nine thirty by the time Dani was finished cleaning the kitchen and loading up the van. She was exhausted and more than half-afraid that she'd fall asleep on the long drive from Scumble River to Normalton, but other than blasting a cold stream of air into her face from the AC, she had no other options.

During the last fifteen minutes of the trip, when Dani had a burst of energy, she was finally able to think of something other than staying awake, and her thoughts turned to the dinner party she'd just worked. Emmy and Simon seemed like such an odd pair, and Dani wondered for the umpteenth time how they'd ended up dating.

While Simon was a good-looking guy and extremely generous — he'd given Dani a very large tip — he appeared oblivious to his girlfriend's feelings. And Emmy gave the impression that she thought that she had to change herself in order for Simon to love her.

That whole conversation about the family burning up in a fire was a good example. How could a man who purported to care for a woman not notice how much that appalling discussion disturbed her?

Dani shook her head. Maybe the couple's relationship bothered her because it was so reminiscent of her own experience with Kipp. Still, it was highly unlikely she'd ever see Emmy and Simon again, and although she was curious about them, as a friend from her church liked to say, she didn't have a horse in that race.

With a sigh of relief, Dani spotted the mansion and pulled into the driveway. After turning off the van's motor, she sat for a few seconds debating whether to leave everything in the back of the vehicle or get it all squared away tonight. She might have gotten her second wind, but she was still exhausted, and with a personal chef gig, there were no perishable leftovers — the client kept whatever food remained. But then again, tomorrow was another busy day. Did she really want to have to deal with the mess on top of everything else she had scheduled?

It wasn't as if she'd have to work in the dark. The LED dusk-to-dawn light attached to the carriage house illuminated the area from the driveway to the back porch. She'd had the automatic fixture installed after the mansion had been vandalized and considered it worth the cost at twice the price.

Hopping down from the driver's seat, Dani was surprised when the back door slammed open and Ivy hurried outside. The girl had on a pair of tiny sleep shorts and a matching camisole, and Dani quickly scanned the area to make sure no one was watching. Between the hedges surrounding the property and the generous lot, it was highly unlikely, but it still made her uneasy to have her young friend outside so scantily clad.

"Hey. Let me give you a hand," Ivy said, joining Dani at the rear of the van. "You're really late. Did something happen at your job?"

"No. It went fine." Dani started loading a cart with her equipment. "Scumble River was just a lot farther away than Frannie told me."

"Didn't you check the GPS before you agreed to take the gig?" Ivy balanced a stack of bins in her arms and dumped them on the other cart.

Figuring it had been a rhetorical question, Dani didn't answer, and Ivy didn't pursue the issue. When they finished unpacking the van, they each pushed a cart up the ramp and into the kitchen.

While they emptied the bins and put away the contents, Ivy interrogated Dani. "What did Detective Christensen have to say about Deuce's murder?"

"Not too much." Dani opened the china hutch near the kitchen table and started to put away the dishes she'd used that night. She'd been nervous to transport the expensive china, but her client had made it worth her while to bring them. "The police have a lead on who Deuce really was, but they have to wait for some kind of clearance from the military to access his records to confirm his legal identity."

"Then why did the detective want to see you?" Ivy waggled her brows. "Or was I right and it was just a ruse to ask you out?"

"Only if your idea of a date is a stroll around the homeless camp." Dani watched in amusement as Ivy's mouth dropped.

"He asked you out to the homeless camp?" Ivy snickered. "Man, that dude needs to improve his game." She paused. "Did you go?"

"Yes." Dani held up her hand to stop Ivy when she started to sputter. "Believe me, it wasn't a social occasion. Gray took me there because he wanted me to walk him through my actions the night we found poor Deuce's body."

"Oh." Ivy gulped. She blinked back tears and her mouth twisted in pain. Her affection for the slain homeless vet was obvious, and Dani put an arm around the girl's shoulders. Finally, Ivy swallowed and asked, "Did you figure anything out?"

"A little." Dani gave Ivy a final hug, then stepped back and told her about the floral scent and the path leading away from the camp, then added, "It's a shame that only one of the camp's residents would talk to us. The others either didn't have anything to say or were unwilling to get involved."

"Who talked to you?" Ivy asked, wrinkling her brow.

"A girl named Atti who had Deuce's dog."

"Shoot!" Ivy put thumped her forehead with her palm. "I forgot about Khan." She frowned. "Is he okay? Will Atti keep him?"

"I think so." Dani started to stack the empty bins inside of each other. "She said she promised Deuce to take care of his dog if anything happened to him. And Khan seemed comfortable with Atti."

"Good." Ivy bit her lip. "Because I'm guessing you wouldn't let me have a dog here? I mean, with the food prep and all."

"You guessed right." Dani looked around. Everything was in its place so she asked Ivy, "Do you want a snack, or are you heading to bed?"

"I wouldn't turn down some of those caramel-stuffed apple cider cookies you were baking the other day." Ivy grinned. "They smelled awesome."

"That was probably the spiced apple cider drink mix." Dani pulled out a plastic container and put it on the table. "I think I'll make some of these for the fall harvest party that I'm catering next month. They turned out pretty well."

"Hmm." Ivy nodded as she bit into a cookie. She caught the melted caramel that oozed from the middle of the cookie with her finger and licked it clean. "That's an understatement if I ever heard one."

Dani smiled and said, "I never asked you about the library's grand opening party. Was Laz's family friendly?"

"I think it went okay," Ivy answered slowly. "His dad talked to me quite a bit, but his mom was really busy mingling." She twitched her shoulders. "Laz didn't mention anything, so I guess everything went fine."

"Good." Dani hid her concern that Laz's mother had ignored Ivy. That couldn't be a positive sign, but she didn't want to say it.

"Uh-huh." Ivy ate another cookie. "So, did you guys find out anything else on your walk around the homeless camp?"

"Just what I already told you." Dani yawned. "Gray would really like to talk to the couple who was in the tent next to Deuce's, the ones who shouted at your uncle and me, but they've disappeared." She yawned again. "I wish I could remember what the woman called the guy. It was something like Tigger or Digger or —"

"You mean Trigger and his wife?" Ivy asked. She was eyeing the cookie container as if looking for the largest one. "He has a job cleaning the equipment at the Train Station. You can find him there in the afternoons between the morning and the after-work rush hours."

"Normalton doesn't have a train station." Dani frowned.

" 'Train' as in 'training,' " Ivy explained. "It's the fitness club near campus."

"And this Trigger from the camp works there?" Dani asked confused.

"Well, yeah." Ivy raised a brow. "Some of the homeless do have jobs, you know. They just don't make enough money to save up first and last months' rent as well as a damage deposit for an apartment."

"Right." Dani's mind was fuzzy with fatigue. She pulled her cell from her pocket. "Okay. I'll let Gray know where to find Trigger."

"He won't talk to the cops." Ivy folded her arms. "But he will talk to me. I gave him and his wife something they needed."

Dani didn't want to know what that "something" might be, so she ignored Ivy's statement. "I'm not about to let you go question someone about a murder victim. Your uncle would kill me."

Ivy shrugged off Dani's concern. "What do you all want to know?"

"Trigger and his wife said they knew Deuce was home because his shirt and pants were hanging on the line," Dani said. "But the police found several other articles of clothing in Deuce's tent, so why did an outfit on the line indicate he was home for the night?"

"Well, since I have no idea why his clothes hanging out would mean he was home for the night, I'll need to ask Trigger." Ivy licked the cookie crumbs from her fingers. "If you want an answer to that question, you can come with me and I'll ask Trigger. Otherwise, you'll never know. Trigger's abusive dad was a cop and he'll never cooperate with a police officer."

263

Dani opened her mouth to say that was the detective's problem but swallowed her words. That wasn't really how she felt. Gray had been extremely sweet to her, and she hated the thought that she might be able to help him out but couldn't be bothered to do so. She wasn't, and didn't want to be, that kind of person.

Plus, Trigger might have the one clue that would find Deuce's killer and bring the murderer to justice. And that information might never come to light if he wouldn't talk to the police.

Besides, Dani and Ivy would be in a public place in the middle of day. It wasn't as if they were meeting a drug dealer in a back alley. Spencer was really protective of his niece and wouldn't be happy if they questioned Trigger, but in reality, how dangerous could a conversation with a health club janitor be?

"Fine, we'll go talk to this guy Trigger together," Dani agreed. She'd just make sure she was between him and Ivy and that they were always near an exit. "Are you free to go tomorrow? I mean, this afternoon?"

Ivy thought about it for a few seconds, then said, "That's doable." She crossed her arms. "But I think we need to pretend that we're actually there to work out. The health club has a one-visit free-trial membership. We can sign up for that, and I'll casually approach Trigger with your question."

"You mean that I have to actually exercise?" That reminded Dani that she really needed to get back to doing yoga. Even if she didn't want to spend the money on classes anymore, she could buy a DVD.

"It won't kill you to lift some weights or something." Ivy narrowed her eyes. "At your age, you don't want your upper arms to get flappy."

"My age?" Dani screeched. "Are you seriously saying I'm old?"

"Whatever." Ivy shrugged. "Anyway, I'll be home by one and we'll head to the Train Station as soon as the lunch-to-go sales are over." She tilted her head. "Who's scheduled to help you?"

"Tippi," Dani answered. "And she owes me some hours, so she can do the cleanup and handle any stragglers that come by later for their meal. She can also do the mise en place for Friday afternoon's faculty tea."

"Great!" Ivy jumped up from her chair. "And as a bonus, we'll both get in a nice workout at the health club. Wear your cutest exercise clothes," she ordered. "Trigger may be married, but he likes to look at the ladies, so we might as well soften him up with our charms."

Dani thought of all kinds of responses to that statement but was still smarting from being called old so decided not to lecture Ivy about women's rights and the danger of objectifying oneself to men.

Instead, she said, "Right, like I have tight shorts and a sexy sports bra in my wardrobe." She rolled her eyes. "Besides, no one will give me a second look with a hot young chick like you around."

"Except Detective Delicious," Ivy reminded Dani. "And of course, Uncle Spence. I wonder what he'd say if he knew you went to the camp with the oh-so-handsome police officer." She threw that last little shot over her shoulder as she flounced out of the kitchen.

The Train Station was just past the NU campus, not too far from Holy Snips, and in the same tiny strip mall as Retro Relics. As Ivy hopped out of the van, Dani admired her low-riding, pink stretch capris and matching ruffled sports bra. Ivy hadn't been quite as pleased to see Dani's gray knit pants and black tank top and had fumed during the short ride from the mansion to the health club.

While they were signing in for their free

trial at the front desk, Ivy finally broke her silence and hissed, "Are those clothes you have on what you consider a cute outfit? Because if so, we need to talk."

"Nope," Dani whispered back. "But this is the best I can do. As a curvy girl, I firmly believe that wearing tight spandex in public is a mistake."

"Seriously? You could rock spandex with that tush of yours," Ivy informed her as they started down a short hallway. "Men like a lush booty."

Dani turned and rolled her eyes at the receptionist who was trying hard to pretend she hadn't been listening to Dani and Ivy's conversation, then looking back at Ivy, Dani said, "Let's get this over with."

"Sure, ignore my opinion about your butt." Ivy headed down a hall and muttered, "Just because I'm a little younger, no one listens to me."

"I do," Dani assured her, following her into the main workout room.

Ivy snorted, then jerked her chin toward a man cleaning an elliptical machine. "That's Trigger."

Dani nodded. The man sure didn't look like she had pictured him from his scary voice. The guy sponging down the machine was short, probably not more than five foot six, and maybe a hundred and twenty pounds after a big meal. He had short brown hair and glasses.

As Dani approached him, his hazel eyes zeroed in on her but quickly flicked away. However, when he caught a glimpse of Ivy, he smiled.

"Hi." Ivy waved. "I don't know if you remember me. I'm Ivy Drake. Deuce introduced us when I brought some food out to the camp."

Trigger stopped what he was doing, wiped his hands on his jeans, and said, "Ivy, uh, sure. What a surprise. Of course, I remember you. What man could forget someone who gave him a box of condoms?"

"I was glad I had them in my car." Ivy's cheeks reddened, then she shot Dani an embarrassed look and explained, "My service club was participating in a high school health fair, and I'd just picked up a carton from the university clinic to bring to that."

"Well, me and the missus appreciate it." He smoothed the sides of his short hair and tugged at the neck of his faded Train Station T-shirt. "We're not in a good place right now to bring kids into the world."

Dani observed the pair without speaking. Either Trigger was ignoring her or he'd forgotten she was there. Either option was okay with her as long as Ivy got an answer to Gray's question.

"Things will get better for you, and then you can start a family," Ivy encouraged. Smiling at the man, she asked, "Are you still living out at the camp?"

"No." Trigger twisted the rag in his hands and sighed. "With Deuce gone, it didn't feel safe no more." He brightened. "We'd been fixin' to move and lucked into an apartment that we only had to pay the first month's rent."

"That's awesome." Ivy beamed. "I know Deuce was really good to the people at the camp. I bet he'll really be missed out there."

"Yeah." Trigger's expression was solemn. "It's going to be hard on some."

He inhaled as if to add something, but suddenly the florescent light overhead crackled, then went dark and Trigger jumped as if he'd been shot. He put his hand over his mouth and trembled.

Dani noticed that his fingers were nicotine stained and his nails were chewed to the quick. The sound of a copying machine whirring to life in a nearby office made him jerk and she wondered why he was so jittery. Maybe he was a vet with PTSD, the same as Deuce.

Ivy waited a second or two, then said in a gentle voice, "Was there any talk of who might have killed Deuce?" She twirled a strand of her hair. "Or why someone would want him dead?"

"It wasn't anyone at the camp." Trigger crossed his arms and frowned. "Doggone it! I think it had to have something to do with where he went every night."

"Where was that?" Ivy asked.

"I don't know." Tigger shrugged. "Deuce wouldn't talk about where or why he disappeared for a couple of hours after supper every night."

"So, you don't have any clue as to what he was doing?" Ivy's tone was light.

"Well . . ." Trigger winked. "He did always come back soaking wet."

"Which is why you knew he was home for the evening," Dani murmured half to herself. "His clothes were drying on the line."

"You!" Trigger's eyes widened as if he suddenly recognized her. "You were the one with the cop who found Deuce."

"I was," Dani confirmed. "But Spencer is head of campus security, not a cop."

"Same difference." Knitting his heavy brows together, Trigger glared at Ivy. "You came here to question me, didn't you?"

"It was us or the police," Ivy said, her

expression sympathetic. "It's important so we can find Deuce's killer."

"Yeah, well . . ." Trigger scowled. "I want to help, but I'm not talking to the pigs."

"I won't tell them where you are," Ivy vowed.

Dani frowned, not sure she could make the same promise.

CHAPTER 17

Spencer pushed his chair back and rolled his neck, trying to get the kink out of his muscles. He'd been sitting in his office all afternoon working on tomorrow's presentation to the faculty. With the entire teaching staff required to attend the tea, it was a rare opportunity to address the whole staff at the same time.

After he was hired, Spencer had made it a point to chat casually with the professors and instructors, and many seemed uninformed about the extent of the campus security officers' duties. While most of the faculty knew that that the security officers patrolled the campus to monitor behavior, secure buildings and property, investigate disturbances, maintain order during events, and enforce regulations, few were aware of the multitude of the officers' additional responsibilities. Spencer intended to educate them.

While he was printing out his speech, Spencer's stomach growled, reminding him that lunch had been a hurried ham-and-cheese sandwich from the lounge's vending machine and that he'd eaten little else all day.

He looked at his watch. It was already past five. That couldn't be right. He checked the computer monitor. The last thing he remembered was the campus carillon chiming noon. Where had the time gone?

His stomach roared again and he sighed. It had been at least ten days since his last trip to the supermarket, and except for a couple of bottles of beer, his apartment's refrigerator was empty. His cupboards were a little better, holding half a jar of crunchy peanut butter, a bag of stale potato chips, and a can of coffee, but unless he wanted to have a peanut butter on potato chip sandwich, he wouldn't find anything to eat at home.

Although Spencer dreaded the thought of another fast-food meal, the idea of going to a restaurant and sitting alone at a table for one didn't appeal to him either.

Spencer searched his mind for an alternative and brightened. Maybe Ivy would be available. It had been a couple of days since he'd met his niece and her friends for pizza and he felt uncomfortable about how that evening had ended. Although as an under-cover officer, deceitfulness had been a way of life, lying to Ivy and Dani about his interest in the carjackers' rubber masks had twisted in his gut like a den of snakes.

The coolness in Dani's eyes was a sure sign that she hadn't believed the reason he'd given them as to why he was asking about the rubber mask and she'd been aloof for the remainder of the night. Knowing how her ex had lied to her, Spencer had worried that any untruthfulness on his part would be the kiss of death for their friendship. But he sure didn't want her, or Ivy, sticking their noses in another murder investigation.

But now, after his meeting with Chief Cleary, he was okay with telling them the truth. With the police following that lead, neither Dani nor Ivy should feel any need to investigate on their own.

Extracting his cell phone from his pants pocket, Spencer swiped until Ivy's picture appeared. Maybe he'd get lucky and she'd ask him to join her and the girls and Dani for dinner at the mansion.

A short conversation later and Spencer was all set. He hadn't even had to drop any hints to get Ivy to invite him to supper.

With the weather changing from the heat

and humidity of the past week to a pleasant seventy-eight degrees, he decided to walk from the security building to the mansion. The cool breeze would feel good, as would the chance to stretch his legs after sitting behind a desk for so long. And it would be easier to pick up a carton of soda to contribute to the meal if he took the footpath across the college grounds.

Once he'd put on the jeans, T-shirt, and athletic shoes he kept in his office, Spencer was on his way. After a quick stop at the campus convenience store, he strolled down the narrow pavement, enjoying the occasional gusts of wind that ruffled the leaves of the hedge maple trees and carried the scent of freshly mowed grass. There was no one around and the peacefulness soothed his soul.

Spencer smiled, realizing that he actually felt relaxed. But a few seconds later he remembered that he would have to repair any rift in his friendship with Dani caused by his deceit on Tuesday night and felt his shoulders tighten. He hoped she'd be as understanding about this issue as she'd been about his extended absence.

The pathway had ended at the mansion's street, and as he walked the remaining three blocks, his mind turned over possible solutions. He needed to figure out a way to tell her about the mask without actually admitting that he'd been less than honest Tuesday night. He was still trying to come up with something that didn't sound lame when the glare of a car's headlights interrupted his reverie and he realized he'd nearly walked right past the mansion.

Backtracking, he scowled as he saw the mansion's driveway. Why were so many cars parked out front? In addition to the girl's vehicles and Dani's van, there was a beat-up blue Honda Civic, a shiny new Maserati, and a black Chevy sedan that looked annoyingly familiar.

Irritation surged through his veins as he hurried toward the front door. What was Christensen doing here? Half a dozen scenarios flitted through Spencer's mind, but the two that were the most probable ones were unsettling. Either the detective was there due to the murder investigation, or he was there because he was interested in Dani.

Several long seconds went by before Spencer was able to paste a neutral expression on his face and ring the doorbell. With every moment that passed as he waited for someone to let him inside, Spencer grew more agitated. He needed to find out what Christensen was up to and nip it in the bud.

Finally, Ivy flung open the door and shouted, "Uncle Spence!" She gave him a hug, enveloping him in the comforting smell of freshly made bread. With her arms still around his neck, she whispered, "You're just in time. That guy is getting pretty chummy with Dani." Then out loud she said, "We're all in the kitchen."

Spencer's stomach knotted and he swiftly followed his niece down the hallway. He needed to warn Dani that the detective could be cozying up to her for underhanded reasons. But after his lie about the rubber mask, would she believe him?

"Be cool, Uncle Spence." Ivy clutched his hand. "But do something. At the rate this guy is sweet-talking Dani, she's going to end up married to him."

Spencer's neck muscles stiffened. Now that he'd admitted to himself that he wanted more than friendship with Dani, just the idea of the pretty chef married to Christensen made him want to either puke or punch someone. He could hear a low-pitched male voice and Dani's responding laughter, and a cold sweat glued Spencer's T-shirt to his back.

Entering the kitchen, Spencer spotted a local newspaper reporter sitting at the table with two males. He recognized the one next to an empty chair as his niece's friend Lazarus Hunter but had no idea about the remaining young man's identity.

The reporter and the unknown guy were clearly focused on the conversation between Dani and Christensen, but Laz only had eyes for Ivy.

Spencer turned toward the stainless-steel island and saw Christensen with a dish towel tied around his waist. The detective was chopping garlic and Dani stood by his side dicing anchovies.

Fuming at the cozy scene, Spencer told himself to relax, but his gut wasn't getting the message. Maybe he needed to take a few seconds to calm down before talking to them. He didn't want to say something stupid and have Dani become even more ticked off at him.

Drawing on his undercover experience of pretending to be someone he wasn't and feeling things that he didn't, Spencer put a genial look on his face, walked to the fridge, and put the carton of soda inside, then said, "What are you guys making?"

Dani flashed him a bright smile. Even under the harsh kitchen lights, which should have emphasized every last flaw, all Spencer saw was the pretty pink flush on her cheeks and her beautiful, warm eyes gazing at him. The feelings he had for her slammed into his chest.

Dani must have remembered that she wasn't happy with him because her smile dimmed and her lips tightened.

In a monotone, she answered, "Bucatini puttanesca." Evidently seeing his puzzled look, Dani explained, "It's an easy one-pot pasta dish with a simple, zesty sauce and kalamata olives, capers, and fresh cherry tomatoes for texture. I wasn't prepared for such a crowd for dinner so I had to figure out something fast."

"I'm sure whatever you make will be delicious." Spencer stepped closer to where the pair was working and asked, "What can I do to help?"

"Do you cook?" Christensen's tone was cordial but his gaze was cold.

"Not at Dani's level." Spencer kept his voice even. "But I've helped her out before and she knows that I follow directions well."

The two men stared at each other until Dani broke the tense silence. "You can slice the tomatoes in half." She nudged the carton toward him, then grabbed a cutting board from a rack behind her and selected a paring knife from a wooden block. Handing both to Spencer, she said, "I know you've met Frannie Ryan, but I don't think you've met her boyfriend, Justin Boward." Dani gestured to the unknown young man sitting at the table. "He's doing an internship in the newspaper's online division."

Spencer and Justin exchanged chin jerks, then Spencer went to work on the tomatoes. As he sliced, he tried to come up with a way to come clean with Dani and Ivy about his interest in the rubber masks without making it into too big a deal.

Deciding to approach the matter in a roundabout way, Spencer asked, "So if you weren't expecting to feed such a crowd, what's everyone doing here?"

"Laz was visiting Ivy, Frannie and Justin popped in to ask Ivy a few more questions about Deuce's experience with the zombies, then Gray stopped by, and then you called Ivy." Dani shrugged. "So, I thought I might as well make us all supper so we can discuss what's happening with the case."

Spencer nodded, wondering what Dani really thought of having people just drop by. He snuck a glance at her, but she seemed genuinely happy to be cooking for the unexpected crowd. He smiled to himself. She was one of those rare people who had a way of making her guests feel at home, even if she truly might have wished they were.

Shooting her boyfriend a proud look, Frannie interrupted Spencer's thoughts. "Justin did some digging on social media and found the kids who harassed the homeless camp the night before Deuce was murdered."

At the reporter's announcement, Spencer saw Christensen's knife still, and he watched as the man processed her statement. Spencer knew before the detective even spoke that the man would take the wrong approach with the young woman.

Christensen wiped his hands, strode over to the couple, and, when he spoke, it was with the resonant tone of someone used to getting their own way. "You'll need to turn over that information to me so I can talk to them."

"No." Frannie crossed her arms. "Journalists are not lackeys of the police department. You can either have your own computer geeks find them, or" — her eyes gleamed — "read about the interview Justin and I conducted with them in the newspaper or online."

"I understand." Christensen nodded and returned to the island. Then as he continued to chop garlic, he said, "And I certainly will take both of your excellent suggestions. But,

Ms. Ryan, can you at least tell me if there's a reason that I should think those people had something to do with the murder?"

Spencer had to give the guy credit. He'd immediately realized his mistake, backed off, and given the reporter a graceful way to cooperate. Not to mention adding some flattery to the mix.

Frannie whispered to her boyfriend, who nodded, then said, "Of the five kids who dressed as zombies and invaded the camp, none admit to having anything personal against any of the homeless."

"That's very helpful," Christensen said, bringing the cutting board of chopped garlic over to the stove top where Dani had a large, high-sided skillet heating over medium heat. "Did you believe that they were telling the truth that their actions were random?"

"We did," Justin answered. "You can read why in our article."

Evidently realizing he'd obtained as much information as he was going to get, Christensen said, "Okay. Thanks for the tip about social media. Our department doesn't have a lot of computer-savvy staff and I never would have thought of locating the pseudo-zombies that way."

Spencer finished the tomatoes and moved

into the space on Dani's other side. She'd poured olive oil into the pan and, once it was hot, added the garlic, anchovies, oregano, and red pepper.

As Dani stirred the mixture, Spencer looked at Christensen and asked, "Did you stop by with more questions for my niece or for Ms. Sloan?"

It was all Spencer could do not to smack him when Christensen smirked and bumped shoulders with Dani, "No, she already answered all my questions when she accompanied me to the homeless camp yesterday. This is more of an informational visit."

Spencer shot Dani a quick glance, and she narrowed her eyes before she said, "Gray came over to let me know that they had a lead. As it turns out, there was a suspicious person near the homeless camp the night Deuce was killed. This individual was wearing a rubber mask that was identical to the one witnesses described the carjackers as wearing. I believe you were asking about that mask just the other night, Spencer, but you assured us that there was no real reason for your questions about it."

Damn! Spencer's gut knotted. This would not turn out well.

"While the standard law enforcement thinking is to not involve civilians, I disagree with that policy." Christensen beamed at Dani. "When the people involved are smart and observant, why not use those resources?" He glanced at Frannie and Justin. "I'm even willing to cooperate with reporters if it will help close a case."

Shit! Shit! Shit! Spencer opened his mouth, but nothing came out.

"An attitude that I really appreciate." Dani stared at him. "And one I thought you shared, Spencer, but I was clearly mistaken."

"I just wanted to —" Spencer started to explain, but Dani cut him off.

"Wanted to what exactly?" Dani demanded. "Keep us all in the dark about your lead on the murderer? Not inform us that the carjackers may have turned violent?" She turned her back on Spencer and added chicken broth and bucatini to the pan. "Lie to us?"

Spencer gritted his teeth to stop from snapping at her, then unlocked his jaw and said, "Not at all. My intention was to pass my information on to the police chief, and if she thought it was pertinent, then tell you and the girls why I was asking about the mask."

Hell! That had sounded better in his head.

"Admirable." Christensen's smirk was evidence that he knew Spencer was in the

284

doghouse.

Racking his brain, Spencer tried to think of a way to put the detective right beside him in the pooch palace. Then maybe he could throw a stick and the guy would leave.

Spencer scowled at Christensen before turning back to Dani. "I came by tonight to tell you all about my meeting with the police chief."

"Now that that's settled . . ." Ivy nudged her way between Dani and Christensen, forever earning Spencer's gratitude. She put her arm around Dani's waist and said, "We should probably tell Uncle Spence and Detective Christensen what we were able to find out."

Dani mumbled something unintelligible as she added the tomatoes and tomato paste to the pan.

"What did you ladies discover?" Christensen asked, looking at Ivy and Dani.

Spencer had been watching the interaction closely and noticed that Dani cringed at the term "ladies." He tucked that bit of intel away and continued to observe the trio.

"Well, first, you have to give me your word that you won't try to find my source." Ivy lifted her chin. "He has a good reason not to trust the police and won't cooperate with you if you do hunt him down."

285

"I completely understand your concern . . ." Christensen's brow creased. "However, I don't want to make you a promise that I may not be able to keep." He put his hand on Ivy's shoulder. "But, if there isn't any real need to speak to him myself, I won't."

"If you can't guarantee me his privacy, then I can't tell you." Ivy shrugged off the detective's hand and marched over to the table.

Spencer noted that Christensen took advantage of Ivy's departure to return to his previous spot at Dani's side. He waited until she tested the pasta for doneness and removed the skillet from the heat.

As she added fresh chopped basil and parsley, pitted and sliced olives, and capers, Christensen said softly, "How about you, Dani? Will you tell me what you two discovered to help me catch Deuce's killer?"

Spencer saw the indecision on Dani's face. Her pretty pink lips pursed and she closed her eyes. It was unclear how she'd respond to the guilt trip that Christensen had just laid on her, until her head jerked up and she shot Ivy an apologetic look.

Dani sighed. "We were able to locate the man who spoke to us the night Spencer and I found poor Deuce's body."

"How did you find him? Where is the guy hiding?" Christensen's smooth facade slipped a little and Spencer silently cheered.

"He's not hiding," Ivy piped up from where she now sat next to Laz.

"No, he isn't." Dani didn't glance up from spooning the pasta dish into a large bowl and shaving parmesan over the top. "Ivy knew who I was talking about and where he worked, so we spoke to him at his place of employment."

Spencer admired how Dani presented the information without giving the detective any information that would lead him to the homeless man.

Christensen must have noticed too because he asked, "Where does he work?"

Dani ignored the detective's question and said, "Ivy had a prior relationship with him so she asked him how Deuce's clothes hanging on the line proved that he was home." Dani grabbed a pot holder and took two loaves of garlic bread from the oven. While she sliced it and arranged the pieces in baskets, she continued, "The man said that Deuce disappeared for a couple of hours after supper every night and always come back soaking wet." Dani took a huge bowl of salad from the fridge. "Deuce always put his clothes on the line to dry once he was home for the night, which was how Trigger knew that his friend was there."

"Where did Deuce go?" Christensen asked excitedly.

"According to Trigger, Deuce refused to talk about his activities." Dani handed Spencer the salad, Christensen the bread, and she took the bowl of pasta. Leading the men to the table, she said, "Ivy, can you please go get Tippi and Starr?"

Spencer's mind raced as he followed Dani. He was pretty damn sure he knew where Deuce spent the hour between supper and twilight. The wet tactical pants and shirt had to mean that he was the Creature from the Blackheart Canal.

CHAPTER 18

Dani observed Spencer from the corner of her eye as everyone helped themselves to drinks from the fridge. He might have claimed the chair next to hers and even brought Diet Coke — proving he'd taken note of the kind of soda she drank — but he'd figured out something and he wasn't sharing his discovery.

As soon as she'd mentioned Deuce's clothes being wet, she could almost see the light bulb pop on over Spencer's head. It was clear to anyone watching that he'd solved some mystery — his relaxed expression and nice manners didn't fool her one little bit — but once again he was keeping information to himself.

Dani was almost ready to forgive him for lying about his interest in the rubber masks — his explanation had been reasonable — but if he didn't come clean about whatever he knew now, she wasn't sure she'd ever trust him again.

A few seconds later, Dani was distracted from her troubling ruminations when Tippi and Starr burst into the kitchen. They were talking excitedly about tomorrow's zombie fun run. Tippi modeled her costume, a zombie judge, and Dani wondered if the girl's choice had anything to do with her mother's occupation.

When everyone was seated, Dani began passing the food around the table. While her guests piled salad, bucatini puttanesca, and bread on their plates, her attention turned back to Spencer. She would give him until the end of the evening to share whatever he'd deduced. Keeping secrets didn't fly with her, and she wasn't about to thaw her freezer-burned heart to even be friends with a guy who refused to share his thoughts.

Tippi waved her pasta-loaded fork in Dani's direction and said, "Any chance you could whip up some breakfast sandwiches and homemade energy bars to sell tomorrow morning during the zombie fun run? You could bring all those cases of juice boxes you were stuck with when that preschool grand opening got canceled. I bet they'd go like hotcakes."

"I thought your club had a vendor," Dani

said, raising her brows.

"That jerk pulled out at the last minute. He claimed he'd provide three food trucks along the route, which was why we hired him." Tippi shot Dani an apologetic glance. "But his company must have been in over its head because I just got at text from him saying that he'd declared bankruptcy and won't be able to work our event."

Dani did a quick mental inventory of the supplies that she had on hand and wondered if she could manage both the fun run and the faculty tea in one day. Figuring that everyone would be on campus for the final orientation week activities, she'd already notified all her usual customers that there would be no lunch-to-go bags available Friday.

She had been a little miffed that Tippi's group hadn't even asked her to put in a bid for their event. But if there was an opening and she could do it, she'd be a fool to let her hurt feelings get in the way of making money.

Turning to Tippi, she said, "Are you willing to help me with the food tonight after dinner?" Tippi nodded, and then Dani looked at Ivy and Starr. "Can either of you work tomorrow at the fun run?"

"Sorry, I can't." Starr used a piece of

garlic bread to corral a stray olive on her plate.

"Me either. Sorry." Ivy glanced at the young man next to her. "I promised Laz that I'd go with him to the alumni breakfast his family is hosting at the country club." She ate a bite of salad, then added, "But I will definitely be there to serve at the tea."

"I can help out," Gray volunteered with a smile. "Officially, I'm off work on Saturdays, but I was going to hang around the campus anyway and see if I could pick up any gossip about the murder." He shrugged. "This gives me a valid excuse to be there, and maybe the students and staff won't realize that I'm a cop."

"Truly?" When he nodded, Dani said, "That would be awesome." She clapped her hands. "Two of us selling will help keep the lines down."

Dani saw Spencer stiffen and noticed that his jaw was so rigid she thought she could hear his back teeth cracking.

He flashed an annoyed glance at Gray, then said, "Dani, you know that I'd be happy to help, but tomorrow is all hands on deck for campus security."

"Of course. I completely understand." Dani hadn't even considered Spencer, knowing he'd most likely be on duty.

"The run starts at eight, so how about I meet you here at six?" Gray asked.

"That would be perfect," Dani said, then went silent as recipes danced in her head.

She'd definitely make breakfast cups. She had plenty of biscuit mix, pork sausage, eggs, milk, and shredded cheddar cheese. Her peanut butter banana protein bars were always popular and she had the quick-cooking oats, wheat germ, ground flaxseed, vanilla-flavored hemp protein powder, peanut butter, and honey in her pantry. Someone would have to make a banana run though.

Did she have time to do her cranberry and raisin granola bars? She had the dried fruit and other ingredients and they stored well if she didn't sell them all. Staying up late might be worth it.

Breaking into Dani's menu planning, Tippi said, "You are a lifesaver." She got up and hugged Dani. "We have the post-party lunch covered — Caleb convinced our group to do a Texas-style barbecue with country music — but no food for the run would be a disaster."

"Well, we can't have that." Dani chuckled. "I should ask though, will your group have a booth ready for me? I don't have that kind of setup available and I think something other than just a folding table would make things go a lot smoother."

"Absolutely." Tippi bobbed her head enthusiastically. "After dinner, I'll call our preparations committee and make sure they arrange a stand for you."

"Is there a fee involved or do I have to give a portion of my profits to your organization?" Dani asked, well aware of how these types of events usually worked.

"My group would love it if you donated whatever percentage you're comfortable with to the charity, but it isn't mandatory," Tippi assured her, retaking her seat.

"I'll be happy to give five percent," Dani offered. It was for a good cause and she could always use a tax deduction.

After Tippi's crisis was averted, they continued their meal, with Tippi, Starr, Ivy, Frannie, Justin, and Laz chatting about the latest movies and music. Dani noticed that neither Gray nor Spencer had much to contribute, and since she hadn't had time for any leisure activities in months, she didn't have anything to add either.

When they finished eating, everyone helped clean up the kitchen. Afterward, Starr went upstairs to study for a final in an online course she'd been taking over the summer, Tippi borrowed the van and headed to Meijer to buy bananas, and Ivy and Laz left to meet up with some friends.

Dani led the remaining group into the back parlor. With the exception of the kitchen, it was the biggest room in the mansion, and once she'd agreed to have Ivy, Starr, and Tippi live with her, Dani had removed the antique furniture, replaced it with a large sectional and a flat-screen television, and started calling it the family room.

Walking over to the large windows across the back wall, Dani drew the drapes against the approaching darkness. It had started raining, and although she appreciated the much-needed precipitation, the drops hammering against the panes were distracting.

Frannie and Justin had claimed the middle sofa cushions of the sectional and the men had taken the two spaces at the end. Realizing that her only option was squeezing into the space between Spencer and Frannie or the space between Gray and Justin, Dani shook her head. Evidently, she needed to check out the secondhand store for a couple of comfy chairs for this room.

Deciding against either of the open spots on the furniture, Dani grabbed a throw pillow and tossed it on the floor. She wiggled until she'd found a comfortable position, then looked around at the expectant faces of her guests.

Not sure why she was the designated speaker, she said, "If Gray agrees, I think we should all put our heads together and make a list of what we know about Deuce and the folks he regularly was around. It's clear we each have information that we haven't communicated to the others and it's time to cooperate."

"Journalists do not share information." Frannie curled her lip, distinctly unimpressed with Dani's suggestion.

"I've told you everything that I'm allowed to tell," Gray protested.

"I don't think . . ." Spencer trailed off. He seemed to have a silent conversation with himself, then said, "Dani's right. It may be the police's job to investigate the murderer, but there's no reason we can't act as a sort of think tank for the cops and help them." He shot Dani a pointed look. "That means imparting whatever knowledge we've come across, not going out to interview suspects with my nineteen-year-old niece."

"That was not my idea," Dani objected. "And Tri—" She put her hand over her mouth and slanted a glance at Gray. "I mean, the man in question wasn't a suspect; he was merely a possible witness."

Gray raised a brow and said, "I thought you wanted us to disclose all our information. You're holding back a witness's name and location."

"But . . . I mean . . . That is . . ." Dani stuttered. "I was trying to keep a promise that Ivy made to the guy, but I'm willing to tell if you all agree to do the same with anything you know." She aimed her gaze at Spencer. "Or think you might have figured out."

"Besides being good citizens, which believe me, as reporters we've heard that argument before, what's in it for us?" Justin asked dryly, pushing up his glasses with his index finger.

"Gray, would you consider giving Frannie and Justin an exclusive if they keep you in the loop with their discoveries?" Dani asked.

"Absolutely." Gray leaned forward. "All I ask is that, if necessary, you agree to withhold certain facts until the killer is caught."

The young couple conferred in whispers, then Justin said, "Deal."

Dani gazed at each person in turn then said, "So everyone agrees to be completely honest and not to keep any information back?"

"Unless I'm under orders from the chief of police or the feds, I'm in," Gray said.

"Me too." Spencer nodded. "I want this guy caught before the violence spills onto the campus. Although I think that may be too late."

"As Justin said, we agree to cooperate in exchange for an exclusive, but I have one more condition." Frannie blew a lock of her shiny brown hair out of her eyes and said, "Dani serves us dessert afterward. Maybe you have some of those awesome cupcakes . . ."

"You have to be kidding me." Spencer's eyebrows rose.

"Hey." Frannie's lips twitched. "A lot of stuff can be decided with kindness, but there are just some things that require dessert."

Gray frowned. "If you aren't going to treat this collaboration seriously —"

"There's not one iota of evidence that proves that life is serious," Frannie interrupted, then snickered. "Loosen up, Detective. You'll live longer."

Dani knew that the truce among the five of them was about as easily dissolved as a dusting of powdered sugar on a hot brownie, so she quickly said, "I'm not sure which cupcakes you mean, but I do have some butterbeer ones in the freezer from a Harry Potter birthday party I catered a couple of weeks ago." Dani jumped to her feet. "If I take them out now, they should be thawed by the time we're done."

"What in the heck is in a butterbeer cupcake?" Spencer asked.

"It's basically a yellow cake mixture with vanilla cream soda and butterscotch pudding," Dani explained over her shoulder as she headed for the kitchen. "The frosting is drizzled with caramel and butterscotch sundae sauce."

"Bring some paper when you come back," Spencer yelled.

As Dani arranged the frozen cupcakes on a tray, her cell phone vibrated. Digging it from her pocket, she saw that there was a text from Tippi.

Meijer bananas are all too green for recipe. Heading to Kroger. Be back to help prepare the food for tomorrow's fun run in an hour.

Dani replied to Tippi's message with a thumbs-up emoji, then went into the pantry in search of the pack of legal pads she had recently purchased during an office supply store's going-out-of-business sale. Tearing off the cellophane, she counted out five pads and grabbed a handful of pens from the drawer near the wall phone.

A few minutes later, when everyone had a legal pad and pen, Dani said, "We have an hour until I have to start cooking, so we need to get cracking. Who wants to go first?" She looked around, and when no one volunteered, she sighed. "I guess that means it's me."

"Seems fair," Spencer drawled. "It is your idea to do this."

"Fine." Dani closed her eyes briefly, then wrote her name in block letters on her paper and said, "I've told you all about finding Deuce's body and why we were looking for him."

"Yes, we've all heard that story," Frannie said, rolling her eyes. "Moving on."

"Okay." Dani bit her lip. "Since I can't remember who I've told what, sorry for any repetition, but here's the rest." She held up her index finger. "One, my hairstylist mentioned that the townsfolk are not happy with the homeless situation and that my helping them might impact my business." A second finger joined the first. "Two, this idea was reinforced when I catered a dinner for the incoming NU band members. I overheard several individuals complaining about the homeless, and later one of them, a Reverend Flynn, told me that if you feed a stray, it keeps coming back."

Frannie jotted down a note and said, "I think I should interview this man of the cloth so he can share his opinions with my readers." She winked at Justin. "I'm sure they'll be thrilled to hear that a member of the clergy is spouting such uncharitable drivel."

"Good idea." Dani smiled at the young reporter, betting stories like that, ones that exposed people in power's true feelings, were exactly why she and her boyfriend had become journalists in the first place. "Okay, let's see what else I know."

"Tell us about your visit to the homeless camp with Christensen yesterday," Spencer suggested with an unreadable expression on his face.

"The only person who would talk to us was a teenager named Atti. Evidently, she was close to Deuce and had adopted his dog." Dani looked at Gray. "Was there anything she said that was important?"

"Nothing significant except that after those college kids scared the campers with their zombie act, Deuce insisted she stay at the homeless shelter until he'd made sure they weren't coming back," Gray said. "I had thought maybe in trying to stop that group from returning to the camp, the vic might've stirred up a hornet's nest that got him killed." Gray looked at Frannie and Justin. "But from what you two have said, that doesn't appear to be the case. Are you willing to tell us about those students now?"

"Yeah." Frannie nudged Justin with her elbow. "You do it. You're the genius that found them."

"All I did was search social media until I found a bunch of posts about the zombies invading a homeless camp. They were all hashtagged 'nobrainstoeat.' " Justin shrugged. "After that, it was easy to find out the group was a bunch of roommates living in some big old house on the edge of the campus." He sneered, "The idiots were happy to talk to us because they want to form their own fraternity like *Revenge of the Nerds.* The morons think if they pull 'cool shit' — their words not mine — like raiding the homeless camp dressed as zombies, others will want to join up."

"But they were all in the hospital for severe food poisoning the night Deuce was killed." Frannie chuckled meanly. "Apparently the geniuses all partook of some oysters they found in a cooler behind a restaurant by the airport. I must say I enjoy witnessing karma in all its magnificent magnificence."

"Yeah." Justin grinned. "Usually it's too slow and you have to move on to the revenge portion of the show."

"Those guys are the kind of half-wits that make me feel sorry for their dog." Frannie crossed her arms. "If they had one, that is."

"Right." Gray looked a little startled at the reporters' bloodthirstiness. "I guess I can cross them off my list." He shook his head. "The other thing we were able to determine was that the guy who said the vic was home because he had his black tactical pants and shirt hanging on the line might have significant information. The crime scene investigators had found a pair of jeans, a couple camo BDUs, and several T-shirts in the vic's tent, indicating he did have other clothing options."

"Right." Dani nodded to herself. "Deuce's neighbor, Trigger, who works at the Train Station, told Ivy that the reason they knew Deuce was home for the night was because of the wet clothes on the line. Deuce's routine was that every evening after supper, he disappeared for a couple of hours, then came back wet."

"And that makes me think that Deuce might be the Creature of Blackheart Canal," Spencer announced. "Both the timing and the soaked clothes suggest he was the one that the kids had been spotting coming out of the canal. Although I have no idea why he was doing it or how that would tie to his death."

"I'm not sure either, but the weapon used to hit Deuce over the head, the long metal pipe with the ends bent into a right angle, turned out to be a vintage military periscope, and we did find a diver's mask among his belongings as well," Gray said thoughtfully. "So, if he was spending time underwater in the canal, he might have been using it to keep an eye on someone. The question is who?"

CHAPTER 19

Dani beamed approvingly at Spencer. He'd come through and told them what he'd figured out about Deuce's wet clothes and nightly disappearance. He produced a faint smile, clearly knowing full well why she was so pleased with him.

Turning to Gray, Dani asked, "If the periscope belonged to Deuce, which I'm guessing from Spencer's deduction about him being the creature is the case, is there any indication as to how the killer got ahold of it and used it against him?"

Gray shook his head. "There wasn't any sign of a struggle, so we figure —"

Before the detective could go on, Frannie snapped her fingers and said, "Clearly the murderer was someone that Deuce trusted."

Gray flashed Frannie an irritated look and said, "That's been our working theory from the outset. Deuce was ex-military with PTSD. There's very little chance he would allow a stranger into his tent, let alone turn his back on someone he didn't know," Gray explained. "And that idea would go along with Dani's memory of getting a whiff of flowers when Drake first opened the tent flap."

Spencer frowned at Dani. "You never mentioned smelling anything."

"I didn't remember until Gray had me walked him through our movements that night." Dani tapped her pen on her legal pad. "At the time, I thought it was a deodorizer or maybe even some wildflowers that Deuce had picked and had in his tent."

"But when our forensics team conducted their search," Gray continued smoothly, "nothing with a floral scent was found in the vic's residence." He smiled at Dani. "After your helpful recollection about the fragrance, I rechecked the CSI report and spoke to the lead investigator. She was certain that there wasn't anything at the scene that would have given off an odor resembling flowers."

Justin leaned forward, dangling his hands between his long legs. "Which points to the last person in that tent with Deuce as being a woman wearing a floral perfume." He looked at Dani. "Or could what you smelled have been an aftershave?"

"I don't think so." Dani shook her head. "I have a pretty keen sense of smell. I think it goes along with having a refined palate. And the scent seemed too feminine for an aftershave or men's cologne."

"Do you think you'd recognize it if you smelled it again?" Frannie asked.

"Actually . . ." Dani tilted her head. "Now that you mention it, I might have remembered the scent when Gray and I walked the homeless camp because I had recently smelled it somewhere else." She chewed her bottom lip. "But I can't put my finger on where it was."

"What events have you worked since we found Deuce's body?" Spencer asked.

Dani shrugged. "Just the college band dinner and a personal chef gig."

"Oh yeah." Frannie bounced excitedly on the couch. "How did that job go? Did Simon love your food? What did you think of Emmy?"

Dani leveled a reproving stare at the reporter. "Well, it didn't start out too well since you severely underestimated how long it would take me to drive from Normalton to Scumble River and I was late."

"Ooh, that's too bad." Frannie made a face. "Simon is a bit OCD." Then she added, "I told you exactly the length of time it takes me to get from here to home. I forgot you were older. I guess we drive at different speeds."

"Seriously?" Dani sputtered.

What was going on? This was the second time someone had called her old in less than twenty-four hours. Evidently, she needed to be more faithful in her application of moisturizer before bedtime.

Dani snuck a peek at Spencer, who was studiously avoiding her gaze while fighting a smile.

Frannie, perhaps realizing that she'd insulted her hostess, tripped over her tongue. "I didn't mean —"

"Whatever." Dani narrowed her eyes at the young women. "Luckily, Simon wasn't there and I was able to make up the lost time and serve dinner when he wanted it."

"Phew!" Frannie exchanged a look with her boyfriend, then said, "My father works as Simon's assistant at the funeral home he owns, and Dad says that Simon doesn't do well when things don't go according to plan."

"I imagine that any delay dealing with grief-stricken family members makes things more difficult for them." Dani might not be quite as obsessed with punctuality as Simon, but she wasn't about to condemn the man for wanting his business to have a good reputation.

Frannie exchanged another look with Justin, then asked, "How did Emmy handle the situation? She's usually pretty laid-back."

"Although she was a bit nervous, she relaxed once we got rolling," Dani answered. "But it was clear that she didn't enjoy the conversation at dinner." Dani cringed. "Not that I blame her. Talking about an entire family burned beyond recognition isn't something most people would be comfortable with while eating."

"Yeah, my friend Skye used to date Simon and she said he had no idea that not everyone wanted to hear the gory details of his profession." Frannie shook her head. "But she seems okay being married to a cop and working on murder cases as a psychological consultant, so she's not exactly consistent."

"You have some interesting friends, Frannie," Dani commented.

"I met Skye and her husband, Wally, a while back," Spencer said thoughtfully. "I think the reason that she may be fine with his job when she wasn't with the other guy's is that she and Wally seemed to be very deeply in love, and maybe that wasn't the case when she was involved with this Simon."

Before anyone could respond to Spencer's speculation, Dani heard the back door open and close. She glanced at her watch and grimaced.

"Darn!" Dani looked around the circle of faces apologetically. "That's Tippi and I really need to start making the food for tomorrow."

"I'll be happy to act as sous chef." Gray stood up and held out a hand to help Dani up from the floor.

"Count me in." Spencer rose to his feet and also held out a hand to her.

"Thanks." She accepted both men's hands and they pulled her upright.

"Well, I only cook when the smoke detectors need to be tested." Frannie grinned and added, "And Justin swore off any culinary endeavors after the turkey exploded, so while we're glad to stay and continue outlining what we know, we'll just sit and watch you guys create your delicious masterpieces."

"Fine with me." Dani led the group back into the kitchen.

Frannie claimed a seat at the table facing the island and Justin grabbed the chair opposite her. He spun it around and straddled it, giving him a view of the proceedings as well.

Dani said to Tippi, who had already put on an apron and was washing her hands, "Get out all the baking sheets and muffin tins that we have. And grab three cans of cooking spray from the pantry."

With Tippi busy, Dani went to her two double ovens and turned all four on. Once they were preheating, she located the trio of recipes she wanted to use.

While Spencer and Gray put on aprons and washed their hands, Dani went out to the carriage house to gather supplies. After piling a cart with sacks of flour, white and brown sugar, protein powder, oats, big bins of dried fruit, an enormous tub of peanut butter, a large container of applesauce, jugs of cinnamon and flaxseed, and a gallon bottle of vanilla, she returned to the house. There, she grabbed several cartons of eggs and blocks of butter from the fridge. They would need all this and more for the numerous batches of goodies required to sell at an event the size of the fun run.

With Gray being the best cook among her helpers, Dani set him up making the biscuit dough and cutting it into circles for the breakfast cups. Spencer's assignment was to spread oats out on a baking sheet in a thin layer, and after ten minutes in the oven remove the pans and allow the oats to cool. Tippi started to peel and mash bananas.

Once Dani had everyone working, she began making the cranberry and raisin granola bars. Realizing Tippi would only interrupt them with dozens of questions if she was left in the dark while they continued to discuss the murder, Dani requested that someone bring her up to speed on what information they'd already gone over.

When Justin finished reading from his notes, Tippi said, "Wow! You guys have really been busy gathering info."

"The rest of them have been busy. I've mostly stumbled onto clues." Dani took a pastry blender from a drawer and started to cut butter into brown sugar. "Who remembers what we were talking about before we got sidetracked chatting about my personal chef job?"

Gray looked up from placing rounds of biscuit dough into the greased muffin pans. "You were trying to remember where you smelled the same perfume as the one in Deuce's tent."

"Right." Dani stirred the butter and brown sugar mixture into flour, oats, chopped dates, raisins, dried cranberries, and ground cinnamon. "It wasn't at the private party, so maybe it was at the band dinner." She wrinkled her nose. "There were a lot of women wearing perfume there." She shook her head. "But I just can't remember if it was one of them or not."

"Then let's move on," Gray said. "Maybe it will come to you later."

"Good idea." Dani was done with mixing together the wet and dry ingredients, and started cracking and separating eggs. She handed the bowl of whites to Spencer, who had finished spreading the oats and was waiting for the oven to get hot enough, and joked, "Beat these eggs like they owe you money."

"Sure thing." Chuckling, he picked up a whisk and went to work.

Dani watched for a second to make sure he was doing it correctly, then said, "Spencer, why don't you fill us in on how the masked carjacker might be related to the murder thing?"

"Okay." The oven dinged, and Spencer put down his whisk and slid the trays of oats onto the shelves. "Some entrepreneur has begun to give tours to spot the Creature from Blackheart Canal. When the creature didn't show the other night, the guide led a bunch of kids to that incline behind the homeless camp and claimed they would see the creature there. Instead, someone wearing a rubber mask, similar to the one that carjacking victims described on their attacker, showed up."

"If the tour guy had spotted the creature near the homeless camp before, that's another indication that Deuce was the creature," Frannie pointed out. "I really think we're onto something."

"True." Dani blended the whipped egg whites with applesauce and vanilla, then added the combination to the oat mixture. "But what does the carjacking have to do with the creature or the murder?"

"I don't think that Deuce intended to be mistaken for some kind of creature." Spencer stood by the oven waiting for the timer to buzz. "Most likely, some kids saw him emerging from the canal in his black tactical gear holding the periscope. And presto, the urban legend was born."

"I agree." Dani put the granola mixture onto two sheet pans, slid them into the second oven, then asked, "Were there any fingerprints on the periscope?"

Gray nodded. "In addition to Deuce's prints there was one other set." He frowned. "Unfortunately, they don't match any in the system, so until we have a suspect, they're useless."

Dani made a face. Noticing that Gray had put dough into all of the available muffin tins, she went to the fridge and took out the ground breakfast sausage. She'd intended to use it for an event on Monday, so she'd have to make a grocery run sometime over the weekend.

Handing Gray the meat, Dani said, "There's a skillet in the cupboard next to the range. Stir this over medium-high heat until it's browned, then drain the fat."

"Gotcha." He immediately set to work.

While he cooked the sausage, Dani headed over to Spencer. The oats were all toasted and she got him started mixing them together with the protein powder, flour, and flaxseed.

Once Spencer had the hang of thoroughly combining the dry ingredients, Dani asked, "Gray, do the police think Deuce was one of the carjackers or mixed up with the carjackings in some way?"

"There was no evidence that he had the kind of money he should have had if he were part of that gang." Gray drained the fat from the meat and began putting a generous dollop of the sausage into the dough-lined cups. "There were only a few dollars in Deuce's tent and no banking records."

Spencer had moved on to mixing peanut

butter and honey into the dry ingredients. Pausing, he looked up from his work and said, "Don't you think that someone like Deuce would have hidden the money?" He pointed the spoon at Gray. "And with most banking being done electronically, he could have accounts all over that we'd never find."

"It had crossed my mind." Gray continued working on the breakfast cups.

"But . . ." Frannie looked up from her notes. "Wouldn't Deuce have been living better if he had the resources?" She chewed the end of her pen. "And he seemed to want to take care of people. Wouldn't he have used the money to do that, rather than taking leftovers from Ivy?"

"That's a likely scenario," Justin agreed. "On the other hand, do we really know that he hadn't been giving the other homeless folks money?" Justin adjusted his glasses. "Think of it. All the vehicles that have been taken have been high-end cars you would expect to be driven by the wealthy. Deuce could have been a modern-day Robin Hood. Stealing from the rich and giving to the poor."

Taking the muffin tins containing the completed breakfast cups to one of the free double ovens, Gray said, "Since none of the homeless will talk to us, it's going to be hard to prove or to disprove that possibility."

"Well . . ." Tippi finally finished mashing the enormous mountain of bananas she'd purchased and walked the bowl over to Spencer, who stirred it into his protein bar mixture. "They may not be willing to talk to you, but I bet the local merchants would be. And they sure would have noticed if the homeless people suddenly had money to spend and were buying instead of panhandling."

"That's a terrific idea." Dani fetched a roll of parchment from a drawer and joined Spencer. As she lined several baking sheets with the paper, she said thoughtfully, "I imagine a lot of those merchants will have a table or booth at the fun run tomorrow, so Gray and I can chat with them once we run out of food to sell."

"Perfect." Gray had already started a second batch of breakfast cups. "And I can have officers canvas the stores and restaurants downtown where the homeless gather to ask for handouts."

Dani watched Spencer's lips tighten as he pressed the dough down onto the parchment-lined pans. She gathered from his uptight expression that something was bothering him. Could he be angry that she was spending time with Gray, helping with the investigation?

She'd quickly learned that with Spencer, it was more about what he didn't say than what he did. Was he upset because he didn't like her to be actively involved with the case? He'd made it clear that he thought civilians shouldn't put themselves in danger.

"If Deuce was embroiled in the carjackings, will they stop now?" Frannie broke into Dani's thoughts with her question.

"Doubtful. There were at least two men going after cars." Spencer waited as Dani took her granola bars from the oven, then slid in his pans. "And with the masks, there could be a lot more."

"The guys who took my BMW were thin," Tippi said. "Was Deuce skinny?"

"No," Dani answered as she started another batch of granola bars. "I would describe him as bulked up, not slim." She paused to think. "Also, I'm pretty sure he had a large knife. Do you know if the police found it on him, Gray?"

"They did." Gray nodded.

"That would indicate that he really wasn't expecting any trouble from his visitor," Spencer said, arranging more oats on a pan to toast.

"You're right." Dani recalled her meeting with Deuce. "He sure seemed ready to pull

318

his knife when he felt threatened by me."

Spencer shot her a thunderous glance and said, "You never mentioned that."

"Hey!" Gray moved closer to Dani. "What were the circumstances?"

She described the scene in the carriage house and Deuce's actions. "I knew as long as he didn't feel I was about to attack Ivy, everything would be fine." She glared at Spencer and added, "Coupled with that, I had 911 ready to hit on my cell."

Gray raised an eyebrow at Spencer. "See. Nothing to worry about." He beamed at Dani and gave her a one-armed hug. "She can take care of herself. I certainly admire that. Don't you?"

Spencer made a noncommittal noise, a deep groove appeared between his eyebrows, then the corner of his lips quirked and he said, "It appears we've covered everything but the most important piece of information."

"What's that?" Gray seemed to sense he wouldn't like what was coming and his spine straightened. "I can't think of anything."

"How about the one vital fact that could mean the difference between solving the case and not ever finding the killer?" Spencer taunted.

"And that would be what?" Gray crossed his arms, his posture stiff.

"Deuce's identity."

CHAPTER 20

Gray admitted he was still waiting for the military to verify Deuce's legal identity and said that he had hoped to have that information confirmed the previous day, but red tape continued to delay the process. He cautioned Frannie and Justin that until the case had been solved, they weren't to reveal that Deuce was probably Special Forces. Or that if he was who they believed he was, he had been discharged because of a personality disorder diagnosis. The pair had reluctantly agreed to hold back that information from their articles.

Soon afterward, the two journalists left and Spencer, Gray, Tippi, and Dani continued making batch after batch of goodies for the fun run. They finished with the food at one o'clock and Dani sent a yawning Tippi to bed, then walked the men to the front door.

Dani unlocked the dead bolt, escorted

Spencer and Gray out onto the porch, and said, "I can't thank you both enough for pitching in."

"It was my pleasure." Gray took her hand and held it between both of his. "I love to tinker around the kitchen, and creating good food with someone is a lot more fun than cooking all alone."

"Are you available for hire?" Dani teased. "Some of the catering events are a bit much for just me and the girls to handle."

"You'd never be able to trust that he'd show up." Spencer moved between Gray and Dani, forcing the detective to drop her hand. "I know from my past experience that being in law enforcement, promises get broken."

Dani watched as annoyance flickered behind Gray's eyes, but the detective's expression was unruffled when he clapped Spencer on the back and said. "Unfortunately, that's true." He turned to Dani and added, "But if you ever want a cooking partner just for fun, I'm your guy." He took her hand again. "And I owe you a big thanks for getting all of us to sit down and share information despite most of us having a tendency to keep our cards close to our chests. It was extremely helpful."

"If I learned one thing in my time in human resources, it's that communication can solve a lot of problems." Dani squeezed Gray's fingers and let go. "So, I guess I'll see you in less than four hours."

"I'll be here. Have the coffee going." Gray waved as he left.

The rain had stopped and Dani took a second to enjoy the cool breeze. She gazed up into the sky and blew out an awed breath. It looked as if someone had bedazzled it with Swarovski crystals.

Spencer's voice rumbled near Dani's ear. "I hope that sigh wasn't for Christensen."

Puzzled, Dani drew her brows together. "Why would it be?"

Spencer shrugged. "He was really turning on the charm tonight with all his talk about cooking with you."

"Nah." Dani shook her head. "Gray just likes puttering in the kitchen. But since I know cooking isn't on your list of favorite leisure activities, I'm even more grateful that you stayed and helped." She couldn't help admiring how Spencer's red NU T-shirt showcased the muscles of his chest and his wide shoulders. Her throat suddenly dry, she swallowed and continued, "Also, I really appreciate that you revealed information to us. I know your first tendency is to protect us and handle it all yourself."

"If the local LEO is willing to share, I realized that it was an error in judgment to withhold whatever I knew or guessed."

"LEO?" Dani asked, distracted by the unfamiliar term and nearly missing Spencer's sweet apology. "Is there a lion involved?"

"Law enforcement officer," Spencer clarified, grinning as he absentmindedly brushed away a curl that the breeze had blown into Dani's eyes.

"Oh." The word left Dani's mouth in a puff of air. Her heart raced at Spencer's touch and it took her breath away. Inhaling deeply, she added, "Got it."

"I'm sorry I couldn't help you out tomorrow at the fun run, but —"

"No need to apologize." Dani place her palm on Spencer's arm. The feeling of his warm skin and corded muscles nearly shorted out her brain and she struggled to recall what she'd started to say. "First, you don't owe me any help. Second, you already explained. And third, one assistant is enough." She gazed down at her feet. "Plus, I don't feel like I'm taking advantage of Gray since he's using the circumstances to sort of go undercover. I don't want to get into the habit of my friends having to rescue me. Clearly, I need to think about hiring some more people for the larger jobs."

"Hiring some additional workers is an excellent idea." Spencer put his hand over Dani's fingers and she looked up at him. "But I am more than happy to help you out anytime and with anything that I can. Understand?"

She nodded, her face heating. "Thanks. And I'm willing to help you out too."

"I . . . I just wanted to make sure you know that I like you," Spencer blurted. Then, his cheeks red, he said, "That is, you as a person, not as Ivy's landlord. I really want us to be . . . uh . . . friends."

There was a thundering beat of silence and Spencer looked as stunned by his statement as Dani felt by it. She processed what he'd said and couldn't fight the smile that crept over her face.

A single, sparkly bubble rose inside of her chest. "Of course." Dani hid a hopeful smile. Was this Spencer's way of taking the first tentative steps toward something more than friendship? "Me too."

"Now that we have that settled, I'll see you tomorrow." Spencer took a hurried step away from her, then turned back and said, "Just remember, Christensen might seem nice, but he could still have an ulterior motive, so be careful. The police chief said he's on the fast track up the ranks in the department and is an extremely driven officer."

"Sounds like a lot of us." Dani raised a brow. "But I'll keep it in mind."

"Good enough." Spencer headed down the front steps. "Get some sleep."

"You too!" Dani called after him. He might not have to be ready quite as early as she did, but she knew he'd be out with his security team on the quad by seven to make sure the fun run participants were behaving.

Dragging herself tiredly upstairs, Dani went into her bathroom and washed her face. Entering her bedroom, she pulled the covers back on her bed, paused, then returned to the bathroom and slathered moisturizer on her face. As she stretched out on the soft mattress, she considered all the information about Deuce that had been revealed that evening.

The five of them had certainly gathered a lot of intel. But was there anything in all the data that they'd shared that would lead to Deuce's murderer?

Dani frowned as Spencer's words of warning about Gray played through her mind. Instinctually, she trusted Spencer a lot more than a detective she'd just met a few days ago. But did Spencer really think Gray was playing her, or was there something else behind his warning her off the guy? Maybe it was jealousy. With that thought, Dani fell asleep smiling.

As promised, Gray was knocking at the kitchen door at 6:00 a.m. Dani greeted him with a travel mug full of coffee and a smile.

It was the first time Dani had seen him casually dressed. Wearing a pair of tan cargo shorts, a plain white T-shirt, and flip-flops, he looked a lot younger than he did in his more formal detective attire. She'd originally thought he was in his early forties, but he might be closer to thirty-five or even thirty.

Earlier that morning, Starr had helped Dani get the food and equipment packed, so it took Dani and Gray working together less than fifteen minutes to get everything into the van. By six thirty, they were parking in the slot the prelaw fraternity had assigned them.

After consulting the little diagram that Tippi had drawn, they headed to the area in front of the Union where Dani's booth was supposed to be located. As they arrived at her spot, she was pleased to see that the stand was actually a rolled-side food truck. Although she had the breakfast cups in a portable warmer, she'd been worried that the batteries would die before all the cups had been sold.

With the food truck, she could use a chafing tray, which wasn't possible on a folding table. Using a piece of equipment with an open flame anywhere that someone could bump it was out of the question. And after her first catering job had ended in a blaze of inglorious humiliation, she was doubly cautious about anything that might result in fire. One event combusting had been enough to last Dani a lifetime.

The quad looked a lot different than it had during the orientation week kickoff. Instead of being covered with booths and stands, the enormous rectangle was a lush green carpet of grass. That is except for the cheerful yellow dandelions that had resisted the university groundskeeper's recent weed patrol.

This time, the vendors weren't lined up down the middle of the quad; they were arranged along the outer edges. The runners were being routed around the quad and the spectators would stand along the opposite sides to view the event's participants.

Dani was positioned at the head of the 5K oval. The course wound its way through the campus, ending up back at the Chef-to-Go food truck. Perfect for sales, but perhaps not as ideal for Gray to chat with the other merchants, who were nowhere nearby.

As she and Gray unloaded the carts and arranged the food on the truck's counter, Dani thought about that obstacle. Just as she was checking to make sure that she had enough change in the cash box and that her credit card reader was getting a signal, an idea popped into her head.

"Gray?" She waited until he stepped closer and lowered her voice. There were already quite a few people gathered waiting to purchase snacks as soon as they opened, and she didn't want anyone to overhear her. "After the initial crowd disperses on the run, how about we load one of the carts with food and juice boxes. Then you can wheel it around to the various other vendors. We're the only ones selling food or beverages, so they might be hungry."

"Sure." Gray shot her a puzzled look. "If that's what you want."

"Well . . ." Dani grinned at his confused expression. "I was thinking that would give you the perfect excuse to chat with them and see if the homeless had recently developed any new spending habits."

"Gotcha." Gray winked, then looked over

his shoulder at the growing throng. "Are you ready for business?"

"One second." Dani grabbed the wooden easel and menu, then descended from the food truck. She stationed the poster next to the roll-up window and retraced her steps.

She'd debated about how to price the items and had finally decided that the bottles of water would go for two bucks a piece, the juice boxes for three dollars, and the breakfast cups, granola bars, and protein bars for five. Now as she watched the people look over her sign, she held her breath. When no one grumbled, she blew out a relieved breath. Then she immediately wrinkled her brow. Could she have charged more?

Reminding herself not to get greedy, Dani smiled at the first customer in line, a young woman dressed in a tattered wedding gown with a dead white face, and asked, "What can I get for you?"

For the next half hour, Dani and Gray were kept hopping serving zombies of every description. There were zombie cops, zombie ballerinas, and an extremely disturbing zombie baby held by a zombie mother. But the weirdest of all was a zombie SpongeBob SquarePants. Dani had never thought of an animated character being turned into the walking dead.

All of them pressed against the food truck. Although they were demanding breakfast, in her imagination, Dani could hear them groaning for brains.

Finally, the fun run started and their line of customers trickled down to the occasional spectator. Dani had a few minutes to think and she remembered that she had wanted to ask Gray a couple of questions that had popped into her head as a result of their group sharing session the night before.

After she sold the last breakfast cup to a one of the fun run workers dressed as a zombie doctor, she turned to the detective and said, "You know, we didn't talk too much about the actual carjackings yesterday. Have any of the cars been recovered?"

"We don't actually expect to find the intact vehicles." Gray rubbed the counter with a disinfectant wipe. "They're usually stripped for parts or shipped to specific buyers in other states."

"Oh." Dani puffed out a disappointed breath. She'd been hoping that finding one of the stolen cars would give them a clue to who was behind the thefts.

"However" — Gray must have noticed her frustration because there was an encouraging note in his voice — "sometimes they get

331

careless, especially if it's something rare." He pulled out his phone and showed her a picture. "Like this 2015 Mazda MX-5 Miata 25th Anniversary Edition in perfect condition that was stolen last week."

"Hmm." Dani studied the photo for a couple of minutes. "Another thing we didn't explore very much was what Deuce might have been looking at from the middle of the Blackheart Canal."

"I was wondering about that too," Gray said. "But it was too late last night and too early this morning to head over there to scope it out." Shaking his head, he made a face. "And it's not something that I want to trust to one of the patrol officers."

"Are you going to bring in a scuba diver?" Dani said, having watched enough crime shows on television to know to ask the question. "Or borrow one from the fire department?"

"Unlike the movies or on TV, Normalton isn't large enough to have a diver on staff, and unfortunately there's bad blood between our chief and the fire chief so getting one from that department would take until hell froze over." Gray chuckled. "We have to go through the state police. That means putting our case on a long list of requests. And since there are no lives at stake . . ."

"Your request would be at the bottom," Dani finished for him.

"Exactly." Gray shrugged. "The canal isn't all that deep, so I may just try swimming out there myself. At least I'd get an idea of what was visible from the spot where the creature was said to be lurking."

"Swimming alone is dangerous." Dani frowned. "Even if it isn't very deep, you can drown in a few inches of water."

"Are you offering to be my swim buddy?" Gray's lips quirked up at the corner.

"Depends on when you're doing it." Dani mentally ran through her schedule. "I have a faculty tea to cater this afternoon."

"How about tonight?" Gray asked. "Probably the best time is right around twilight. That's when the creature was supposedly there."

"Sounds like a plan." Dani prepared the juice, granola bars, and a cash box for Gray to sell to the vendors he wanted to chat with along the route. She was keeping the water and remaining protein bars to sell when the participants returned from the race. After she handed the merchandise off to Gray, she went back inside the food truck, leaned out the window, and asked, "When is twilight anyway?"

Gray thought for a moment and answered,

"Between six and eight."

"Okay." Dani dug out her cell phone and entered it into her calendar. "I'll meet you at Blackheart Canal at six." She grinned. "Did I mention I can't swim, so I'll be the one with the water wings?"

"You're too much." Gray laughed as he pushed the cart down the sidewalk.

Dani started to clean up. Business had been so good they hadn't had much time to keep things tidy. As she restocked the ice chest with water bottles, she kept wondering what Deuce could have wanted to see every night.

She didn't have any brilliant flashes of inspiration about what the homeless vet might have been looking at, so she moved on to cutting the remaining pans of protein bars into two-inch squares. Fifteen minutes later, she was interrupted by the first few participants returning from the run.

They were clamoring for water and food and as she served a zombie Snow White, she overheard a pair of zombie pirates discussing a job opening. Only half listening, Dani made change for her customer, but as she put the fifty underneath the smaller bills, she heard the words *rubber mask* and tuned in.

Zombie Blackbeard had lowered his voice,

but Dani could still hear him when he said, "The boss is looking to replace one of the crew."

The female pirate whispered something Dani couldn't make out.

But the male's answer was crystal clear. "The previous guy is no longer around."

CHAPTER 21

"Judging from your expression, I'm guessing none of the merchants have seen any increase in spending among the homeless," Dani said as Gray returned to the food truck, his smile dimmer than usual and his shoulders slumped.

"Correct. Not one report of anything unusual." Gray handed Dani the stuffed cash box. "And the bakery guy told me that Deuce was still a regular every morning for the shop's day-old bread and pastries."

"Well, shoot!" Dani's frustration bubbled to the surface. "When I heard this zombie pirate couple talking about a job opening up because the previous guy wasn't around anymore, I thought for sure they were referring to the carjackings and Deuce's death."

"I wouldn't rule out that possibility just yet."

"Okay . . ." Uneasiness prickled the back

of Dani's neck. They were missing something.

As she and Gray headed toward her van, she saw a flurry of activity as the fun run volunteers began their cleanup. The participants had been herded toward the post-event party at the other end of the quad.

"Maybe Deuce wasn't involved in the carjackings." Gray gazed off into the distance. "But there's got to be some connection between them and his murder."

"It's a shame that I couldn't stall those pirates. It would have been great if you could have talked to them." Dani sighed. "I went as slow as possible. I even pretended that the machine didn't accept their credit card the first time they swiped it through, but when they offered to pay cash, I had to say it worked."

Gray stopped and said, "You have their credit card information?"

"My machine has it." Dani nudged him to continue walking. The van was only a few feet away and she needed to get back to the mansion to prepare for the tea. "But I have no idea how to get that kind of data." She raised a brow. "I'm assuming you do."

"Uh-huh." Gray's smile was triumphant. "All I need is your permission to access your account."

"Sure," Dani said, then felt a flicker of unease. Spencer had warned her not to trust Gray. Was this a stupid move on her part? "I mean, you have my authorization to look at that one transaction."

"That's all I need." The skin around Gray's eyes crinkled. He was clearly amused at her caveat.

Dani placed the empty containers in the back of the van, using that as an excuse not to meet the detective's gaze as she explained, "Not that I have anything to hide, but I feel that I should preserve my customers' privacy as much as I'm able to, without standing in the way of your investigation."

"I understand." Gray and Dani got into the van. "I'm very grateful for your assistance and would never take advantage of your good-heartedness."

Dani patted Gray's arm. "I appreciate that."

"Was the pirate couple's purchase the last one of the day?" Gray asked.

"Not quite. I think there was a couple after them."

"Do you remember the name?"

"Sorry, no." Dani bit her lip. "But if you go back three or four names, I'm sure you'll find them. Their total was fourteen dollars."

Dani was silent the rest of the short trip,

concentrating on the road. Traffic was still heavier than usual, and if she went by all the sudden stops and turns of the other vehicles, a lot of drivers weren't familiar with the area. She'd be happy when orientation week was over and things settled down.

As she parked the van in her driveway she said, "Thank you for your help today at the event."

"My pleasure." Gray grinned at her. "It was fun to see you in action." After he helped Dani get all her gear inside, he said goodbye and stared for the door, but before he stepped over the threshold, he said, "I'll see you at the Blackheart Canal tonight."

"Right." Dani waved, already pulling out what she needed for her next event. "I'll be there at six with my life jacket on."

It was nearly eleven and the tea was scheduled for two, so Dani hurriedly washed and dried the empty containers and reloaded them with the food for the next gig.

After a quick shower, she secured her hair in a loose bun and put on her chef jacket and a pair of black slacks. Once everything she needed was in the van, Dani headed back to the university. Some of the streets were still blocked off due to the fun run and others were crowded because of the redirected traffic, which had her counting the hours until orientation week was over.

The tea was being held at Hawk Hall. It was the oldest structure on campus and its Collegiate Gothic Revival architecture made it unique among the other more modern buildings.

The hall's massive size and stone walls, combined with the castle-like towers, stained-glass windows, pointed arches, buttresses, and spires had doubtlessly inspired many a potential student to choose Normalton University. Dani had heard numerous undergraduates talk about how the Hawk had a real collegiate feel to it, unlike the rest of the campus.

Having been fascinated by NU since she was a teenager growing up in nearby Towanda, Dani could understand their admiration. NU had always felt like it was "her" school and she was proud of its history of diversity. Normalton College, which became Normalton University, had always been one of the most progressive schools in the Midwest. It had invited black students to enroll as early as the 1860s and women in the 1870s.

Attending NU had been a no-brainer for Dani, and catering the faculty tea at Hawk Hall made her feel as if the university was giving her and her business its stamp of approval. She was sure that the NU administration wouldn't hire just anyone for the momentous event that kicked off every school year.

When Dani drove behind the impressive building and parked the van near the rear entrance, she saw that Ivy was already waiting beside the door. The girl hurried to help Dani, and between the two of them, they wheeled all the supplies into the hall's spacious lounge where the tea would take place.

The hot weather had returned and Dani took a deep breath of the pleasantly cool air. Her senses were immediately flooded with the wonderful scent of old books and beeswax furniture polish.

Looking around, she was pleased to see that long serving tables with white cloths had been set up as per her directions. Not all of her clients followed her instructions and she often had to improvise.

Dani and Ivy quickly began laying out the serving equipment Dani had rented. They put the two silver services at opposite ends of the table — each contained the necessary paraphernalia for tea and for coffee. Ivy would pour from one service and Dani from the other. The guests would help themselves to sugar, cream, and slices of lemon.

Lifting a stack of small plates and a pair

of silver baskets containing crisply starched cloth napkins folded into tiny fans from her cart, Dani arranged them next to each beverage service. Once the guests had their coffee or tea, they would move toward the center of the table, choosing from a trio of savory selections.

Dani had made pistolettes stuffed with a ground sausage mixture containing onions, bell peppers, celery, and cheddar cheese. She also had pumpernickel-and-egg-salad sandwiches and triangle buns containing a delicious peppery steak filling.

On the sweet side, she had five options. On various tiered trays were buttery madeleines, canelés — small rum-and-vanilla-flavored pastries with a custard center and a caramelized crust — tiny squares of carrot cake, moelleux au chocolat — a chocolate cake with liquid chocolate inside — and, of course, several types of scones. She'd been determined to leave no scone variety untried.

The water was just starting to boil for the tea when the doors to the lounge opened and Dani heard the clicking of hard-soled dress shoes on the polished wood floors. She had been told to expect from 160 to 175 guests and had been preparing food for several days. Seeing the seemingly unending stream, she prayed she had enough.

Dani watched as the college faculty crossed the expansive lounge and headed toward where she stood.

It was obvious which professors had previously attended the event. The old hands made a beeline for the serving table before the newbies even realized that food was being served. Within seconds, a queue had formed and Dani and Ivy were kept busy for the next hour pouring tea and coffee and replenishing the food on the trays.

Finally, the line dwindled to a few stragglers and the university president asked everyone to take a seat. While the guests were occupied, Dani walked over to where she'd put the remaining cartons of food to check her supplies.

She'd been informed that after the president's short welcome speech and the keynote address, there would be a break in which attendees would have the chance to refill their cups and plates. She just hoped she had enough food for a second wave of people through the buffet line.

Dani was astonished to find that they were completely out of the pistolettes and triangle buns. Good thing the pumpernickel and egg salad sandwiches hadn't been as popular. There was another full container of each of them, so at least they had something to fill the platters.

The canelés, carrot cakes, and moelleux au chocolat were also gone. Luckily, they still had a decent supply of madeleines and an entire container of ginger-orange scones that somehow hadn't made it onto the original serving platters. Unfortunately, there was no more clotted cream, but thank goodness there were still a few jars of strawberry jam left.

Dani glanced around the lounge. Since everyone was seated and listening to the university president, she told Ivy she could take a break. Cautioning her helper to be back in fifteen minutes, Dani leaned against the rear wall and checked her phone.

She was thrilled to see more inquiries for catering and personal chef jobs. Evidently, all the warnings that her food donations to the homeless camp might hurt her business had been wrong.

Engrossed in an email from a client requesting a bid on a huge corporate dinner, Dani only vaguely heard the president end his speech and introduce the keynote speaker. But as soon as that person spoke, she jerked her head up.

Why hadn't Spencer mentioned that he was presenting at the tea? Dani was pretty darn sure she'd told him she was catering the event.

After last night's goodbye, she'd thought they were making progress and she'd been happy that Spencer was willing to share information with her, the reporters, and Gray. Now, seeing something else he hadn't told her, she narrowed her eyes. His habit of playing everything so close to the chest was getting old fast. Her father was the same way, and it wasn't a trait she found at all attractive or conducive for any kind of relationship.

Pushing that troubling thought away, Dani put her phone away and turned her attention to Spencer. He'd thanked the president for inviting him to speak and was now glancing down at his notes.

Clearing his throat, Spencer flashed the audience a charming grin, then said, "My goal this afternoon is to make you aware of the range of campus security's duties. While most of you know that we patrol the campus to monitor behavior, secure buildings and property, investigate disturbances, maintain order during events, and enforce regulations, few of you probably are cognizant of the extent of the officers' additional responsibilities."

Dani listened intently as Spencer spoke

about security's role as first responder for any violent incidences on campus and how his officers were trained to handle reports of rape or stalking or hate crimes. He also informed them that security was tasked with providing primary prevention and awareness programs for all incoming students and employees, as well as his part in any resulting disciplinary proceedings. He concluded by stating that he personally wrote all the reports containing these statistics to the U.S. Department of Education's Office of Postsecondary Education.

The faculty had a lot of questions and Dani was impressed with how smoothly Spencer answered all of them. During the Q&A, Ivy returned from her break and Dani took the opportunity to visit the restroom. She refastened her bun, washed her face, and put on a little lip gloss, all the while telling herself that it had nothing to do with Spencer's presence.

Returning to the lounge, Dani put Ivy to work brewing more coffee and then put an urn of water on to boil. Just as the first bubbles appeared, the university president stepped up to the podium and announced that there would be a brief intermission, then a few housekeeping matters before the tea ended.

Ivy and Dani braced themselves for the rush as the crowd rose and descended on the refreshment table. Either the treats she'd made were really good, or the faculty was determined to take advantage of the free food. Probably a little bit of both.

Several of the female professors had cornered Spencer, and Dani watched as a muscle ticked in his jaw. She couldn't hear what he was saying, but his responses to the women appeared to be short and clipped.

As he tried to edge away, his gaze met Dani's and his expression brightened. Pointing at her, he said something to his admirers and headed her way.

Walking around Dani's end of the table, Spencer put his arm around her shoulders and she stiffened. After his statement last night declaring that he wanted to be her friend, she wasn't sure what was going on with him.

Leaning down until his lips were at her ear, he whispered, "Play along." He kissed her temple and said, "I didn't realize you were going to be catering this event, sweetheart. We could have driven over together."

"Oh well." Dani's heart thudded from the feeling of his lips on her skin and she gulped. "Next time."

Spencer beamed, stepped back, and said,

"Well, you're busy so I won't get in your way." This time he kissed her cheek. "See you tonight, honey."

Dani waved her hand, then caught Ivy's delighted expression and shook her head. She returned to pouring cups of tea and coffee, making a mental note to clear up Ivy's misunderstanding of the scene she'd just witnessed as soon as they were in private.

The platters were nearly bare when the last couple of women strolled up to the table. The blond paused to reach for one of the few remaining sandwiches but jerked her hand back and said, "I'd better not. I put on ten pounds these past couple of months and I need to get it off."

Chuckling, the brunette said, "My philosophy is that the more you weigh, the harder you are to kidnap." She took the sandwich and put it on her friend's plate. "Here. Better safe than sorry."

"Hey, that's not funny." The blond woman frowned. "I just told you what happened to my brother."

The two women lingered in front of Dani as they continued their conversation.

"Oops! Sorry." The brunette snatched a lone madeleine from the tiered tray. "You're right. To serve his country and have his wife do that to him is horrible."

The blond's hand hovered over a scone as she said, "What I don't understand is why she just didn't divorce him. He wouldn't have fought it."

"Maybe she didn't know that." The other woman scoured the table for any hidden treats. "Maybe she was frightened."

"Nah." The blond, seeing her friend's gaze fall on the scone, grabbed it. "My brother is a big softy. He might be a tough marine when he's on duty, but he gave that woman anything she wanted."

"Couldn't she have gotten a part of his pay or his pension if she stuck around?" The brunette held out her cup to Dani and said, "Coffee, please."

"I'm not sure." The blond waited impatiently for Dani to finish pouring, then asked her for tea. "But I think I remember reading that there's no such thing as military divorce benefits unless the service member was in the military for at least twenty years and that they were married during those entire twenty years."

"Not even for the boy?" The other woman asked as she added cream and sugar to her cup. "Wouldn't he have to provide for his son?"

"He'd be glad to pay child support if the

witch hadn't disappeared and taken the boy with her." The blond scowled. "My brother's hired a private investigator but the guy said not to get his hopes up. If my ex-sister-in-law changes her and her son's names and gets decent fake IDs for them both, they'll be almost impossible to find."

"So nothing like those television shows and movies, huh?" the brunette said as the two women turned and walked back toward their seats.

"Sadly, no." The blond's voice carried as she sat down. "And even sadder is the fact that he isn't the first military spouse this has happened to. He's heard of several others."

Dani swallowed the lump in her throat. Those poor, poor men and women. Serving their country, only to come home to their loved ones being gone.

CHAPTER 22

Spencer Drake, you are an idiot! Regret punched Spencer in the gut with an iron first as he sat in his truck scrubbing a hand over his face. Why in the world had he pulled a boneheaded stunt like that?

Hell! It wasn't as if he had never had a woman come on to him before. Maybe it was because there were so many of them invading his personal space, leaning too close, touching his chest. Now he knew what a tasty crumb being swarmed by a colony of ants felt like. He really needed to sign that whole group of female professors up for harassment awareness training.

Still, he should have handled the whole situation in a businesslike manner. Announcing that Dani was his girlfriend and putting her in the spotlight like that while she was working was unforgivable. Spencer blew out his cheeks. So why had he done it?

Did it have anything to do with the fact

that he'd detested seeing her laughing and having a good time cooking with Christensen?

Yep. Spencer rolled his eyes. He was jealous all right.

Spencer turned the key in the truck's ignition, and when the engine roared to life, he put it in gear. Pointing the pickup toward his office, he considered what he wanted to accomplish before quitting time.

First, he needed to go over how his team had handled the fun run and make a list of anything they could improve on. Then he'd talk to them about adding extra patrols to the campus perimeter. Finally, he'd caution them to be aware of any unusual activity near the road leading to the railroad overpass by the homeless camp.

When Spencer arrived at the security building, the guards on duty were all out on their rounds. After checking in with the dispatcher and telling her he wanted to talk to everyone at the end of shift before they went home, he retired to his office and got to work. Pushing all other thoughts aside, he settled down to analyze his team's performance at that morning's event.

The remainder of the afternoon passed swiftly, and before he knew it, his stomach was growling. He'd had a light lunch, thinking that he would get some of Dani's amazing food at the faculty tea, but that hadn't worked out as planned and now he was starving.

Staring out his office's tiny window, he thought about his options. Only one appealed to him. And it would kill two birds with a single stone. He could apologize to Dani for his actions at the tea and ask her to join him for dinner, thus having a companion for the meal and clearing up any issues about his behavior.

Spencer made a quick stop in the bathroom to wash his face and comb his hair. Whistling, he headed for his truck. This would be a good time for them to start getting to know each other away from both the girls and the investigation. Where would a gourmet cook like Dani enjoy eating? Maybe Revelation Farms. He'd heard that restaurant was a foodie's paradise with fresh farm-to-table entrées and everything made from scratch. One of his guards had brought in a gigantic pumpkin muffin from the place, and he had moaned and groaned as he'd consumed every single bite.

It was a few minutes before six when Spencer pulled into the mansion's driveway. His shoulders drooped when he saw that Dani's van wasn't there. She'd already worked two events that day. Surely she hadn't scheduled a third one.

The downstairs windows didn't have any lights shining from them, but Spencer rang the doorbell anyway. It wasn't dark yet and Dani could be saving electricity. Or maybe everyone was in their rooms.

He waited impatiently for a minute or so, then rang the bell again. This time he could hear faint footsteps running across the hardwood floor and his niece's voice yell, "Just a minute."

Ivy flung open the door and Spencer blinked. Her hair was encased in thick white glop, she had shiny black gunk covering her face, and she smelled like mayonnaise, eggs, and coconut.

"Uncle Spence." Ivy stepped back so he could enter. "What's up?"

"Uh . . ." He realized he should have thought his plan over before turning up on the mansion's doorstep. Stalling, he asked, "What's that goop on your face?"

"It's a mask to make my skin look better," Ivy explained. "And the stuff on my hair is to make it shinier." Ivy put her hands on her hips. "But you didn't come here to find out about my beauty regimen."

"Not specifically," Spencer equivocated. "Is Dani around?"

He didn't like the knowing smile that spread across his niece's face. Even under the black mess, he could tell he was in trouble.

"Ah." Ivy crossed her arms and nodded in understanding. "You're here to make up for this afternoon."

"No." Spencer's denial rang false even in his own ears. "Just to clarify what happened."

"Okay." Ivy jerked her chin. "What did happen? Dani claimed it was all a joke."

"Not exactly." Spencer sighed and said, "I was trying to politely tell some ladies that I wasn't interested in them and they weren't getting the message, so I implied that I was dating someone else."

"Dani." Ivy raised a brow. "You know, you could make that be the truth."

"I'm barely divorced." Spencer shook his head. "Definitely not ready to date again."

"Uh-huh." Ivy rolled her eyes. "Well, to answer your question: Dani went to meet that hunky detective. So she may be taken by the time you're ready."

Spencer frowned. "Did she say where they were meeting?" He had to nip that in the bud.

"At the Blackheart Canal." Ivy smirked. "The perfect place for a romantic stroll."

"Shit!" Spencer muttered under his breath. "When did she leave?"

He'd bet a year's salary that the detective hadn't taken Dani there to romance her. After what they'd figured out last night, Christensen was headed to the canal to investigate what Deuce had been looking at.

Ivy glanced at the grandfather clock against the foyer wall, scrunched up her face, and shrugged. "Maybe ten minutes ago."

"Okay." Spencer waved and rushed outside. "See you later."

Yanking open the door to his pickup, Spencer leaped inside. He quickly backed out of the driveway and sped toward the canal. If Christensen insisted on involving Dani in his investigation, then Spencer would be there to make sure she was safe.

A few minutes later, Spencer had a sense of déjà vu as he parked his truck in the same spot he'd used when he had been here to stake out the site where the creature appeared. Following that same path, he set off through the woods that separated the canal from the campus. He could have used one of the lots at the southern part of the canal's access, but that would have meant hiking the entire trail to the north end of the channel, where the creature had been spotted rising out of the spraying water. And that would have taken more time than he wanted to spend before getting to Dani.

Tangled weeds grabbed at his ankles, snagging his suit pants, and his dress shoes sank in the claylike soil that had turned to mud from the recent rain. His wingtips were probably ruined, but he couldn't care less as he hastened his steps.

The wetness from last night's storm sharpened the odor of earth and decaying leaves that he'd only caught a hint of on his previous visit to the canal. It reminded him of fall and he wondered if summer was truly coming to an end.

Emerging from the trees, he spotted the aerators spurting jets of frothy droplets toward the sky. Picturing Deuce dressed all in black with a diver's mask on his face surfacing with his periscope in his hands, Spencer could understand why the college students thought they were seeing a creature holding a bent sword.

Spencer surveyed the area. Where was everyone? No kids walked the path. No detective swam in the canal. And Dani was nowhere to be seen.

Was she really on a date with Christensen? Had she lied to Ivy about where she was going? Spencer scratched his head. But why would she do that? She was a free woman and could go out with anyone she wanted.

Unless Dani was trying to spare his feelings. Could it be that his behavior last night and then this afternoon had made her uncomfortable revealing to his niece that she was actually involved with someone else?

The sound of footsteps on the asphalt path to his left interrupted his thoughts and he turned in that direction. An instant later, he heard Dani's giggle and then a male chuckle joining her laughter.

Realizing that he'd beaten Dani and Christensen to the canal, Spencer leaned against a nearby tree and shoved his hands into his pockets. His expression firmly neutral, he waited for their arrival.

When they rounded the bend and caught sight of him, he lifted a casual hand and said, "What took you two so long to get here?"

Dani yelped and clutched Christensen's arm, then quickly released it and narrowed her pretty amber eyes at Spencer. "What are you doing here?"

"I stopped by the mansion to talk to you, and Ivy mentioned you guys were going to check out the canal." Spencer straightened. "Since it's on campus, I decided that a representative from NU security should join your little expedition."

Now it was Christensen's turn to narrow his eyes, but his tone was unconcerned when he said, "If you want, but it's no big deal."

"Great." Spencer jerked his chin in acknowledgment of the other man's acquiescence, then turned to Dani and said, "Ivy thought you had left several minutes before I arrived, so where were you two?"

"Gray wanted to cordon off the access points to the canal's path, so we had to go to both ends," Dani explained. "You know, so students didn't wander down here and get in our way or spread any more rumors."

"Keeping a lid on the gossip is a good idea." Spencer nodded toward the detective, who had moved closer to the water's edge.

"Hard to do in a college town," Christensen said. "But I try."

"So how did you get here?" Dani wrinkled her cute little nose.

He pointed his thumb over his shoulder and said, "I took a shortcut."

Evidently unimpressed with Spencer's woodsman skills, Christensen asked, "Can you swim? Dani's supposed to be my backup, but she says she isn't too good in the water, and truthfully, neither am I."

"I was a lifeguard in high school." Spencer looked between Dani and Christensen and asked, "Doesn't the police or fire department have a diver for this sort of situation?"

"We have to request help from the state." Christensen shrugged. "And with no lives at stake or missing people, we're not any kind of priority. But I really want to figure out what Deuce was looking at."

"How about I do it?" Spencer asked. "You two can be my backups."

"Do you have a swimsuit?" Dani asked. When he shook his head she said, "Maybe you could borrow Gray's."

"It would never fit. Christensen is a couple of sizes smaller," Spencer said. "I'll just leave on my boxers. They cover pretty much the same thing."

"Not once they're wet," Dani blurted, then her cheeks turned a pretty shade of pink and she put her hand over her mouth.

"If it bothers you, you can close your eyes when I come out of the water." Spencer smiled at how adorably flustered she appeared.

After he kicked off his shoes, pulled his shirt over his head, and unzipped his pants, Christensen handed Spencer a pair of binoculars and said, "You better take these."

"Thanks." Spencer hung the Bushnells around his neck and said, "Here goes."

Unsure of the depth of the canal, Spencer waded in and swam to the aerator. Climbing into the center of the three jets, he realized why Deuce had chosen that spot. It would give him perfect cover. No one would see his periscope sticking up and ask questions.

Peering through the binoculars, at first all Spencer could see to the right or left was a privacy wall for the upscale neighborhood directly behind the canal. But as he scanned the area, he noticed that in the center, there was a significant dip where the wall didn't rise as high as it did along the rest of enclosure.

Cupping his hands around his mouth, Spencer shouted to Christensen and Dani, "The only thing I can make out is the back decks of a few houses. We'll have to check a map to figure out those addresses."

CHAPTER 23

Dani averted her eyes as Spencer returned to the canal's shore and dried off with the towel Gray provided. While he re-dressed, he elaborated on what he had observed from the aerator.

"Thanks, man." Gray clapped Spencer on the shoulder. "I'll figure out which houses you were able to see, and once I have that information, I'll give you both a call."

"Great." Spencer nodded, then looked at Dani and asked, "Have you eaten yet?"

"I grabbed something before coming here." Dani tilted her head. "Why?"

"Uh." Spencer shrugged. "Just wondered if you guys wanted to grab a bite."

"I'll take a rain check." Gray was clearly anxious to leave.

"Thanks, but me too." Dani smiled. "I still have stuff to do for tomorrow's birthday party."

"Okay." Spencer waved and disappeared

among the trees.

Dani and Gray walked to their separate vehicles, said their goodbyes, and headed home. For the remainder of the evening, Dani concentrated on blocking the image of Spencer's muscular chest, washboard abs, and firm rear end from her thoughts. Seeing him nearly nude had not helped her accept that they were only friends one little bit.

The next day, while Dani prepared for the Newcastle birthday party, loaded the van, and drove to the address Hilary had given her, flashes of Spencer in his black boxer briefs kept flickering though her head. As she pulled into the driveway of an impressive two-story redbrick house, she allowed one last image of the hot security chief, then pushed thoughts of him aside and put on her chef face.

Staring at Hilary Newcastle's home, Dani's mouth dropped open. She hadn't expected anything quite so large or imposing. It had to be five thousand square feet and, from what she knew about real estate prices in Normalton, worth close to a half-million dollars.

Hilary's hair salon must be doing really, really well. Or maybe she'd inherited the place. Considering her own good fortune, Dani couldn't rule that out.

Shaking her head, Dani reminded herself that Hilary's financial situation was none of her business. She was there to feed the party guests and nothing else. And because this wasn't a paying job, she was handling it alone, which meant she had to serve the food as well as prepare it. She needed to get moving.

A large party rental company truck occupied a good part of the driveway, but Dani was able to edge past it and park on a section of concrete next to an oversized storage shed. Running her to-do list through her head, she got out of the van and hurried up the walkway to the front porch.

Before she could ring the bell, the door swung open and Hilary stepped out, dressed in a long-sleeved pink cotton blouse, and tailored navy Bermuda shorts. "Hi. Did you have any trouble finding the place?"

"Thanks to my GPS, no, but I doubt I could have done it otherwise." Dani chuckled. "The streets in this subdivision certainly wind round and round."

"It's because the lots were laid out to maximize those with access to campus." Hilary jerked her thumb over her shoulder. "Can I help you carry anything?"

"No, thank you." Dani glance into the front hallway. "Do you want me to bring things through here or is it easier to get to the kitchen from the garage?"

"Probably the garage." Hilary stepped back inside. "I'll meet you over there once I open the big doors."

Dani returned to the van and loaded the supplies onto a rolling cart, pushed it across the driveway and into the now-open garage. Hilary stood at the door leading inside and helped Dani lift the cart up the steps and into the back hallway, then led the way to the kitchen.

After Dani had stowed the perishables in the fridge and turned the oven to preheat, she looked at Hilary and asked, "Where do you want the food?"

Hilary gestured to a pair of sliding doors. "Outside." She added, "There's another set in the living room so the guests won't bother you going through the kitchen."

"Great. Mind if I take a look?" Dani was anxious to see how things were arranged and to make any necessary tweaks.

"Of course not." Hilary led the way.

Dani followed, pausing to admire the huge multi-level deck that spanned the entire length of the house. In the center of the largest deck, well away from the railings, a man was using an air compressor to inflate a bouncy castle that had been surrounded by thick foam mats while other workers were putting up tables and chairs.

Hilary touched Dani's arm and said, "Excuse me for a minute. I need to make sure the arrangement is the way I want it."

When Hilary headed toward the workers, Dani wandered over to look at the view. She had thought the bouncy castle would be in the yard, but saw that there really was no lawn. Wooden steps led to a gravel trail that wound down a steep incline to a door in a large privacy wall.

Dani lifted her head and found herself staring at the Blackheart Canal. She could see the aerator shooting a fountain of droplets into the sky. Turning to go back into the house, she froze as her mind raced.

Could this house be what Deuce was surveilling every night from his watery perch, or was that too much of a coincidence? Spencer had said he could see three decks so maybe the homeless vet was spying on one of the neighbors.

She shook her head at herself. Why would Deuce be watching Hilary's house? Unless the salon owner made a habit of sunbathing in the nude or having sex outdoors, Dani doubted there was anything interesting for him to see.

Chuckling at the absurdity of something actually criminal going on at Hilary's, Dani tore her gaze away from the canal. Still, she bit her lip. It wouldn't hurt to give Gray a call once everyone was fed. She'd have to find a private spot so she could tell him what she'd discovered. And after that, any follow-up was in his hands.

Returning her focus to the party, Dani noted that the castle piñata was hung on the deck to her left, and the banner reading *Happy Birthday, Princess Crystal* was suspended above a long table that held party favors, pink plates, napkins, and cutlery, and a treasure chest cooler filled with ice and cans of soda.

Although Hilary was busy directing the men setting up tables for four scattered among the various deck levels, she waved Dani over and asked, "Does everything look okay?"

"Absolutely." Dani nodded, then checked her watch. "Your guests should be arriving shortly, so I'll just get back to the kitchen."

"Okay." Hilary trailed Dani inside. "When do you want to serve the food?"

"I'd say in about an hour," Dani answered. "I'll put out some snacks for people to nibble, but the kids will want to play before they eat." A thought suddenly occurred to her. "By the way, where's the birthday girl?"

"Crystal likes to make an entrance, so she's staying in her room." Hilary's chuckle was affectionate. "I'm supposed to go get her when everyone's here. I'll bring her through the kitchen so you can see her in her princess outfit."

"I'd like that," Dani said. The doorbell rang and Hilary hurried away.

With Hilary busy greeting her guests, Dani grabbed the cheese and fruit trays she'd prepared that morning. Taking them outside, she placed them on the buffet table and returned to the kitchen.

She'd already brined the turkey legs in the refrigerator overnight using a mixture of water, salt, brown sugar, and bay leaves, so all she needed to do was apply a combination of chili powder, paprika, and onion salt. Once the rub was spread all over and under the skin, she placed the legs into the four-hundred-degree oven, then washed her hands at the sink.

As she walked back to the counter, Hilary and an adorable little girl entered the kitchen. The child was wearing the costume that Dani had seen delivered to the hair salon, and both mother and daughter were beaming.

Hilary led the girl to where Dani was standing and said, "This is my daughter, Crystal."

"Nice to meet you, ma'am." Crystal waved her scepter in Dani's direction. "You are now under the protection of the crown."

"Thank you." Dani sketched a small curtsey. "Happy birthday, your majesty. I hope your party is wonderful."

"It will be." Crystal grinned. After a moment, her expression grew sad. "But it isn't perfect because my daddy isn't here." A tear slid down her cheek. "I don't even remember him. He died when I was only two."

"I'm so sorry." Dani patted the girl's arm. "What hap—?"

"We don't talk about that," Hilary interrupted. She looked at her daughter and said, "He'd want you to have a good time today, so no more thinking about him." Without another word to Dani, Hilary steered Crystal to the french doors and out to the deck.

Dani's heart broke for the little girl and she resolved to do all she could to make her birthday special. While the turkey legs roasted, Dani started the flatbread pizzas. She'd made the dough, marinara sauce, and cooked the toppings at the mansion before leaving for the party, so all she had to do was assemble and bake the pizzas. After lining several baking sheets with aluminum foil, she spread out dough on each one, then topped it with the sauce, crumbled bacon, and mushrooms. Once she had sprinkled all the pizzas with mozzarella and asiago cheese, she placed them in the oven and set the timer for fifteen minutes.

As Dani prepared the food, the doorbell rang almost continually. The sound of giggling children and excited shouts coming from the deck and the rest of the house made Dani smile and she hoped Crystal was having a blast.

While she waited for the pizzas and turkey legs to finish cooking, she turned her attention to the dessert. She had searched for a kid-friendly recipe and come up with mini caramel apple tarts. She'd baked the tarts that morning, but she wanted to make the caramel sauce just before serving them.

Taking out a large saucepan, she measured in dark brown sugar, heavy whipping cream, and unsalted butter. Then bringing the mixture to a boil over medium-high heat, she whisked constantly until the caramel thickened.

When the timer beeped, Dani covered the caramel sauce with a lid and placed the pan in the oven's warming drawer, then checked the turkey legs and pizzas. Both were done, and after wrapping the bottom of the legs in foil for easier handling, she placed them on the huge platter she had sitting on the top of her rolling cart.

Next, she cut the pizza into small squares and arranged it on the second large tray that she then put on the bottom shelf of the cart. Pleased with how the food had turned out, Dani wheeled everything out the sliding glass door and onto the deck.

Catching Hilary's eye, Dani jerked her chin toward the buffet table. Hilary nodded and quickly followed Dani. Between them, the two women hefted the heavy platter of turkey legs and then the tray of pizza squares.

While Dani put the nearly empty fruit and cheese plates on the cart, Hilary raised her voice and announced, "Will Princess Crystal and her friends please come to lunch."

As the children hit the buffet, Dani kept a close eye on the food and was glad to see that she had estimated their rate of consumption correctly. While most of the kids had dressed in the prince and princess theme, the last little boy through the line was wearing a hideous rubber mask that consisted of a mass of tentacles in place of a face.

Shuddering, Dani opened her mouth to say something, but Hilary beat her to it. With her nostrils flaring, the salon owner screamed, "Andrew Konrad, where did you get that mask?"

The boy shrank back. With a withering look, Hilary ripped the mask from his head and stalked away.

Disturbed by the scene, Dani waited until the child's mother rushed up to comfort him, then returned to the kitchen. In Dani's previous encounters with Hilary, the salon owner had seemed so calm and collected; it was shocking to see her lose her temper like that.

Shrugging, Dani finished up the caramel apple tarts, all the while wondering what there was about that mask that seemed familiar. She'd never seen one before, but something tickled at the edges of her mind.

After the tarts were ready, Dani took them out to the deck. As she arranged the trays on either end of the dessert table, Hilary came out of the living room's sliding glass doors carrying an enormous dragon birthday cake. She placed it in the center of the table and gazed at it with a gratified expression.

Although Hilary seemed back to her usual genial self, Dani was still a little hesitant when she asked, "Can I help with anything else?"

"Thanks." Hilary smiled sweetly. "Give me about fifteen minutes to get the device going that makes the smoke pour from the dragon's mouth. Then I'll round up the kids, and once Crystal blows out the candles down his back, I'd appreciate you slicing and serving the cake."

"Sure thing," Dani agreed.

She was heading back to the kitchen when it clicked. The rubber mask that the boy Andrew had been wearing was just like the one that the victims of the carjackers had described.

Shoot! She wasn't sure how everything went together, but between the mask and the deck being in the sight line of the canal, there had to be some connection. She needed to call Gray ASAP.

Setting her watch for fifteen minutes, Dani rushed out of the house. She wanted privacy and her van was the only place she could think of where she wouldn't be overheard.

Dani hurried past the storage shed, but something inside caught her eye. After retracing her steps, Dani pressed her face against the glass and blinked. The small building was entirely taken up by what looked like a 2015 Mazda MX-5 Miata 25th

Anniversary Edition. Gray had shown her a picture of the carjacked vehicle, and what she saw sure looked like the car in that photo. It was the unique metallic red that he'd said was only on that particular year's car.

Okay! Three strikes, you're out. The location of the house might be a fluke. The mask could be a coincidence. But the car . . . it had to mean something.

Wanting a better view, Dani went to the storage building's door and saw that whoever had been in there last hadn't quite clicked it shut. Dani stepped inside and gasped. The car definitely looked like the picture on Gray's phone.

She looked through the windows to examine the car's interior, and on the driver's-side front quarter panel, she saw a twenty-fifth anniversary badge. This had to be the stolen car, but just to be sure, she took her cell from her pants pocket, snapped a photo of the license plate, and sent it to the detective.

After making sure the image went through, Dani dialed Gray's number, but it went straight to voicemail and she was forced to leave a message.

Heck! She needed to run her discovery past someone right now. Spencer seemed like the most logical choice and he answered on the first ring.

Before she could speak, he said, "Glad you called. Christensen just texted me. He finally got confirmation on Deuce's legal identity. His name is Roy Lee Olhouser and he's originally from Clay Center."

"That's great," Dani said, quickly explaining where she was, what she'd seen, and her conclusion that Hilary was somehow involved in the carjackings and possibly in Deuce's death.

Spencer asked her to repeat the address, then said, "Get out of there right now."

"But my equipment and my —"

"You can get it later." Spencer's voice was urgent. "Just leave."

"You're right." Dani turned to go and caught a glimpse of Hilary at the window. "I'll try, but I think I might be trapped."

"I'll be right there. I'm only a few minutes away," Spencer said, then added, "Don't hang up. Put it on speaker."

"Done." Dani's heart thudded as the storage building's door squeaked open.

"Leave the line open," Spencer ordered.

"Okay, Spencer." Dani begged, "But please get here as fast as you can."

"I wouldn't count on your boyfriend rescuing you." Hilary stormed into the shed, holding a gun.

Dani's pulse raced, and for an instant, she froze, then for the benefit of Spencer listening on the other end of the phone, she said loudly, "Hilary, what's up with the pistol?"

Ignoring Dani's question, Hilary shook her head. "I must have forgotten to lock this door when I came in here to hide the mask. That was a stupid mistake." Hilary advanced, glaring at Dani. "You figured it all out, didn't you?"

"Figured what out?" Dani stalled giving Spencer time to arrive.

"I could hear you from the window telling someone, who I presume is a cop, everything. I should have gotten rid of you when I saw you staring at the canal, but I thought we could be friends." Hilary shook her head. "Then when the kid found the mask and you kept staring at it, I was sure you knew something." She rolled her eyes and made a disgusted clucking sound with her tongue. "Why didn't I burn that mask?"

Dani took a step back and said quickly, "I really don't know what you're talking about."

"Right," Hilary sneered. "That's why you're in here snapping pictures of my car. Another thing that I shouldn't have kept."

"I only took a photo to show my boyfriend," Dani lied. "I always wanted one of these kinds of cars and hoped he'd buy it for me." She widened her eyes and lied like her life depended on it — which it probably did. "That was him on the phone. I mentioned the mask to him so he could get one for Halloween and the canal because I want to go for a walk there after I finish here."

"Right. And I'm Queen Elizabeth." Hilary moved closer, shaking her head. "You know, I used to be good at getting rid of things that had the potential of causing me trouble, but raising my precious little girl has made me soft." She waved the gun in Dani's direction, her voice controlled and as cold as her expression. "You wouldn't understand."

Dani took another step back and hit the car. She had nowhere left to go.

Seeing Dani was cornered, Hilary pointed the gun at her chest, and eyes burning with contempt and determination, she said, "You've left me no choice. I have to kill you. Then, just like before, I'll have to grab Crystal and start over."

"Just tie me up and go," Dani pleaded.

"This is all your fault. We were supposed to become friends, but you had to be nosy." Hilary's expression darkened, and her eyes glittered with malice as she leaned closer. "You deserve to die."

CHAPTER 24

Bracing for the pain of being shot, Dani closed her eyes and inhaled. The fragrance of Hilary's perfume filled her lungs and Dani's eyes flew open.

"It was you!" Dani gasped. "It was your perfume that I smelled coming from Deuce's tent when Spencer and I found his body."

At Dani's accusation, Hilary staggered back and stuttered, "I . . . I . . . Don't be silly." Straightening, she said, "I was there because we were partners in the carjacking, but I didn't kill him." Narrowing her eyes, she shrugged. "Oh. What does it matter? It's not as if you'll be alive to tell anyone."

"The police will figure it out," Dani whispered, breathless with fear. "You left your fingerprints on the murder weapon."

The news that there was evidence against her seemed to stun Hilary, and when the door behind them squeaked, she turned her head to look over her shoulder. Seeing her opportunity, Dani launched herself at the woman.

The salon owner hadn't been prepared for Dani's tackle and fell to the floor with Dani on top of her. Fighting to keep Hilary pinned to the ground, Dani frantically tried to pry the weapon from the woman's clenched fingers.

For once, Dani was thankful that she'd put on a few pounds since becoming a professional chef. Her not-inconsiderable weight helped her hold down the much smaller woman, but Hilary's grip on the gun never wavered.

An instant later, Spencer ran in, pressed his Glock to Hilary's temple, and roared, "Drop it!"

Dani had never seen Spencer look as angry or as lethal as he did holding his weapon to Hilary's head. His face was a combination of fury and determination. It was clear that he'd reverted back to his undercover officer persona, willing to do whatever it took to keep the public safe from criminals.

Hilary twisted her head to look at Spencer, evidently saw the same thing that Dani had in his expression, and released her gun.

Spencer helped Dani get off the woman

and then flipped the salon owner over onto her stomach. After securing Hilary's hands behind her back, he got her to her feet.

Dani was wondering what came next when her cell rang. It was Gray returning her call. When she explained what had happened, including the fact that Spencer had been an "ear" witness to the whole incident, he told her to wait right there. He was on his way and would transport the prisoner to the station.

Several hours later, Hilary was in police custody and about to be questioned. Before Gray took her away, Hilary had begged Dani to make sure that her friend Serena, who was attending the party, took her daughter home with her.

Dani had given her word, and once she had fulfilled that promise, she and Spencer had spent the rest of the time between Hilary's apprehension and her interrogation writing up their versions of the events. When she'd handed the statement to Gray, Dani had jokingly said to him that she wished she could watch him question Hilary. Much to her surprise, he'd agreed and allowed Spencer to join her.

Now she and Spencer were standing in the area behind the one-way glass, along with a fortysomething man who had introduced himself as a prosecutor from the McClean County State's Attorney's Office. He had seemed somewhat surprised at their presence but hadn't voice any objection.

Dani didn't really care what the prosecutor thought of her being there; her attention was riveted to the scene in front of her.

Hilary was seated at a metal table and looked a lot worse for wear. Her blouse was missing a sleeve, and her shorts were torn from when Dani had wrestled her to the ground.

Gray entered the room carrying a folder, which he placed on the table. After taking the chair opposite Hilary, he said, "We are taping this interview. Do you have any objections?"

"No."

"Then state your full name and address."

Hilary complied.

Gray read her the Miranda warning and said, "Would you like a lawyer?"

"I don't need one." Hilary shook her head and widened her eyes. "I'm innocent."

"It's all here." Gray tapped the file in front of him. "You might as well confess."

"All you have is some story made up by a disgruntled caterer and her boyfriend." Hilary crossed her arms. "I have nothing to confess."

"We have your fingerprints on the weapon used to murder Roy Lee Olhouser" — Gray pulled out a piece of paper and put it in front of Hilary — "a.k.a. Deuce."

She didn't respond, and as the silence grew, Dani stared at the scarring on Hilary's exposed forearm. She'd never seen Hilary in anything but long sleeves and she wondered if the scars were the reason.

Spencer must have noticed Dani's interest and murmured, "It looks as if Hilary suffered a bad burn at one time. Probably several years ago."

Finally Hilary spoke, "It's not what you think." Her tone had changed and it was clear she was trying to sound pitiful. "He was stalking me."

"Why would Mr. Olhouser do that?" Gray's expression was impassive.

"I . . . I tried to be nice to him." Hilary shrugged. "He took it the wrong way."

"You told Ms. Sloan that Mr. Olhouser was a part of your carjacking ring." Gray selected another page from the folder. "We have proof that the car in your storage shed was stolen, and the rubber mask we found in its trunk has been identified by the carjacking victims."

Hilary wrinkled her nose. "Maybe that

caterer planted the car and the mask at my house."

Dani growled and Spencer patted her shoulder.

"Did she also force the young man we have in the interrogation room next to this one to admit that you had recently brought him into the gang?"

"The zombie pirate," Dani muttered.

When Hilary didn't respond, Gray changed gears and said, "So you're claiming that Mr. Olhouser was stalking you. Do you have any proof of that?"

"What kind of proof would I have?" Hilary's lips curled. "I only recently found out he was watching my back deck from the Blackheart Canal."

"Hmm." Gray stroked his chin but didn't say anything more.

With neither Hilary nor Gray speaking, Dani searched the corners of her mind. She'd forgotten something important that had to do with the name Olhouser. Systematically, she reviewed her activities the past week. There was the orientation, the band dinner, and her personal chef gig.

That was it! The answer burst from where it had been hiding and slammed her in the chest.

Tapping Spencer's shoulder, she lowered

her voice and said, "Where did you say Deuce was from originally?"

"Clay Center." Spencer shot her a puzzled glance.

"And you're certain that those scars on Hilary's arm are burns?"

"Absolutely." Spencer jerked his chin in Hilary's direction. "See how white and leathery they look, and their thickness?"

Dani nodded, then said, "You know that personal chef job that I had in Scumble River? The client was a county coroner and he was talking about a couple, their daughter-in-law, and granddaughter that were nearly completely incinerated in a fire in Clay Center about four years ago. It was deemed a homicide because the fire turned out to be arson." She paused, then added, "The name of the family was Olhouser."

"Okay." Spencer was still clearly confused.

"Hilary mentioned having to take her daughter and start over again." Dani's heart raced. Could she be right about this? "And they didn't find the victims' bodies. They had to use the DNA from a few teeth and some bone fragments to make the identifications. Hilary could have been burned starting the fire."

"And the teeth that were found?" Spencer raised a brow.

"Let's face it." Dani shrugged. "If Hilary was determined enough to disappear, pulling a tooth from herself and her daughter wouldn't have been beyond her capabilities."

"Okay. But how could you prove it?"

"Well, Hilary's last name is Newcastle, which is pretty much the opposite of Olhouser," Dani mused. "And her daughter is the right age."

The prosecutor broke into Dani and Spencer's conversation. "If they had DNA from something to make the comparisons for the fire victims, we can certainly see if Ms. Newcastle's matches."

"And we can also see if her daughter's DNA is a combination of Ms. Newcastle and Mr. Olhouser."

The attorney narrowed his eyes. "But the question remains: Why would Hilary burn down her in-laws' house, take her baby, and disappear?"

"I overheard a couple of women talking about that kind of thing yesterday." Dani shook her head. "It seems that some military husbands and wives use their spouse's deployment to disappear because they're afraid of a custody battle if they ask for a divorce."

"And if Deuce found Hilary and his

daughter, he might have been able to get full custody because of Hilary's prior actions," Spencer said slowly. "Even if Deuce didn't know she set the fire that killed his parents, her disappearance would provide him with a lot of ammunition in a court case. Which would certainly give Hilary a motive to get rid of Deuce."

"Not to mention if Hilary set the fire that murdered her in-laws, she'd already killed once, and it probably gets easier," Dani reminded him. "She didn't seem to have any trouble deciding to kill me."

The prosecutor excused himself and seconds later there was a knock on the interrogation room door. Gray answered and Dani could see the attorney whispering to him. As soon as Gray nodded, the prosecutor returned to the observation room.

When Gray returned to his seat, he smiled and said, "It seems as if you knew Deuce a little better than you said, Ms. Newcastle." He folded his hands in front of him. "Or should I say Mrs. Olhouser?"

"How did you . . ." Hilary gasped, her face stained by an ugly flush, then shook her head. "That's not my name."

"I think that the DNA from the Stanley County's forensics lab will prove that it is." Gray raised a brow. "And that Deuce was your daughter's father."

"You don't understand." Hilary crumpled. "Every time he came back from deployment he was a little more erratic. A little more paranoid. A little crazier. I had to protect Crystal from him."

The prosecutor muttered, "That's right, try to justify your criminal actions."

"So you decided to make him think you and your daughter were dead, then disappear." Gray's tone was encouraging. "Did it take you a long time to figure out how to do it?"

"Uh." Hilary seemed to realize belatedly the path she had started down, then twitched her shoulders as if to say *fine, I'll tell you.* "I got the idea from a movie and that's when I started squirreling away cash. I worked as a hairstylist in a salon in Joliet and the owner was in love with me so he was happy to pay me off the books. I told my in-laws that business was bad and they picked up the slack on bills and living expenses."

"That was generous of them," Gray murmured. "And, of course, you had your husband's military salary since I'm sure you had a joint account where his pay was directly deposited."

"Yeah." Hilary rolled her eyes. "That was

my one mistake. A few days before the fire, I emptied the account so I could buy my own salon once I relocated. When Roy Lee discovered that, he realized that I wasn't dead."

"You didn't consider that?" Gray asked.

"I'd hoped he'd think that I was planning to leave before the fire but didn't get a chance before I was killed in the flames." Hilary twitched her shoulders. "I had to take a chance. My little girl and I needed that money so we could start over and have the life we deserved."

"She doesn't even grasp what she's admitting." The prosecutor's smile reminded Dani of a cartoon shark. "I love it when they're too arrogant to realize they need an attorney," he murmured, turning his attention back to the one-way glass window.

Gray fiddled with a slim silver pen. "So you had the money, and I'm guessing you stashed your daughter in the car with your packed bags. Then what?"

"That's not what happened." Hilary finally seemed to tumble to the fact that she was admitting to arson and tried the wide-eye trick again. "The fire was an accident. I was lucky to get Crystal and myself out. I tried to rescue my in-laws, but it was too late."

Dani held her breath and nervously jiggled

her foot. Was Hilary going to get away with it? Was the only charge against her that would stick be the one for holding Dani at gunpoint?

"Now. Now." Gray's smooth tenor was mocking. "Don't try to lie now. You've already admitted that a movie gave you the idea and that you pulled out the money right before the fire and that you're one mistake was taking the money, which resulted in Deuce knowing you were still alive."

"I . . . I was planning on leaving and that's why I had the money, but I didn't deliberately set the fire." Hilary lifted her chin and stated, "I just took advantage of the situation."

"If that were the truth," Gray said slowly, "then the forensics team wouldn't have found a tooth belonging to you and one belonging to your daughter. A jury might believe the rest, but they certainly won't believe that in the heat of the moment, you managed to pull out your own tooth and one of your daughter's teeth *and* plant them in your beds." Gray pounded on the table making Hilary jumped. "And don't forget, we have your prints on the weapon that killed Deuce and our 'ear' witness, who" — Gray's smile widened — "is *not* Ms. Sloan's boyfriend but is the head of campus security. Which makes him a very credible witness."

Hilary's mouth dropped open, then closed, and her lips tightened. "Roy Lee attacked me. It was self-defense. You know all those vets come home crazy. Hell! He wasn't even honorably discharged."

"Those men and women give up their lives to protect your ass," Gray thundered.

Dani had never seen the detective like that before. He was truly outraged at what Hilary had done and how she was defending her actions.

"But that doesn't make being married to them any easier," Hilary whined. "I didn't sign up to be the wife of someone who screamed and hollered in his sleep. Or who could never find a job. Roy Lee promised to support me and Crystal and buy us nice things."

Dani's stomach churned. How could someone be so evil? Burning up two innocent people who had been so good to her. Killing her child's father. And for what? So she and her daughter could live the good life. Clearly in Hilary's world, there were two kinds of people: those whose lives didn't matter and herself.

"Keep going, Detective," the prosecutor

crooned. "You almost have her."

"So what happened when Deuce found you?" Gray's smooth tenor was back.

"I'm not sure how he tracked me down." Hilary chewed on her thumbnail. "I think the creep I bought my new identity from told him. I should have used someone who wasn't local, but how do you go about finding that kind of professional? Put an ad on Craigslist?"

"Sorry being a criminal is so hard," Gray sneered.

"Anyway." Hilary huffed at the interruption. "Roy Lee came to the salon and demanded to see Crystal, or as he knew her, Twyla Faye." Hilary shuddered. "Can you believe he insisted on such a hick name? I was so glad to be able to switch it to a more elegant choice. And changing my name from Estelle was no hardship either."

"I take it you didn't allow him to see his daughter." Gray's voice was low and deathly quiet.

"Of course not." Hilary blew out a raspberry. "But then he started spying on me and figured out my side business."

"You mean the carjacking," Gray clarified.

"Yeah. The two nitwits who worked for me allowed themselves to be followed." Hilary sighed. "After Roy Lee snapped pictures of them turning over the cars to me, he told me I had to close down that business and let him see Crystal or he'd turn me in. I couldn't have that."

"Why not?" Gray gripped the table edge, perhaps to stop himself from punching the woman.

"I needed the money." Hilary grew more composed and her words held utter conviction. "My little girl and I deserve to live the life we see on those *Housewives* TV programs. We're as pretty as those women, so we should have the same kind of nice things they own. I made sure Crystal went to a good private school where she could meet the right people and end up married to a doctor or a lawyer. She won't have to settle for a common soldier like I did. If I had to kill her daddy to accomplish that, it was a small price to pay."

"And we have her," the prosecutor crowed.

Dani watched as Gray's body went rigid with outrage. Then he relaxed and smiled.

"You might have been able to pull it off if you just knew when to stop." Gray gathered his papers and tapped them into a neat pile before inserting them into the folder. He stood up. "But I'm thankful you didn't. We have enough evidence to put you away for good."

"What?" Hilary squealed, appearing suddenly to come out of a daze. "But . . . but I had to do it all." She grabbed Gray's fingers. "Putting me in prison for taking care of my daughter isn't fair. What will happen to her?"

"You should have thought of that before you started killing people." Gray shook Hilary off, then opened the door to the interrogation room and said to the officer standing on the other side, "Lock her up. I need a whiskey." He blew out a long breath. "Make that a double."

EPILOGUE

Dani had intended to have a meeting with her employees several days ago, but between the orientation week events and Deuce's murder, she hadn't been able to find the right opportunity. Now that things had calmed down, she couldn't find a good reason to put it off any longer.

When she returned from church that morning, Dani rounded up her three boarders and asked them to take a seat at the kitchen table. Promises of a sublime brunch had lured them from their beds, but they all clutched cups of coffee and looked as if they were still barelyconscious.

Dani smiled to herself as they grumbled about being roused before noon on their last chance to sleep in before classes started the next day. Dani couldn't even remember a time when she wasn't awake, and usually in the midst of food prep, by 6:00 a.m.

Clearing her throat, Dani waited for them

to stop complaining, then announced, "We're here to discuss some recent problems with your work habits." She held up her hand to stop Ivy's and Starr's protests. "Yes, Tippi has been the worst culprit, but all three of you have been slacking off."

Starr opened her mouth to respond, but the doorbell rang and she snapped her lips closed. Ivy jumped to her feet and yelled, "I'll get it."

Dani blew out an exasperated breath and tapped her foot, waiting for Ivy and their mystery guest to return.

Hearing Spencer's voice, Dani fought the feeling of warmth filling her chest. Yesterday, after Hilary's interrogation and subsequent arrest, Spencer had driven Dani home and asked a friend to bring her van back to the mansion. He been so sweetly concerned for her, worried that the experience of being held at gunpoint might cause a delayed reaction, that he'd stayed, making her tea and ordering takeout.

However, once Starr returned to the mansion and said she was in for the night, Spencer had left with just a kiss on Dani's cheek and no mention of seeing her again.

So what was he doing here now?

Evidently, Ivy had filled in her uncle on what was happening, because after greeting them, he said, "Don't let me interrupt your meeting."

"If you're sure you don't mind waiting," Dani said, assuming that he had come to take his niece out for breakfast.

"Nope." Spencer walked over to the coffee maker and poured a cup. "Carry on."

"Okay." Dani made eye contact with each of the girls. "As I was saying, things have gotten too lax around here. From now on, there will be consequences for arriving late for your shifts or running off early, for checking your phone while on duty, and for leaving the kitchen a mess." She snuck a peek at Spencer and saw him nod his head in agreement. "Too many infractions and you will be asked to move out."

The girls gasped, but Dani's resolute expression didn't falter.

"What kind of consequences, and how many slipups are too many?" Tippi demanded in her best prelaw voice.

"First time, you will be fined thirty additional minutes of work." Dani crossed her arms. "Second time, you owe me an extra hour." She took a breath. "Three times and it's an entire shift."

"How about four times?" Ivy's voice quavered. "What happens then?"

Dani's swallowed the lump in her throat.

"Sadly, that would mean you would need to find other living accommodations." She would truly hate for any of the girls to leave, but she knew she'd been far too easy on them and they had taken advantage of her.

"What do you think about that?" Tippi turned her big brown eyes on Spencer and gave him a puppy-dog look.

"I think that Dani is being more than fair." He stared at each girl in turn, then added, "She took you in when you were in a tight spot and you all made her a promise. She's given you several months to adjust to your new circumstances, but now you have to pull your weight. She doesn't have parents paying her way and she is counting on you to help her make her business a success."

The three girls were silent for a moment, then Ivy got up, embraced Dani, and said, "I'm so sorry. I promise to do better."

Starr and Tippi made it a group hug and vowed that they would turn over a new leaf too. Dani was blinking back tears when the front doorbell rang again.

"Are you expecting anyone?" Spencer asked, scowling as if he'd like to punch whoever had arrived.

"I'm not." Dani glanced at the girls. "Any of you have friends coming over?"

"This early?" Ivy giggled. "All our friends are still in bed."

While Starr and Tippi nodded their heads in agreement, Dani heard a knock at the kitchen's door. Evidently whoever had been out front had grown impatient and walked around to the side of the house.

Glancing out the window, Dani saw Frannie waving at her. Justin was a few steps behind his girlfriend, and when he saw Dani looking at him, he jerked his chin in greeting.

Dani got up and unlocked the dead bolt, then opened the door, waved in the reporters, and said, "Let me guess why you're here. Gray gave you your exclusive, but you want to hear my version of the events." She glanced at Spencer. "And lucky you, the other witness is here too."

"Yeah!" Frannie's eyes were bright. "We have a terrific story already, but a little human interest never hurt."

"Fine. Take a seat." Dani raised a brow. "Anyone mind if I cook brunch while Spencer and I answer your questions?"

"Absolutely not." Frannie beamed. "We hoped we were in time for breakfast."

Although Starr, Ivy, and Tippi had heard it before, the three girls listened quietly as Spencer, and then Dani, told the young reporters their experiences with Hilary. While they talked, Dani started making Farmhouse Benedicts. First, she whipped up a batch of cornbread and got it into the oven, then made the rosemary hollandaise sauce.

When it was Dani's turn to talk, she started poaching the eggs. While they cooked, she took mangoes, nectarines, kiwifruit, strawberries, pineapple, and a honeydew melon from the fridge and started slicing and dicing.

Drizzling orange juice on the fruit salad, she finished her account with, "Then I put together everything and realized that Hilary was actually Deuce's wife and had set up things so he would believe she and their daughter was dead."

During Spencer's and Dani's explanations, Justin had slouched in his chair, resting his notebook on his knees, but now he said, "I have a couple of questions that I didn't think to ask Detective Christensen."

"Fire away." Dani placed the bowl of salad on the table and began assembling the Benedicts.

"Okay." Justin shoved his glasses up his nose. "Who did that girl sitting behind the homeless camp see that night?"

"That was Hilary," Spencer answered, getting up and setting the table. "She was wearing black tights and a black shirt in order to sneak in and out of the camp without being noticed, and she had the mask in her purse because she'd stuffed it there after firing one of her henchmen. After she killed Deuce, she put the mask on so no one would see her face."

"And Deuce was never involved in the carjackings," Frannie said.

"Only to the extent he knew about them and was trying to use that knowledge to gain access to his daughter." Dani finished placing a piece of Canadian bacon on each cornbread square and started gently spooning the poached eggs on top.

"So Deuce was homeless because Hilary had emptied his bank account," Justin said thoughtfully. "How did he find Hilary and his daughter?"

"It took Deuce years to unravel Hilary's trail, but once he found the guy who sold Hilary the fake identifications and persuaded him to reveal their new names, he asked an army buddy to use his computer expertise to locate them," Spencer explained as he poured glasses of juice for everyone. "And no, I have no idea how he got the forger to give him the information. My guess is that he beat the crap out of him."

Dani narrowed her eyes at Spencer's assumption but didn't say anything since he probably was right. Taking up the story, she said, "Once Deuce knew where his wife and daughter were, he moved here and started watching for his chance." Dani ladled hollandaise sauce over the eggs Benedict and brought the platter to the table. "He must have known that if he showed up with no ammunition against her, Hilary would just disappear again."

"Deuce was a lot smarter than people thought." Ivy sighed. "I don't understand why so many folks are so mean about the homeless. This is supposed to be such a liberal area."

Dani slid into the chair Spencer held out for her and said, "Sometimes, there are none so intolerant as those who preach tolerance."

"I'd have to agree." Frannie screwed up her face. "No one really wants to hear the truth. People keep trying to bend my words as a journalist to suit their own perspective so that it falls in line with their own beliefs."

"That's right." Justin straightened. "We report the facts, but others try to skew them to fit their biases."

Everyone was quiet after that and when they'd all finished eating and the kitchen was clean, the girls excused themselves and went up to their rooms.

Justin and Frannie headed toward the door, but Justin paused with his hand on the knob and asked, "Any idea how Deuce got that nickname?"

Spencer chuckled and said, "Best guess, it's because his given name was Roy Lee. You know a double name, or a deuce."

Once Dani and Spencer were alone, she wasn't sure what to do. He didn't seem to want to leave, but he wasn't saying anything.

Dani smoothed the skirt of her peach sundress and waited for him to speak.

He stepped closer to her and whispered, "It's probably too soon for both of us, but after yesterday, I don't think I can wait any longer."

"What do you mean?" She looked up and saw that he was only a hairsbreadth away.

"You know what I meant." His finger traced her lips. "I thought she was going to kill you before I could get there."

"Me too." Dani breathed, her lips tingling from his touch.

"If that had happened, I would have regretted never telling you how I really feel. Never acknowledging the chemistry between us." Spencer's mouth was an inch from hers. "Never doing this."

"What?" Dani knew what, but that was the only word she could force from her suddenly dry throat.

Spencer nuzzled her nose and said, "This." Then he claimed her lips.

It was a soft kiss, gentle, but in no way tentative. It was tender and Dani was unprepared for her body's response. Part of her wanted the kiss to remain exactly what it was, perfect. But another part, long-dormant passion, wanted it to deepen.

Before she could decide which desire was stronger, Spencer pulled back, resting his forehead against hers. They stood there like that, Dani with her eyes closed, breathing in Spencer's wonderfully masculine scent, trying to memorize it.

If he changed his mind about their relationship and went back to insisting on friendship only, she wanted to remember every smell, every touch, and every sensation of this magical moment.

ABOUT THE AUTHOR

Denise Swanson is the *New York Times* bestselling author of the Scumble River mysteries, the Deveraux's Dime Store mysteries, and the Chef-to-Go mysteries, as well as the Change of Heart and Delicious Love contemporary romances. She has been nominated for *RT*'s Career Achievement Award, the Agatha Award, and the Mary Higgins Clark Award.

CPSIA information can be obtained
at www.ICGtesting.com
Printed in the USA
BVHW072145070721
611417BV00001B/6